Demons and Darlings

EMILY BLACKWOOD

7 years ago

"Stay quiet," my mother ordered. "I don't want to hear you say another word. Understand?"

I nodded through the pain that pierced my back and my neck. It didn't matter if I had said anything or not. It never did. This punishment was *mine*.

She tightened the chains around my arms, making sure I would hardly be able to move. "If you can't be a good daughter and do as you're told, I'll have to ensure you stay here by chaining you up. This is your fault, Lyra. You did this to yourself. Remember that."

This time, I stayed quiet. I obeyed. My thin wrists ached from the iron shackles; the scabs beneath hadn't had time to fully heal since the last time I had been chained up. I tried not to think about my raw skin underneath or the cold cement floor I had been unable to get away from.

I tried not to think about any of it.

"When I can trust you to do as you're told," she hissed in my face, "I'll let you go. This world is depending on you.

You don't *get* to live a normal life like the other girls. I don't know how long it's going to take you to understand that."

I looked anywhere but her makeup-covered face. *Stay quiet, Lyra. Stay quiet and she'll leave you alone.*

She always did. She would leave me here while she returned to her seemingly perfect, pristine life.

"Now, tell me again," she pushed. She knelt before me, gripping my chin with her long, perfectly manicured fingernails as she forced me to look into her golden eyes. "Tell me why you're here."

"*I am the secret,*" I repeated through gritted teeth. "*My blood is the key, and my life has one purpose.*" The words ignited a deep numbness in my chest.

"You forget so quickly," my mother sighed. Her eyes softened, just like they always did every time she pretended to feel sorry for me. Her ice-blonde hair fell over her shoulder as she cocked her head sideways. "You are fulfilling a great destiny, child. Stay quiet, stay hidden away, and when your time comes, *save the world.*" The same estranged edge in her voice sent a chill of disgust down my spine.

She let go of my chin and walked out of the basement, clicking her designer high heels on the cement floor and closing the heavy door behind her.

One singular trail of light came through the tiny basement window. Nobody would come for me. Nobody ever had before. Nobody would even miss me.

My life's purpose was to stay hidden. To stay quiet.

I closed my eyes and tried to picture myself anywhere else but the freezing, empty room I was trapped in. I imagined a warm beach with sand under my feet. A forest with the crisp smell of grass. I missed the real world, but pretending to be elsewhere was the only way I could survive these days, imprisoned in an underground room shrouded in darkness.

This was my life. Stay hidden. Stay quiet. I was my mother's weapon to the world. My mother, the Goddess of Light, had a very dark secret.

Her own daughter.

CHAPTER

One

I never expected to graduate college. I never even expected to *attend* college, but since online programs were becoming more and more available, my mother —Theia—had eventually broken down and let me attend simply to keep me occupied.

Over the last four years, I didn't mention that I would never *need* a degree. I already knew exactly what my life had in store. But in some ways, those online classes had been my only portal to the real world.

That, and Netflix.

Sheltered was an understatement. Theia had lightened up over the past four years, but I was still hardly allowed to leave my camera-monitored studio apartment. I took a long, calming breath and settled my rising heart rate. *I should be grateful*, I reminded myself. Grateful that I even had this apartment. Grateful that I wasn't locked in Theia's basement with chains holding me inside.

Good behavior had earned me this freedom, and I needed to appreciate that.

I kicked my feet up on the white couch and closed my eyes. Theia was out of town until next week, which meant I could relax for once. I wouldn't have to worry about her dropping by unannounced just to make sure I was still behaving.

With my last final exam behind me, I had nothing left. Nothing to look forward to. I could get another degree, I supposed, if Theia agreed to pay for it. Or I could start some sort of hobby. Knitting, maybe. Or yoga.

I shook my head and rubbed my temples. The dark, looming shadows of doubt began creeping closer and closer to my sanity. I hastily shoved them away.

Losing my mind wouldn't help me survive.

Staying quiet would. Staying obedient would.

A rapid knock on my window made me jump from the couch. I quickly crossed my small living room and peeked out of the glass into the darkness of night.

Natalie's face peered back at me with a wide smile and her brown, puppy-dog eyes as she motioned for me to open the window.

I slid the frosty glass open, letting the cool winter air rush inside. "What do you want, Natalie?" I grumbled. "It's late."

Natalie ignored my question and maneuvered her slim body through my window, her chocolate curls falling around her face as she hauled herself through. I stepped back to give her more room.

"Sure," I muttered, "come on in. You can use the front door, you know. As the one person who is allowed in my life, I don't think Theia would mind seeing you on the security camera."

It wasn't until she was inside that I noticed her skin-tight mini dress and ridiculously tall high heels.

I shook my head before she could even speak. "Don't even ask," I blurted.

"Come on, Lyra!" she argued. "We're *officially* college graduates now. Doesn't that call for some sort of celebration?"

"No way. Theia will freak if she finds out. You go have all the fun you can, but leave me out of it."

"But look at this!" Natalie reached into her purse and pulled out a small envelope. She opened it up and handed me the card inside.

You're Invited!
Night Raven is hosting a special night for college graduates! All graduates are welcome to come drink, dance, and have a night they'll never forget.
Use this invitation as your ticket inside.

"This is a once in a lifetime opportunity," Natalie continued as I pushed the invitation back into her hands. "Night Raven never hosts events like this. We have to go!"

Night Raven? I tried to think of why that name sounded familiar, and then it hit me. I grimaced. "Night Raven, as in the *demon* bar? Seriously, Nat?"

She gave me a pointed look. "All the more reason why it's so exclusive! This is a good thing for us, Lyra!"

Night Raven was the demon hotspot in town. From what Natalie had told me in the past, it was essentially the hideout for the supernatural creatures. To any humans, the bar would look completely normal.

But Natalie and I weren't lucky enough to be regular humans. Both of our mothers were goddesses, which put us in that small category of people who knew things that the humans didn't—including the fact that Night Raven would be crawling with demons.

"Demons aren't as evil as we've been told," Natalie emphasized. "They blend right in with the rest of us. You won't even notice them, I swear it. Besides, my mom told me she and Theia are gone for a few days. The timing is perfect! Please, Lyra?" She pursed her full lips, giving me the best pout she could muster. "This might be our only chance."

I tried not to let my anger take over. Of course, it was possible that Nat and I could sneak out through the window, have a great night without anybody ever finding out who I was, and then sneak back in through the window before my mother noticed I had left.

But the other possibility? The possibility of my mother finding out, realizing I had been lying to her, and then deciding to take her punishments out on me once again?

It wasn't worth it.

Natalie could beg all she wanted to. The fear of going back to that place was what kept me in this apartment for the last four years.

It wasn't going to stop now.

But even with my confident answer, even with the fear and the memories and *her*, I heard a voice. It was that same voice that had been creeping into my mind for some time now. At first, it had been easy to push away. To decline. To ignore. But over time, the words grew louder and louder.

And I actually started to listen to them.

Stop letting fear control you, the voice said. *She'll control you forever if you let her.*

Similarly enough, Natalie had made the same argument. "College is over," she pointed out. I snapped my attention back to her, biting my lip. "If you want to sit back and let your entire life pass you by, fine. But I'm trying to help you, Lyra. I've seen you shrivel away in this apartment for years. You aren't getting any younger."

I shoved my fingernails into the palms of my hands. *No, no, no.* Don't listen to that voice. Don't listen to it.

It was a dangerous, poisonous thought—that I could be *free.*

Those thoughts didn't belong to me. They would never be mine.

And neither would freedom.

"It's too risky," I whispered. But Natalie didn't give up. She held onto my shoulder and leaned in until her big brown eyes were directly in front of mine.

"I won't force you to go," she said. "But I wouldn't be able to live with myself knowing I didn't try my damned hardest to get you to live like a normal fucking girl for one night."

A normal fucking girl.

I pressed my nails harder into my palms. I expected pain. I expected a sharp reminder of reality, because clearly, I had lost my mind.

Was I really considering this?

No, absolutely not. Think of the basement. Think of the chains.

My obedience had earned me this apartment. This might be the most freedom I was ever going to get in this life.

My chest tightened. Deep down, I knew it wasn't enough. It had worked for a while. Hell, I had been thrilled when my mother gave me this apartment to live in.

It had been four years. Four years down, and the rest of my life to go.

No fucking way.

"Lyra? Are you listening to me?"

"Sorry." I shook my head. "What were you saying?"

A grin spread across her face once more. "I was saying, it's one night. We'll be back before midnight. You owe it to yourself to at least try."

I glanced around my small studio apartment, taking in the perfection. It took me a long time to stop seeing this place as my prison and to begin seeing it for what it really was—my freedom. I had collected a bookshelf full of my favorite novels; my personal, miniature windows to the outside world when I had none. The framed photos of Natalie and I hung in a perfectly spaced gallery wall above my fluffy white couch.

My chest tightened even further as I looked at the pictures. Every single one of them was taken in this apartment.

One night out. That's all it was.

Natalie was right. My mother would never find out.

Shit.

"Fine," I said before I even registered the words. "You want to go out? Let's go. Theia doesn't have to know every-thing, right?"

Natalie squealed as her face morphed from shock to excitement. She immediately began rummaging through my closet.

"I don't think you'll find much in there," I reminded her. "I don't have a need for party clothes, remember?"

She gave me a sympathetic smile and turned to dig through her own purse. "Here," she said, tossing me a tiny black dress. "Put this on."

I stared at her, my mouth falling open. "Are you kidding? You keep spare dresses lying around in your purse?"

"I came prepared! Besides, you never know when you need a backup. Now, grab some heels and let's get to work!"

I rolled my eyes. The dress *was* tiny, but something inside of me flickered with excitement at the thought.

When was the last time I relaxed and let myself be a young college student? When was the last time I wore something provocative? Although Natalie would argue that the dress wouldn't even fit into that category.

Never, I thought. I had *never* allowed myself to do any of those things.

"I'll wear this, but I'm wearing my tall boots and a jacket. You can't take my warmth away from me."

She snorted. "Deal!"

I spent thirty minutes curling my thick red hair, something I hadn't done in years, and slipped on the black dress Natalie picked out for me. Even when I tugged on the bottom, it only came to my mid-thigh. I dug the tall black boots out of my closet, the ones that passed my knees, and pulled them on. With my matching black leather jacket that I had owned for years, most of my skin was covered.

But the crisp fall nights were quickly turning into spine-chilling winter days in the city. It would still be cold as shit outside.

"This better be worth it," I hissed. Natalie held my face still while she plastered red lipstick on my mouth that matched my amber hair.

"Trust me, honey," she said before putting the lipstick on herself, "tonight will be epic. I can feel it."

Natalie and I walked the few blocks to Night Raven.

I tried not to think about how long it had been since I last left the apartment. If Natalie felt how nervous I was to be outside, she didn't show it. She continued to fill our conversation with rumors she had heard about the bad boys that dwelled within the club.

After a while, I didn't mind it. Hearing Natalie talk about semi-ridiculous topics had been one of the few links I had to the outside world over the last twenty-two years. In many ways, Natalie had saved my life. I nodded along as she continued talking, debating whether or not a demon would be a better kisser than a human boy.

She landed on yes, the demons would be better at kissing.

Before I could second-guess my decision, we were approaching the bouncer.

"IDs and invitations, please," the ridiculously large man barked.

Natalie handed hers over first, along with the Night Raven invitation. I followed right after, mimicking everything she did.

My heart skipped a beat as he took the thin plastic and surveyed it closely, even bending it slightly while he examined it. He glanced at me, his shadow-covered eyes soaking in my features, before returning his gaze to my ID.

This is it. I'm screwed. I accepted my fate that this bouncer would recognize my name. My cover would be blown. The one secret I had tried to keep my entire life would be outed in front of this single-story, run-down building with white paint chipping off the bricks.

"Go ahead," the bouncer mumbled.

I hardly had time to register his words. I took back my ID just before Natalie grabbed my arm and yanked me through the cracked doorway.

"Relax," Natalie whispered. "You look like you could pass out any second! Remember, you're a regular college graduate. Act like one."

I nodded, unable to form words.

"Drinks," Natalie demanded, glancing around. My eyes adjusted more with every second. "We need drinks."

Natalie held my hand while we made our way through the body-filled club. Neon lights flashed through the darkness, matching the beat to the music that played so loud, I could feel it in my body.

The nerves I felt earlier slowly morphed into an adrenaline-fueled excitement. This was what *living* looked like. The lights were so dim, nobody would ever get a good look at my face. Natalie had been right about one thing—nobody knew who I was. How could they?

She elbowed her way up to the front of the bar. "Two shots of tequila, please!"

My jaw fell open in shock. "Natalie!"

"What? I might never get you to come out with me again! We have to make the most of it while we're here! Besides, rule one of drinking is to start with shots. That way we get drunk faster, and we don't spend as much money!"

I rolled my eyes while she turned back to the bartender. Natalie didn't have to worry about money. Her mother was one of the wealthiest and most powerful goddesses of our time. That was the reason Theia had taken up an interest in her and had finally let Natalie become my friend. I always assumed my mother had no idea about Natalie's *extracurriculars*. There was no way in hell she would let me be friends with her if she did.

The bar around us was absolutely packed. It seemed smaller than I expected, with just enough room for a bar, a pool table, and a dance floor.

I looked around at the people. How many of these men were demons? How many were regular humans? My gaze landed on one man in particular who stood on the other side of the bar. He appeared to be about our age, but tattoos covered the majority of the skin on his arms, even peeking out of his slim t-shirt onto his neck. He looked... *mean*. Menacing. If anyone in this bar was a demon, my money was on him.

His blazing green eyes found mine, only for a second, before I ripped my eyes away and turned back to Natalie.

"Do you think there are any demons here?" I yelled in her ear.

Natalie traded her credit card for the shots and passed me one. "I hope so." She smiled wickedly. Her glass clinked against mine, and I watched as she tossed the entire shot into her mouth.

Aside from a couple bottles of wine with Natalie in the confines of my apartment, I never drank. There was no need. I wasn't allowed to act like a normal college student, so I missed out on the partying and the sloppy nights. Most of the time, I didn't mind it. I had focused on reminding myself of my *life's purpose*. Sometimes, though, I felt a tiny ball of grief building inside of me. Grief for the life I could have lived.

Natalie shook her head and bit into the lime slice that had been waiting for her on the rim. "Woo!" she cheered. "Your turn, Lyra!"

I debated my options. I could reject the shot and spend the entire night worrying about all the ways my mother could possibly find out about this.

Or I could drink it and actually live my life for once.

"Don't be afraid!" Natalie yelled to me.

Don't be afraid. Those were the words Natalie had been repeating to me since we met. Only now, they sounded different. They *felt* different.

I held my breath and took the shot.

The tequila burned as I downed it in one gulp, just like Natalie had. I nearly gagged on the sharp flavor before I squeezed the lime juice into my mouth.

Another cheer of excitement came from Natalie.

"Are you happy now?" I asked her as I set my empty shot glass onto the bar. The line of people waiting behind us in the club slowly pushed forward. Natalie and I were now being shoved from every angle.

"Ecstatic!" she hollered back. She turned to face the bartender again. "Two more, please!"

This time, I didn't fight her on it. We took the second shot, and by the time we set those small shot glasses back down on the bar, I was already feeling more relaxed.

"I can't believe I'm actually doing this," I said to her.

"It's about damn time!" she laughed. "You have no idea how many times I've wanted to drag you out to bars with me!"

"Well, don't get used to it," I reminded her. My chest physically ached as the words left my mouth. "This is a one-time thing."

She grabbed my wrists and began tugging me with her to the dance floor, waggling her eyebrows suggestively. "Then we better make the most of it!"

My first instinct was to fight her on it. To decline her invitation. But there I was, inside of a demon bar, no less, with two shots of tequila burning in my stomach.

Natalie was right. This might be my only chance.

My feet were moving before I even agreed to it, as if my body knew exactly how much I needed this. Before I knew it, Natalie and I were in the middle of the crowded dance floor. A small, lifted stage with massive black speakers and cascading neon lights stood at the front of the room. This close, I could feel the vibrations of the music as the loud beats filled the room.

"Relax!" Natalie reminded me. "Let go of everything you're worried about. This is what we do to forget."

I watched as she closed her eyes and began moving to the beat. Natalie effortlessly blended in with the people around her as she swayed from left to right. I had to remind myself that Natalie had spent the last four years doing things like this; she was used to it.

Me, on the other hand? I had absolutely no clue what to

do. I took a long breath and tried to remove some of the tension in my body. I had always been tense, something I had my mother to thank for.

But tonight, I could be anything I wanted. I could be anyone I wanted. That scared, sheltered girl who feared her mother more than life wasn't here tonight. *No*, tonight I could be free.

Natalie danced senselessly. She blended in with the others—people dancing to get lost. Or maybe it was to find themselves. Either way, they felt *something*. I could see it all over their faces.

Bodies shoved me from each side as the music morphed into an even more upbeat, contagious song. The room was filled with mostly women, but a few men also blended in around us, dancing just as closely as everyone else. Instead of fighting the frequent shoves from every angle, I became one with them. I became part of the crowd.

I focused on Natalie. I focused on relaxing.

And before I knew it, I, too, was moving with the electric pull of the music.

"See?" Natalie yelled to me with a grin. "It's fun!"

For once, I agreed with her. I let my head fall back as I looked up at the flashing lights that hung from the ceiling. Natalie pulled me closer to her, holding my hands as we both jumped and swayed to the beat. The music controlled us—fueled us.

Laughter bubbled in my chest as the song switched from one beat to the next. Once I got used to it, I didn't have to think so hard about dancing. My body took care of that on its own, almost as if it were instinct.

Natalie laughed, too. Her chocolate curls bounced with her as she jumped up and down to the music with her arms in the air. Together, we shared that feeling of euphoria, that feeling of freedom. If this was what Natalie was experiencing every time she came to a party like this, I now understood her lifestyle.

I would kill for more moments like this one. It felt so *right*.

I wasn't sure how long we stayed like that, but I became addicted to the pure joy that grew and grew as we danced. Natalie and I took small breaks to take more shots of tequila, which only pulled me further into that place of bliss.

This was the version of me I had dreamt about. This was the version of me that I had quit believing in, because *this* Lyra was never supposed to see the light.

Yet here we were.

I became so used to bodies bumping up against mine that I didn't even notice the man moving to dance behind me.

Natalie was already enthralled in the hands of another man, dancing in his arms as if she belonged there all along.

This should have scared me. It should have felt inappropriate and foreign and downright wrong, but it didn't.

The stranger's hands fell on my hips, lightly at first, as if he were asking for permission.

To him, I'm sure it was a simple gesture. He had probably danced with hundreds of women this way. To me, though, his touch was intoxicating.

The lightest movement sent a thrill of excitement through my body. Even over my leather jacket, I could feel every centimeter of space where he touched me.

I didn't turn around, not at first. Instead, I continued dancing how I had been; letting the music control my movements. The body behind me did the same, blending with me until we became one force on the dance floor.

After a few minutes, I leaned deeply into him. The heat of his body only turned up the level of exhilaration still rolling through me. That, and the subtle scent of sandalwood.

"You're a great dancer," the stranger murmured into my ear. His breath kissed my cheek as he leaned in to talk, sending a pleasant shudder down my spine. I decided to turn around, to finally look at the man I had been dancing with for the last few minutes.

And my jaw nearly dropped.

Dancing behind me had been the sexy man I made eye contact with across the bar earlier. With his face just inches from mine, his sharp bones made him look dangerous and threatening, his bright green eyes even more intense.

"Thank you," I replied. I had never been that close to a man before. Only a couple of seconds passed before I became very aware of the fact that his hands were still resting on my hips.

Maybe it was the tequila, or maybe it was that shadow of a voice that had been screaming at me to *live*. Either way, I took a small step toward him and placed my arms over his shoulders as we continued to dance.

A small smile from the stranger told me it was the right move.

More euphoria. More dancing.

Adrenaline fueled me as I stared into those neon green orbs, completely enthralled by the man before me.

He seemed just as interested. His menacing eyes didn't leave mine as the song flickered from one to the next, over and over again until sweat rolled down my neck.

I never wanted that moment to end.

"Care for a drink?" he asked. We were both out of breath

and glistening in sweat. I didn't want to stop, but I reluctantly agreed and let him pull me out of the crowd and back to the bar.

"Wow," I said once we got there. "This is incredible! I didn't know dancing could be so much fun."

The stranger smiled at me, which elicited another thrill of excitement.

"Not a big dancer?" he asked. He quickly ordered two shots of tequila from the bartender without having to ask what I was drinking. I stared at him, eyebrows raised, until he noticed. "What?" he asked. "I'm observant."

"I can see that," I replied. "I think some people would call that creepy."

"I believe some people would also say that drinking and dancing in a room full of strangers is considered creepy, but we let things like that slide here at Night Raven."

He had a point. I picked up my shot of tequila. "You come here a lot, then?"

The man shrugged. I watched the visible parts of his tattoos flex under his now-sweaty black t-shirt as he picked up his own shot. "You could say that," he said. When the bartender returned, the stranger flagged him down. "Put her tab on the house," he ordered.

"Yes, Sir Alek," the bartender replied before scurrying away.

In the midst of my tequila fog, I froze. "Sir Alek..." I repeated. He put our tab on the house? And the bartender called him Sir?

Natalie had mentioned the name of the owner in her ramblings on the way here. She had called him... Alekzander Black. He also happened to be the notorious *prince of demons*. Not a real prince, of course. Just like his father wasn't a real king. But together, they ran the underground legion of demons in the area.

And now, the demon prince was standing right in front of me.

The stranger—Alek—stared at me expectantly, as if waiting for me to piece it all together.

"You're Alekzander Black?" I questioned. "As in, the owner of this bar?"

He nodded and clinked his tequila glass against my own. "The one and only." A smirk played on his lips.

I was too stunned to down my shot. I watched as he took his without so much as blinking.

"That means you're—"

"A demon?" he finished, raising a dark brow. "Considering you know that, you must not be human, either."

"No," I stuttered. My mind raced for an answer. I couldn't tell him who I was—who my mother was. Nobody could ever know that. The only reason I knew about demons was because of her, but he didn't know that. I had to lie. "My mother works with gods and goddesses. She's let me in on a few secrets."

He looked me up and down with raised brows.

"I've never met a demon before," I said, desperate to change that topic. My heart was pounding so hard in my chest, I was certain he could hear it. After a few seconds, though, the smile returned to his face.

"Today must be your lucky day, then. I take it you're here to celebrate college graduation?" His arm brushed against mine as he leaned closer. The bar was so crowded around us, I had to lean in to hear what he was saying.

"My best friend dragged me here. She couldn't turn down an *exclusive* night at Night Raven."

"Well, I'm glad she dragged you along," he teased. "It's not often that we see many newcomers around here. Especially newcomers who know about us."

I finally took the shot of tequila I had been holding. It seemed to taste hundreds of times better than the first shot of the night. I didn't even need the lime as I turned back to Alek.

"Do all demons have eyes like yours?" I asked. It was blunt and forward, but the alcohol was turning me into a brand-new Lyra.

"Demons have brightly colored eyes," he started. He leaned in dangerously close before finishing, "but you'll never find another pair like mine." His voice dripped with seduction, whether he meant for it to or not. I stared into his eyes, and he held my gaze like an unspoken promise.

"What's your name, new girl?"

"Lyra," I answered. "Lyra Sol."

"Lyra," he replied, his lips slowly spreading into a smile. "I like that name."

"I'll send your compliment to my mother," I joked, but the mention of my mother sent a harsh bolt of reality through me. I immediately stiffened. If Alek noticed my blunt change in attitude, he didn't show it.

"I have a proposition for you, Lyra Sol," he said after a few seconds.

"Oh, really?" I questioned. "What's that?"

"My father's been on my ass for quite some time. He insists that I find a date and settle down, something about what's best for the family and all of that." I waited for him to continue. "I know we just met, but would you consider being my date to a small event tomorrow night?"

My first reaction was to laugh, mostly because this entire

situation was so ridiculous. But Alek didn't know that. He didn't know how sheltered my life had been and now rare this was for me.

"Sorry," I started, "but I have a very strict mother. There's no way she'll let me do something like that."

Alek moved even closer—close enough that I could see each one of his thick, dark eyelashes as he stared into my eyes. "What if I swore to you that she would never find out? Demons can be very sneaky, you know. You're the perfect girl to help me get my father off my back."

I opened my mouth to object but stopped myself.

"Besides," Alek added, "nights like these are nothing compared to what I can show you. It's clear you're new to having fun like this. If you agree to help me, I'll do you a favor and take you out. I'll show you everything you've been missing."

I couldn't believe I was actually considering it. Alek had found me at the perfect time, though, because I had just experienced the best night of my entire life. My heart was still racing, either from the adrenaline of dancing or from the thrill of Alek standing so close to me.

I swallowed.

"She can't know," I repeated. "My mother must never find out about any of this."

"Easy," Alek answered with a shrug.

"And you'll show me more of this?" I waved at the bar. "You'll show me what it's like?"

"I'll show you the world, Lyra Sol," he whispered sarcastically. But I felt the underlying truth in his words, even beneath the smirk that curved his lips.

The smile on my face gave it away. This was everything I

had been searching for, and Alek only needed me to help him get his father off his back.

Alek leaned even closer, as if that were possible. "Deals with demons are sealed with a kiss," he whispered. "Kiss me, and change your entire life as you know it."

I froze. I wanted this. I wanted this so badly. Alek was right here, offering me the world on a platter.

Kiss him, that voice whispered to me. *Kiss him and experience more nights like this.*

I had never kissed anyone before. It should have seemed dangerous to me, but it didn't. My heart rate sped up as I leaned in—just an inch.

Alek's eyes scanned my face. His hand fell to my hip.
Kiss him and live.

"Is this a good idea?" I whispered.

"Don't worry about good or bad. What do you want right here at this moment? What does your heart tell you?"

I closed the distance between us with a single movement and I pressed my lips softly against his.

Aside from his hand on my hip, he didn't move. I had no idea how to kiss a man, let alone a demon.

But this kiss was nothing other than transactional. The flicker of heat I felt from his lips against mine lasted only a second. Alek barely kissed me back before pulling away.

That didn't stop my heart from nearly exploding. Nerves erupted through my body, even though I tried to force them down.

My first kiss. And it was with *him*.

"The ball tomorrow starts at eight," he said. "Meet me here. I'll have my assistant send you something to wear."

"That's it?" I asked. "We're actually doing this?"

A wicked smile grew on his face. "Oh, we're doing this, sweetheart."

He walked away, leaving me alone at the bar and completely disheveled.

What the hell just happened?

"Who was that guy?" Natalie asked as she elbowed her way over to me. "He was totally into you!"

"Alekzander Black," I answered, ignoring her second comment. "I agreed to be his date to some event tomorrow night."

Natalie's jaw dropped. She put a dramatic hand over her chest as she asked, "What are you, and what have you done with my best friend?"

I laughed and threw my arm around her shoulder. "He agreed to show me the world. I'm doing what you told me to do, Natalie. I'm actually living my life for once!"

She turned to face me. "Are you telling me you made a deal with that demon? Not only *a* demon, but the *demon prince*?"

A laugh bubbled in my chest. "Yes, ma'am!"

I half expected her to get angry, but she only laughed along with me. "You're full of surprises tonight, Lyra. Come on. Let's go dance."

CHAPTER
Three

One day later, I walked toward Night Raven with my long black coat secured tightly around my body. There was no way I was going anywhere tonight without it covering me.

The route to the bar was fairly simple and easy to remember after last night. Sneaking out of my window with a long dress on, however, had been difficult.

Alek had sent a package with a small, hand-written note about wearing the very revealing, black silk dress that was included.

Both of which only increased my nerves.

After the tequila wore off, the doubt began to set in. This entire plan was absurd. It was risky, impulsive, and idiotic.

But either way, I had no choice. We made a deal.

Natalie had stayed with me all day. She curled my hair into long, loose waves that met my waist, and she tried her best to fill me in on everything she had heard about the demons.

It wasn't much. Demons had a reputation of being exclusive, cliquey, and out of sight. The humans in town didn't know Night Raven was crawling with demons. Of course, the humans didn't even know demons existed, so they would never expect an entire demon bar.

While Nat and I didn't have magic like our mothers, we weren't human. Not entirely. Some children of gods developed special abilities later in life, but that was rare. I didn't expect anything special for myself, and neither did Natalie.

"And even if you wanted out of the deal," Natalie had explained, "it's impossible. You kissed him, and the deal was sealed. Deals with demons have some sort of magic attached; it's what makes them so dangerous. Neither of you could back out, or else your soul could cross to the veil."

The veil.

Yet another fun piece of information that came with being non-human. Similar to humans, our afterlife was like two sides of the same coin—that coin being the veil. The downside was similar to hell with the supernaturals being forced to live an eternity without finding peace.

But if you were good enough and your soul deemed worthy, you could pass to the upside, where supernaturals find true peace. Supernatural creatures would be forced to live in eternity without finding peace.

The difference between the two was something called the veil, the supernatural wall that separated the other side from our world.

An eternity of misery was enough to rid me of any thoughts about backing out.

An hour later, I walked up to the front doors of Night Raven. I couldn't make myself walk inside, though. Not yet. Walking through those doors meant I was doing this. I was committing.

If my mother ever found out about this, I would be locked away forever. *Shit, where was Natalie with the tequila shots when you needed her?* I reminded myself that I didn't have a choice. We kissed, and the deal had been sealed.

God, I wished I had thought this through before I kissed the demon prince.

Rolling my shoulders back, I bit the inside of my cheek and stepped inside.

"That's not what I told you to wear," the familiar voice echoed through the nearly empty bar as soon as I walked through the doors. I stiffened immediately, silently cursing myself for having any reaction to his presence at all. "That's a winter coat. Where's your dress?"

Play it cool, Lyra. Calm and collected.

I flipped my red hair over my shoulder and made my way to the bar.

"You dressed me like a prostitute," I said once I was there. "If I were to walk here dressed like that, I would have been arrested."

Alekzander approached behind me, but I didn't turn to look at him. The warmth of his body alerted me to his closeness before his words did. "You're early."

"You make some great observations," I replied blandly. "Just as I remembered from last night."

I turned and looked at him for the first time. The tattoo along his neck snaked below his blacked-out tuxedo, leading my eyes lower to the expertly toned muscles etching through his tight-fitted shirt.

I tried not to stare, but I knew my face was already turning pink. Alek was used to this. Someone like him probably dated hundreds of girls.

But considering he needed my help to settle his reputation…

This was just a deal to him. I needed to keep that in my head. Blushing at the sight of him standing before me wasn't going to help me.

I cleared my throat, my fingers absentmindedly running across the smooth surface of the bar. "What exactly is expected of me tonight?"

Alekzander huffed and leaned down on the bar. "Just being there should do the trick," he started. "I'll have to introduce you to my father, of course, and plenty of other high-ranking assholes. That will be the fun part. We'll make sure we're seen together, and then you'll be back in your cozy little bed."

My fingers stilled. The entire room stilled. "I'm meeting your father? As in… as in, the demon king?" I stumbled over my words, which only made the situation worse. There was no way Alek would introduce me so soon. I wasn't ready for that. *Right?*

Alek's emerald eyes locked with mine. "Yes. He has to see I'm in a relationship and am no longer available for him to pawn off as he pleases. And he's not a real king, you know."

"Just like you're not a real prince," I muttered.

Alek's laugh surprised me. "No, I'm not. But you flatter me."

"And who exactly does your father think I am? I can't imagine he thinks we've been dating that long."

"As far as he knows, you're an ordinary girl I met at the bar. We just started seeing each other, but things are getting very serious. Serious enough to take me off the market, and serious enough that I'll turn down any more *propositions* from him."

"I guess that's close enough to the truth."

Silence passed between us, but I could feel him looking at me. "Are you afraid?" He smirked.

I met his stare again. "Should I be?"

"Don't worry." He paused, his smirk ticking up into a grin before leaning closer to whisper, "Don't leave my side, and you'll be the safest woman in the entire world."

Heat rose to my cheeks. Not because he was now just inches from me, but because he blatantly offered his protection.

I could count on one hand the amount of people who would protect me.

It would take way more than two hands to count the people who would exploit me.

"Fine," I said. "Let's get this over with, then." I stood up and peeled off my coat, letting Alekzander see the dress he had so diligently picked out for me. Or *lack of a dress*, rather.

His eyes flickered down my body, snagging on my cleavage before lowering to my hips. The outline of my body was entirely revealed to him, cut out by the thin black silk. His mouth twitched as his gaze scorched a path back to my eyes.

"The dress fits you well," he praised. "You'll definitely be turning heads."

What is that supposed to mean?

"Come on," he said, clearing his throat. "I have a ride waiting for us. I'll fill you in on the specifics on the way."

Alek grabbed my coat, and I followed him out the front of the bar where we slipped into the long black limousine that had just arrived.

Alek opened the back door. "After you," he insisted. I tried to keep my composure as I slid into the back seat. The white leather interior was a shocking contrast, and the entire roof glittered with magical twinkling lights.

I moved across the seat, giving Alek plenty of room to follow.

As soon as he shut the door behind himself, Alek grabbed the bottle of what I assumed to be champagne and filled two glasses. "Here," was all he said before handing me one. I watched as his tattooed throat bobbed, swallowing his drink in two gulps. He filled it again while he took a deep breath.

"This ball is going to be that bad?" I joked, taking a small sip from my own glass. The liquid was fizzy and sweet, definitely more appealing than the tequila.

Alek's eyes found my own. "The ball will be fine. It's my father who drives me to drink." He signaled to his now-empty glass and filled it again. "Every year he pushes me to find a suitable match. This year in particular, though, he's been rather pushy. He's threatening to remove my inheritance. He doesn't think I'm worthy of being part of this family or some shit like that. I'm hoping seeing you will finally shut him up."

I stiffened. "Does your father care that I'm a random girl you picked up at the bar? What if he doesn't believe we're actually in a relationship?"

He nodded. "That's why this is just the first of many events you'll be attending with me. This will take some work."

"*What?*" I replayed his words, making sure I heard them right. "You mean I'll have to attend *multiple* events with you? That wasn't our deal!"

"Our deal was that I'd show you the world if you help me fool my father. Fooling him will take time."

I silently cursed at myself for being so ignorant. I should have known a deal with a demon wouldn't be so simple.

"Your mother won't find out," Alek said after a second. "Us demons like our secrets. There are no cameras, no photos. These events are very exclusive. Anyone bringing a guest, like me, has to receive my father's approval. And he's not very generous, if you can imagine."

His voice morphed to a whisper as he finished the sentence. Natalie had emphasized that particular fact about demons and their secrecy, but it was a relief to hear it from Alek.

Although, I knew the itching paranoia would never completely vanish. There were too many questions still echoing in my head—ones I couldn't really explain to Alek. Not if my mother was just someone who worked with goddesses.

What if there are spies within the demon society? What if my mother has people reporting directly to her? What if someone has been following me this entire time?

A cool hand fell onto my wrist. "Relax, Lyra," Alek said. "I can feel you worrying from over here."

I took a long breath, but my exhale was audibly shaky.

"Your mother is really that strict?"

Where did I even start? "I've just begun to get on her good side," I sighed, which wasn't entirely a lie. "I don't want to screw anything up."

Alekzander's brows drew together, but he didn't push any further.

Twenty minutes later, we pulled up to a massive glass

building. Alekzander straightened in his seat and brushed his shirt down, ensuring there were no wrinkles.

It was bizarre to see a demon prince so disheveled. Alek was clearly strong and powerful, and after what I saw in the bar yesterday, I knew he held respect. Yet here he was, nervous to see his own father. Half of me wondered what had happened between the two of them to get to this point. It had to be something.

"Ready?" he asked. I nodded. "Let's go."

The driver swung the door open, and the silence of the car was immediately flooded with the roar of the crowd. Dozens of people suddenly started shouting Alekzander's name.

He held his hand out for me to join him.

This was it. This would be the moment that the public saw Alek was no longer on the market for a suitor. This would change everything for him, and it would be the start of me upholding my deal. The last twenty-four hours had completely changed everything for me, and this was going to be my new normal.

You're not the same Lyra you used to be, I reminded myself. *You can do this.*

I grabbed his hand and stood up out of the limousine.

When I moved to let go of his hand, though, he only squeezed tighter. "Here goes nothing," he whispered to me.

I took a long breath and attempted to relax. The screaming never stopped, nor did the amount of people yelling his name. I held my hand up to my face, attempting to hide from the dozens of eyes lingering on our every move.

"Who is that?" I heard a few people say. The crowd then filled with murmurs and whispers as to who the demon prince had shown up with.

"A human, maybe?" a few guessed. "She can't be that important if we've never seen her here before."

Alekzander pulled me close to him as we walked toward the large glass doors. I was suddenly grateful for how tall he was; he easily towered over every other person in the crowd, which made it easy to maneuver through them.

"Let me do the talking," he reminded me. *As if that would be an issue.*

And then we were inside.

Long, black diamond chandeliers hung from the towering ceilings of the ballroom. Ice sculptures and circular tables surrounded by red velvet chairs littered the space ahead, accompanied by a massive stage with a throne centered upon it.

I had never seen anything so elaborate—so *regal*—and it took a ridiculous amount of effort to maintain my composure.

The rest of the people inside were already busy mingling, eating, and dancing. We were clearly late, but Alek didn't seem to mind. Violin music drowned out the shouting that echoed from outside.

"What is this event for again?" I asked.

"It's the tenth anniversary of my father's reign as king of demons," he whispered back.

I nodded as Alek tugged on my hand, pulling me further inside.

"Alekzander!" a young, female voice yelled toward us. I spun my head around to find a tall blonde woman with the same eyes I was now realizing belonged to most demons. "I didn't think you'd actually show. Who's this?"

The girl's eyes hovered over every single inch of me, lingering over Alek's hand still holding mine. Normally, I would flinch away from such direct attention, but Alek's date needed to be convincing, which meant I had to act like I belonged here. I lifted my chin and stared back at the woman.

"This," Alekzander announced, "is my date. Lyra."

Shock and disbelief flashed across the woman's face. "Lyra," she muttered. "It's a pleasure to meet you." I shook her outstretched hand with a smile before the woman turned back to Alek. "I wasn't aware you were bringing a date." The words were cheerfully forced through a fake smile of gritted teeth.

Alek's hand moved to my waist. I tried to relax under his touch, but every ounce of my body was aware of him. I had never allowed anyone to touch me this way. *Can he feel it? Can he feel how nervous I am?*

"Lyra and I have been seeing each other for a while now," he stated. "I figured now was as good of a time as any to introduce her."

Her jaw fell open. "So things are pretty serious with you two?" she asked. Alek nodded. "Wow, I have to say, you'll be breaking hearts all over the city tonight."

Alek's body vibrated as he chuckled. "It was nice seeing you," he said as he began to turn us away. "I have a few others to introduce Lyra to. Please excuse us."

Her romantic interest in Alek was clear in her long glance after him, and I couldn't help but smile. Maybe this night wouldn't be all that bad, after all.

"There are plenty of snakes in the grass, Lyra," Alek whispered to me as we walked through the crowded ball-room. "One down, hundreds to go."

And he wasn't wrong.

Over the next hour, Alek introduced me to dozens of

different high-standing individuals—some I recognized from Natalie's ramblings about demon politics, but most were strangers. We walked from table to table, and I stayed silent as Alek did the talking. He repeated the same speech every time, discussing how we met and how our relationship was quickly growing more serious.

My nerves eased over time. I soon relaxed into my role as Alek's fake date.

While the shock on everyone's faces was worth it, I began to wonder what type of person he really was if everyone was *this* shocked that he brought a date.

And in the very depths of my mind, the thought of my mother's face kept rearing its ugly head. She would be much more shocked than anyone here—and much more enraged.

I clenched my jaw. My mother would kill me if she knew I was doing this. *I was ruining the family name,* she would tell me. *I should be more careful, someone will find out who I really am.*

"Up there," Alek whispered to me, pulling me from my thoughts. "That's him."

I looked to where he was talking about, and my stomach sank.

At the end of the ballroom on the stage, sitting on a massive red and black throne with iron snakes surrounding it, was the demon king. Alek's father.

"I'm going to vomit," I mumbled.

"Stop it," Alek hissed, moving his hand up to grip my upper arm. "This is what we came here for, Lyra. Hold it together. This has to be convincing. For both of our sakes."

I nodded and gulped down the rush of emotion. He was just a man. A demon man, no less, but a man. And he was Alek's father.

That shouldn't be scary. Other than Alek, though, I couldn't remember the last time I'd had a real conversation with a man.

What if word got around that this entire thing was a sham? What if he knew I was a fraud?

I shut my eyes and fought against the panic. *Calm and collected*, I reminded myself. *You're Alek's mysterious date. Act like it.*

"Fine," I said. "Let's get this over with."

Alek eyed me for a second longer, almost to see if I was really up for the task, before leading me up to the front of the stage. My dress flowed on the steps behind me as we moved up and up, closer to the king of demons.

"Look who decided to show their face around here again," the demon king stated as we approached. I kept my eyes down, looking anywhere else but him.

Alek stepped forward.

"Father," he greeted. "I'd like you to meet my date, Lyra Sol."

I bowed my head in greeting. "It's a pleasure to meet you," I said.

When I lifted my head again, Alek's father was staring directly at me. His eyes—the same emerald green as Alek's—stared straight into my soul.

"Why are you here?" he snapped.

It took me a second to register his question. "Oh," I stammered. "I—"

"She's here because I invited her," Alek stepped in. "Lyra was nice enough to accompany me. We're getting to know each other quite well, actually."

He grunted a response. We both waited for him to speak, but he said nothing. Alek stood frozen next to me.

"If you need nothing else, Father, I suppose I'll get back to the party."

Alek turned to walk away, taking me with him, before his father barked his name. "Alek." We both turned, and I watched as his father grabbed Alek roughly by the arm. "Don't forget what you're really doing here."

What the hell was that supposed to mean?

Alek only nodded, and before I could even look at the demon king again, he was immediately pulling me back into the crowd.

"That went well," Alek whispered in my ear. "Better than I expected."

I scoffed, "You call that going well? Is he always so..."

"Yes," he finished. "He is."

"He didn't seem happy that I was here with you," I noted. Unless that was how he typically expressed his happiness.

Alek guided me to the champagne table and grabbed us both a glass. "He's just worried about me. That's all." He shrugged.

"Worried about you how? Because you're with me?"

Alek shrugged. "Something like that."

"You're very cryptic."

Alek looked at me again for the first time since we talked to his father. "And you're very curious. Curiosity killed the cat, you know." He took a sip, gazing at me over the rim of his glass.

I rolled my eyes. "It's a good thing I'm not a cat. And excuse me for wanting to know more about the man I'm forced to date."

The tattoo on his neck flexed as he took another drink. "The less you know, the better. Trust me."

Somehow, I didn't quite believe that.

"Can we leave now?" I asked. "Or do you have anyone else you'd like to parade me around for?"

I tried not to look at his mouth as he smirked. "Almost," he said. "Dance with me first."

The ballroom began filling with couples swaying closer together, moving their bodies to the sound of the music.

"Are you crazy?" I hissed. "I can't dance! And this is very different from dancing at the bar!"

"I'll show you." He finished his drink in one gulp. "It's not that different, and you seemed to be very competent at dancing last night. Come on."

I didn't have time to resist. Alek grabbed my wrist and pulled me after him, only stopping when we were in the middle of the crowd.

"Put your arms around my neck," he whispered. Heat was already flooding to my face, but I did what he said anyway. My hands fell awkwardly on the back of his neck.

Alek gripped my waist and pulled my body to his. I hated the way I gasped under his touch. Did he feel it, too? The electricity of his touch? *Of course he doesn't,* I thought. He was used to this. *I* was the odd one. *I* was the sheltered one.

"Good," he whispered. "Now, relax. Follow my lead."

"What does that even mean?" I hissed back. "I'm going to look like an idiot!"

That damn smile. "Trust me, you'll look even worse if you don't at least try. My father needs to believe we actually like each other, and everyone's watching."

A long breath escaped me. *Relax, Lyra,* I told myself. *He's just a guy. One dance won't kill you.*

I softened under his touch, letting the warmth of his hands on my bare back guide me. Our chests were nearly pressed together as he began to move, just barely, around the dance floor.

"Natalie told me magic would enforce a deal with a demon," I started, looking all around the dance floor but never at Alek. "What does that mean?"

I felt his breath on my cheek as he took another step, pulling me with him. "It means we're connected now. Imagine a small, invisible tether connecting my soul to yours. I'll be able to… sense you now. It's to ensure you could never escape our deal. You won't be able to run away."

I stole a glance at him. "That sounds… scary," I mumbled.

"Maybe," he said, his lips twitching with a smile, "but it could come in handy."

"Do you feel anything?" I asked. "Like, right now? Can you feel the tether?"

When he didn't respond, I met his eyes. It took all of my willpower to not look away. His gaze was as strong and intimidating as ever, but I was supposed to be his date. I was supposed to stare into his eyes, especially if his father was going to believe this.

His finger traced a small circle on my back. I shivered. "Do you want me to feel something?" he whispered. He traced another circle.

My mouth fell open. *Was he trying to flirt with me? Or was he just being an arrogant asshole?*

He glanced above my head for a second before saying, "We're being watched. Follow my lead."

He took one more step and dropped my body backward, pulling us into a low dip in the middle of the dance floor. My heart stopped beating.

I didn't even flinch as he brought his face down, sending chills through every inch of my body as he brushed his lips against my jaw.

But before I could panic, Alek's strong arms brought me back to his chest.

I didn't have to fake the laugh that escaped me. A thrill of adrenaline flushed my body. My arm hung over Alek's shoulder as he laughed, too.

To anyone else, I'm sure we looked like a romantic couple. My face was only inches from his, and I didn't back away as he spun us around once more.

I was certain he could feel how I reacted to him. To his touch.

"Do you think we convinced them?" I said after the song had ended. I pulled out of Alek's grasp.

"I think that was a pretty good start."

We finished up the evening after two more glasses of champagne and an endless amount of fake conversations with strangers.

The people, or the demons, did more than just fear Alek. They respected him. Almost everyone bowed their heads, just slightly, before approaching him to say hello. It was a subtle act, but I noticed.

I also noticed the way hundreds of eyes followed me around the room the entire night. I was half-tempted to cross my arms over my chest and cover up more skin, but Alek's hand in mine caused me to resist.

The hand in mine that didn't budge for the entirety of the night.

It was well past ten o'clock when he finally agreed to take me home. Alek helped me tighten my coat around my shoulders before holding open the glass doors.

"Hope you're okay with walking," Alek said, typing something on his phone. "My driver had an emergency. It's just a few blocks."

"Just a few…wait—how do you know where I live?"

He smirked. "You don't think I did my research on you, Lyra? I know a lot of things about you."

Alarms went off in my mind. If he knew about me… *no*. It wasn't possible. If he knew who my mother was, we would be having a very different conversation. He certainly wouldn't have brought me to meet his father. I was just paranoid.

We strolled down the dark street. "That's disturbing," I said. The words fell out of my mouth before I could stop them. "And once again, creepy."

Alek smiled, but I noticed how exhausted he looked. Dark circles now hung beneath those emerald eyes. When he didn't answer my snarky comment, I turned my attention toward the city around us.

Tall, sky-scraper buildings surrounded us. I couldn't help but stare at the scattered apartments that still had lights on.

I hardly left my apartment after dark. I hardly left my apartment at all, actually. Unless I were heading to school, which was mostly online these days anyway. Natalie was the only one who forced me to get out every once in a while.

The city was pretty at night. I had never noticed before.

My thoughts were interrupted when I stepped in a small crack in the pavement, twisting my ankle and completely busting my ass. My knees cracked against the concrete as the fabric around my knees ripped. Pain shot through my knee.

Alek was next to me in a second. "Shit, Lyra! Are you okay?" The genuine concern on his face shocked me. A hand was instantly on my knee, examining the blood that was already dripping from my skin. "Does it hurt?"

"No." My lie was easily discovered when he wiped the dripping blood away from my skin, causing me to hiss in pain.

"Come on," he insisted. "We're almost to your place."

I started to stand but Alek threw my arm around his neck and picked me up.

"I can walk!" I insisted. The remaining distance wasn't short, but it would definitely be difficult for him to carry me the entire way.

"No way," Alek argued. "I don't need you dripping blood everywhere. This is supposed to be a secret, remember?"

I shook my head and turned my attention back to the city, even as my entire being was electrified at every place my body touched his.

I tried to ignore the way his muscles flexed under my grip.

And the way I wanted to feel more.

"Not the front door!" I interrupted as my building came into view. "We have to go through the window. It's to the left."

He stopped walking. "Are you serious?"

"My mother has a camera set up to watch the front door. She doesn't know I left tonight. Window, please!"

He shook his head in disbelief but eventually carried me through the grass and over to the window. He lifted me up and through it with ease.

I only backed away from the window when Alek started crawling through. "You don't have to come in," I insisted. "I'm fine."

He ignored me entirely.

"Nice place," he said once he was inside. He pushed past me and surveyed the interior of my small living room.

It was weird hearing him say something so casual. "Um, thanks."

His eyes lingered on the photos of Natalie and I, and for a second, I could have sworn I saw him smile. "Sit up here so I can look at your knee." He motioned to the kitchen counter.

"I promise you I can take care of myself just fine," I repeated. Once again, he ignored me.

When I got close enough, Alek gripped my waist and lifted me onto the counter. I was absolutely certain I could have done that myself, but I also didn't stop his hands from lingering on my waist.

"Band-Aids are in that cabinet," I breathed.

Alek swiftly followed my instructions to find the Band-Aids but set them down beside me and grabbed a paper towel instead. He ran it under the kitchen water to dampen it. When he turned back to me, his face was completely serious. "This might hurt," he said. He slid one hand to the back of my knee, and with the other, lightly dabbed the bloody skin.

Yeah, it hurt like a bitch.

I instinctively kicked out, but he gripped my bare leg with strong fingers and held it down. "Easy there," he teased.

"Sorry," I whispered.

Alek smirked and returned to cleaning the wound. His brows drew together in focus as he wiped away every drop of blood. When he was done, he placed the Band-Aid on my knee carefully.

Goosebumps electrified my skin at the soft touch of his fingers.

"All done," he announced. His hands lingered on my knee, sending floods of heat through my thigh. "Do me a favor and don't tell your mother you were bleeding all over the city with me tonight."

His dark eyes met mine, the deep green in them seeing straight into my soul.

I laughed. "Theia won't be hearing about any of this. Don't worry."

"Theia?" he repeated. "You're on a first-name basis with your own mother?"

Shit. A chill ran down my spine. I cursed at myself for letting her name slip, but Alek didn't seem to register anything. He had no reason to be suspicious, anyway. I'm sure there were plenty of women named Theia living in the city. Why would mine be the Goddess of Light?

If only he knew. I hadn't considered that woman a mother in a very long time. "Something like that."

Alek's eyes darkened. I could tell he was curious, but he didn't push, and I didn't add anything else.

"I should get going," he said. "Are you okay here?"

"I'll be fine."

"Good," he said, walking toward the window. "I'll pick you up here tomorrow for your side of the deal. I'll have another demon event for you to attend later this week."

A groan escaped me. "How many events am I going to have to attend with you?"

"What?" he teased. "Tonight was so terrible?"

I questioned his words. "No, actually." *Shut up, Lyra.* "It wasn't."

Alek's eyes twinkled, and his mouth flashed a smile. "Good. I'll call you with the details."

"No way, my mother will know if you call me. That won't work."

Alek fished into his pocket and pulled out a small, ancient-looking cell phone. "Here," he said. "This is for you. My number's in it, and feel free to add your friend's."

I stared at his hand for a second, my mouth practically on the floor. "You're giving me a cell phone?"

"Consider it a loan. Your mother doesn't need to know everything we're up to, right?"

My chest warmed.

If Theia found out about this, I would no doubt be back in that basement with chains around my wrists.

But a small ball of fire in my soul told me to take it. Take the risk. Take the cell phone.

I reached out and grabbed it from his hand, pretending not to notice the way my skin brushed against his.

"Good girl." He smirked.

And then he was gone.

My knee was still warm where his hands had been.

Shit. I was in trouble.

Four

My eyelids grew heavier with each passing second until the darkness came back to me. I welcomed it as always and surrendered to the deep, peaceful sleep.

"You know you are a fool," my mother said to me. "You've been acting like you are in control, but you're not, are you? You are nothing, daughter. You don't have control here. You never will!"

I opened my mouth to speak, but something cold and heavy kept it shut.

My mother only smiled in amusement. "That's what you get for speaking up. Good luck telling your secret to anyone with your jaw bolted closed."

No, this couldn't be happening. The panic had already set in, spreading through my chest and clawing at my lungs. My mother had clamped a cold, metal mask over my face that restricted any movement in my jaw. I could hardly breathe, let alone talk.

I pleaded to her with my eyes. I wasn't going to tell anyone my secret! I had nobody to tell, and certainly no reason to tell them!

She began humming a song as she secured tight chains around my wrists and around my ankles. I looked for the window, the familiar window that had kept me sane all those times I had been chained up in the basement. But there was no window this time.

There was no light.

I looked to my mother again, but her face had morphed. She was no longer the achingly beautiful blonde woman who had raised me. Her face was gone entirely, replaced by a demonic, evil face of hatred.

The scream in my mouth became muffled by the iron shackles around my face that seemed to be shrinking.

"Not to worry, darling," she said, but her voice had changed, too. The words became a low roar of terror as she crawled closer to me. "Nobody will ever find you down here."

I tried to scream louder.

Nothing changed.

I pressed my back against the cold cement of the basement wall. I couldn't move far enough away from her—from it. The demonic creature that used to be my mother threw its nasty head toward the sky and laughed.

It didn't stop laughing. Not as I clawed at my ears. Not as I covered my eyes and tried to disappear.

This was my hell. This was my torture.

This was my punishment for being born.

▭

I woke up with a racing heart. My white bed sheets had been soaked in sweat, and the memory of my nightmare came to me in flashes of panic and horror.

Just a dream, I reminded myself. I wasn't going back there. I was safe, I was in my apartment. I wasn't in a basement. There was no metal mask over my face.

I ran my trembling hands over my mouth to make sure.

You're okay, Lyra.

My phone buzzed on my nightstand. When I picked it up, I had a message from Theia.

"Sleep well, daughter. Remember your purpose. – T"

Five

I spent all day wondering what Alek and I would be doing tonight. Another nightclub? More dancing? Drinks? Something entirely different?

After finishing a new book and cleaning my entire kitchen, I was antsy. I practically tore a hole in my kitchen floor from pacing back and forth before Alek texted me that he was waiting outside.

To avoid any questions from my mother, I snuck out the window again. If she ever put a camera out there, I would be totally screwed. Lucky for me, though, she hadn't thought of that yet. As long as she didn't come home from her work trip early, I would be safe.

Alek waited for me as I walked up. It was a little past eight and the sun had set, but I could still see him leaned against his matte black car with arms crossed. "Ready?"

"Ready for what? Are you going to tell me where we're going?"

"Nope," he said with a smile. He opened the passenger

side door and waited for me to get in. "You'll find out when we get there."

I rolled my eyes and tried to hide my bubbling excitement as I climbed inside.

Alek shut the door behind me before walking back to the driver's seat. "We have a bit of a drive, so I figured we could discuss what type of things you've been wanting to experience. What haven't you done before?"

I shrugged. "Everything, honestly."

Alek glanced over at me, his brow creasing. "What do you mean?"

"I haven't done much of anything. I rarely leave the apartment. I took college online. My mother monitors my apartment with a camera pointed directly at the front door. So any suggestions you have, it's likely that I haven't experienced it."

He shook his head and let out a low whistle. "Well, it's a good thing you met me, then. We'll start with the basics."

I snorted. "Basics?"

"Sure. We'll start with all of the stupid, reckless things everyone did in high school. The rites of passage that you missed out on."

"Really?" I questioned. "Like what? I can't imagine a food fight in the cafeteria is on the list."

Alek laughed. "No, what I have planned for us is much more fun than a food fight."

I relaxed into his passenger seat. "I have to say, I can't picture you throwing spaghetti at anyone."

He lifted his chin and surveyed his reflection in the rearview mirror. "No? Is it because I'm too polite and courteous?"

"Why do I have a feeling you're not as polite and courteous to everyone else you meet?"

When he smiled this time, my stomach flipped. "I'm as nice as I need to be. Us demons have a reputation to uphold, anyway."

"Is that what the tattoos are for, too?"

He glanced at me again as we drove out of the city. "Some are for looks. Others have deeper meaning."

I know I shouldn't have pushed, but I did anyway. "Like what?" I asked.

"You sure do ask a lot of questions."

I shifted in the seat. "I have years of information gathering to catch up on. Can you blame me?"

"No," he said after a few seconds. "I guess I can't."

"So? Your tattoos?" I pressed.

Something dark washed over his face. "That's a conversation for another time."

I nodded, picking up on his hint. We drove in silence for the next thirty minutes. I didn't prod him with any more personal questions for the rest of the ride, although my brain erupted with them as the car rolled to a stop.

We were in the middle of nowhere, definitely outside of the city. Towering trees shadowed the bright moonlight that filtered through the dying leaves. Not a single light from the city surrounded us. The surrounding forest bustled in a darkness that became oddly comforting.

"We're here," Alek said.

"Are you kidding?"

"Not in the slightest." He grabbed a bag from his backseat and flung it over his shoulder before getting out of the car. "Let's go."

In the midst of the darkness, I could see the moon's reflection on the water in front of us. He had driven me all the way to the lake.

"This looks like the type of place you take a girl when you're about to murder her and dump her body where nobody's going to find it!"

"If I killed you now," he said with a grin, "what would my father think? You're safe, Lyra. You have a deal to uphold, remember?"

I knew I should have been alert about being in the woods with practically a stranger, but all I felt was excitement. I crawled out of the car and shut the door behind me. Alek was already spreading a blanket out on the grass before us.

"What is this?" I asked.

"This is tonight's date."

The way he said *date* made my chest tighten. I knew this was just part of our deal, but I would never experience a real date. I would never be taken out. I would never be normal. My mother had made sure of that.

But I could pretend. That's all we were doing, anyway. Pretending. For tonight, I could be someone else.

Alek sat on the blanket and motioned for me to join him. I obliged, moving to sit on the other side of the thick quilt. The fabric was smooth compared to the rough grass poking underneath. I picked at a loose thread, unsure of what to do with my hands.

In silence, the forest around us illuminated. Some sort of animal howled in the distance, not far enough away to make me any less uncomfortable. Other critters scavenged the foliage around us but stayed hidden from sight. I didn't blame them. I'd been doing a lot of hiding recently, too.

Once the lights of his car flickered off, I could hardly see a thing. Alek fumbled for a second and turned on a small lantern beside us. As soon as he did, my stomach erupted in butterflies. It wasn't just that we were sitting so close together on this quilt, although I was acutely aware of exactly how much space sat between his hand and mine. It was also a small, thrilling trickle of adrenaline releasing into my veins.

I wasn't nervous at all, I realized. I was excited.

A cool breeze rustled the sticks and leaves around us. A stray piece of my red hair flew in front of my face, and I froze as Alek picked up his hand, reaching for it.

But he stopped himself and returned his gaze to the moonlight reflecting off the water ahead. I immediately stiffened, returning my attention to the loose thread on the blanket.

"Sitting in the dark?" I asked. "That's what we drove all the way out here for?"

Alek leaned back, laying down and stretching his long, toned legs out over the quilt. "Stargazing," he said quietly. "Look up."

I waited a second longer while I stared at him. In the dim lighting of the lantern, I could only see half of his face. His hands tucked into the pocket of his black sweatshirt, and his eyes flickered around the sky as he continued to look upward.

He must have felt me staring, because he said, "Eyes up there, not on me."

Red-hot embarrassment crept up my neck, and I was suddenly grateful that he couldn't see me blushing.

I mimicked him, lying backward on the quilt and staring up at the sky.

When my eyes settled on the sky, an audible gasp escaped me.

"It's beautiful, isn't it?" Alek whispered. But beautiful didn't come close to describing the view. The sky drowned in stars. Orbs of light of every size littered the darkness, creating a maze that turned and weaved throughout the entirety of the night.

It was breathtaking, and yet it was also deeply, deeply sad.

I fought back tears as they approached. Twenty-two years of living, and I had never seen the stars. Not like this.

"You have to leave the city to see them this bright," Alek explained. "I come out here every once in a while just so I don't forget what they look like."

I understood that. My chest tightened even further at the thought that I would forget this. Maybe not tomorrow, maybe not next week. But years and years from now, tucked tightly in Theia's grasp, I would forget about this sea of magic before me.

"What do you think is out there?" I whispered.

Alek hummed as he thought. I could feel the vibrations of his rumbling voice. "Peace," was all he said.

I didn't ask him another question. He didn't say anything, either. We stayed that way, staring off into the darkness for what felt like hours.

I could have stayed there my whole life.

But after a while, Alek sat up. "What are you doing?" I asked.

He began pulling his hoodie up and over his head. "The second half of the evening. Considering we don't have years to bestow experiences upon you, we have to double up." He threw his hoodie onto the blanket and began fumbling with the belt on his jeans.

"What the hell are you doing?" I sat up but I didn't look away. My eyes lingered on his sculpted abs until he actually began pulling his jeans off.

"Going for a swim," he answered. "Come on."

"What?" I shielded my eyes with one hand as I heard his jeans hit the quilt. "It's freezing out!"

"All the more reason to hurry!" he yelled, but he was already running toward the lake. I looked up just in time to see him splash into the dark water.

"Are you crazy?" I hissed, although I wasn't sure why I was trying to keep my voice down. We were likely the only people for miles.

"Yes," he answered, splashing around in the water. "But that's irrelevant. Get in!" He sent a wave of water in my direction with his hand.

"I can't swim, you idiot!" I tried to dodge the water as it flew in my direction but failed miserably.

"Look," Alek said, standing up in the lake. Half of his chest rose up from the surface. "It's not deep at all. Come in, or I'm coming to get you."

Part of me wanted to get back in the car and drive away immediately. But the other part of me—the dark part of me that longed for adventure—screamed for me to jump in.

I chose to listen to that voice.

I looked around us, making sure we were actually alone before pulling my sweater over my head. I threw it on top of the lantern, making sure Alek couldn't see me as I stripped down to my bra and underwear.

The night air was absolutely freezing. I avoided thinking about how cold that water would be as I ran forward.

And jumped in.

As soon as my body hit the water, I wanted to scream. The cold temperature froze me immediately, shocking my system. I forgot how to move, how to breathe, how to think.

Until Alek's hands found me in the water and pulled me up.

"Hey," he said as I broke the surface. He held onto both of my shoulders. "Are you okay?"

I nodded, too stunned to speak for a few seconds until I caught my breath. His hands were shockingly warm, even in the frigid water. "It's cold in here," I said.

Alek laughed. "Yeah, it is. So swim around a little and we can check this off the list before you get hypothermia."

"How are you not freezing?" I asked. As soon as he removed his hands from my body, I missed their warmth.

"I'm not human, remember?" he said, clearly amused at my question.

I stuck my hands out, feeling the frigid water around me. I had to admit… something about floating in the dark water in the middle of nowhere felt liberating. The cold water numbed my senses and halted my thoughts. For once, I wasn't concerned about getting caught. I wasn't thinking about that basement. I wasn't picturing those chains.

I was just… swimming. Half-naked in ice cold water with a near stranger.

And it felt damn good.

Alek swum up next to me and grabbed me around the waist before hauling me through the air. I screamed and landed in the water a few feet away.

When I broke the surface again, Alek was laughing.

"You jerk!" I yelled. I pushed myself over to him and

jumped onto his shoulders, sending both of us under the water.

This time when I surfaced, we were both laughing. "See?" Alek questioned. "This is what fun looks like. It's not so bad."

"Maybe not," I replied. "But I'm freezing cold."

"Alright, I guess this counts. Although, typically you should stay in until your lips turn blue."

"I can't even feel my lips," I retorted. "They're definitely blue."

Alek surprised me by reaching out and grabbing my chin with one hand, holding my face still while he took a long, deliberate look at my lips. The heat of his hand on my face spread through my core like a wildfire.

I stared at him in awe while he took his time observing the color. "Yep," he said after a while. "Definitely blue."

I splashed him and pushed myself back toward the edge of the lake.

As the two of us crawled out of the water, I became acutely aware of my now soaking-wet bra and underwear. I only caught Alek staring once, and the heat in his eyes nearly made me melt. He waited a few seconds before he jogged ahead of me, running to the trunk of his car. I followed.

"Here," he said, pulling a towel from the trunk. I stood, shivering, while he wrapped it around my shoulders. "We'll dry off a little and then hit the road. It'll be late by the time we get back to the city." He got a towel of his own and wrapped it around his own body before starting the car. We both dried off for a few minutes before pulling our clothes back on and heading back into the city.

On the way home, I stared at the stars out the window until the city lights drowned them out. I promised myself I would try to remember.

Until I could see those stars again, I would try to remember how beautiful the middle of nowhere could be.

I ordered a pizza for delivery, making sure the security cameras caught Natalie coming inside before it arrived. My mother hadn't seen me on the camera in a couple of days, and she had been suspiciously quiet over text.

That part sucked the worst. Not knowing if she was going to bust through my front door at any given moment.

What if she had known what I was doing? What if she knew where I was last night?

There's no way, I thought to myself. If she knew what I had been up to, I would already be back in her basement with chains on my wrists.

Everything was fine. Everything would be okay.

"I've never seen you like this," Natalie said with a mouth full of bacon pizza. "I mean, look at you! You're glowing!" She waved a hand at my face.

"Oh, shut up," I muttered. "I am not!"

"You totally are!" She uncrossed her legs and leaned

closer to me on the couch. "Tell me, what was it like? Did he kiss you again?"

"No, we didn't kiss. And we won't. This is all part of the deal I made with him, nothing more."

She squinted her eyes. "A man doesn't take you stargazing and skinny dipping at night because it's part of some deal. He does it because he likes you."

I could feel my cheeks heating, but I couldn't stop it. Natalie and I had never had conversations like this before. Not when I was the subject, anyway. We had spent days and days gossiping about Nat and whatever poor soul had been sucked into her traps lately, but I was always the listener. I was always the bystander.

"He was nothing but respectful," I said, taking another bite of my pizza with a noncommittal shrug. "And I don't foresee anything changing in that regard."

Natalie finally leaned back on the couch, but I could feel her lingering eyes. "Can you imagine what Theia would think if she found out?" I stopped chewing and snapped my attention to her. "What?" she asked defensively. "I'm just saying!"

"No, I can't even think about that. Thinking about Theia finding out would literally paralyze me at this point."

"What happens when this is all over?" she asks. "When your deal is done and Alek goes back into the shadows of the demon world?"

I shifted uncomfortably. "I don't know. I try not to think about that, either."

Natalie nodded and picked up the remote for the TV. "I just don't want to see you get hurt. By Theia or by Alek, for that matter."

Her words warmed my chest in a way I couldn't even explain. "I know you don't," I said after a few seconds. "Me, neither."

58

When Alek told me that our next outing was at a shooting range, I nearly fainted.

"Absolutely not," I groaned.

"It's fun. Trust me. I go all the time, and if you're going to be hanging around demons, you need to learn how to be around a weapon. This could be a great experience for you."

"Trust you around a room full of loaded weapons and strangers shooting? No thanks."

"You won't have to shoot anything. My father will be there, and so will plenty of the Night Ravens. We'll make an appearance, I'll shoot a gun once or twice, you'll pretend to be completely encapsulated by my skills, and we'll leave."

"I have a feeling it won't be that simple."

"I'll pick you up at five."

And at exactly five, I was crawling out my window once again to get into this demon's car.

What the hell is my life turning into?

I had chosen to wear a casual pair of jeans and a black

hoodie. For whatever reason, I felt like I fit in more with Alek when I was wearing dark clothing.

Alek must have noticed this too, because he smiled as I walked up to the car. "Now you definitely look like you're prepared to shoot somebody."

"Don't get any crazy ideas. There's no way I'm even touching one of those things."

He opened the door for me with that same stupid grin on his face. "We'll see."

This shooting range, as Alek described it, was another one of the demon-owned establishments. It was only a few blocks away from Night Raven, and it was exclusive to legion members only.

Alek explained that the legion was essentially the pack of demons under his father's rule. They formed a tight-knit brotherhood, and they conveniently called themselves Night Ravens. Together, they ran a few businesses. Some legal, and some not-so-legal. Although he refrained from diving into detail when I asked him to explain the illegal parts of their operations.

Even in the cold temperatures, my nerves heated my body. I reached forward to turn the air off in Alek's car, but he did the same. Our hands collided in the center, and his rough fingers intertwined with mine. His touch electrified me before I yanked my arm back, even more blood rising to my face.

Alek chuckled, which only caused me to blush further. "If you wanted to hold my hand, you could have just asked."

I rolled my eyes, and we drove in silence the rest of the way as I tried to calm my breathing.

"What if I get shot?" I asked as we pulled into the

parking lot. "What if someone misfires or tries to get rid of me?"

"There's barely anyone here," Alek said. "And we all shoot at targets. It's very safe." He got out of the car and walked around to open my door.

"Fine," I conceded, biting back nerves as he extended a hand to me. Taking it, I climbed from the car, adding, "But if anything goes wrong, I'm out of here."

"Great," he said. He walked to the trunk and grabbed a black bag. "Good plan." He winked at me and began heading toward the small brick building.

I could see how this place was kept so discreet. From the looks of it, anyone else would think this was a worn-down, abandoned brick building. It was small, too, only one story high in the midst of the city.

Alek pulled the rusty white door open and waited for me to walk through.

The loud sound of guns firing in the distance only increased my nerves. I logically knew these things were probably safe for most people, but these were *demons*. They didn't play by human rules.

Deadly creatures with deadly weapons.

I pushed my fingernails into my palms, focusing on the sharp pain rather than the nerves that built inside of me.

But Alek threw his arm around my shoulders and pulled me close to his side as we walked into the dark building. "Don't forget, we're in a loving, committed relationship."

"How could I possibly?" I said with an annoyed tone, but heat flushed to my face.

The small room we entered was some sort of viewing room. Glass windows covered the far side of the wall, and through those, we could see small stalls with targets. Three demons were inside shooting—including Alek's father.

"Come on." He pulled a large, bulky pair of headphones from his black bag and secured them over my head. "These should help with the noise."

I gave him a small smile and adjusted them over my ears as we walked to the entrance of the range.

As soon as the door opened, all eyes turned to us.

"Father. Kylar. Blade. Nice to see you." Alek spoke differently when he addressed them. The tiny hint of humanity that I had identified was gone, glossed over by an emotionless mask. The two demons, Kylar and Blade, seemed absolutely dumbfounded at our presence. Alek's father, however, didn't even blink. He rolled his eyes and returned to shooting.

"Wow," Kylar said. "How long has it been since you've practiced your shooting? It's been years since I've seen you in here."

"I don't need the practice," Alek replied smoothly. He walked over to one of the booths, not removing his arm from my shoulders until we were there. Dropping the bag on the small, metal chair, he unzipped it and pulled out a few weapons—more than I anticipated.

Anxiety bit at me and I turned away just in time to nearly bump into Blade as he approached, leaning a shoulder on the doorframe.

"And who's this?" Blade asked. "Bringing your toys to the shooting range now?"

Alek set his gun down and turned to face them, shielding me partially with his body. "Lyra and I are together now. She's welcome anywhere I go."

"Together?" The boys blinked. I tried not to cower as

both pairs of bright eyes slid over to me. They were nothing like Alek's eyes, though. Nobody's could be. "As in…"

"We're dating," Alek said. "Does that answer your question?"

The two demons stiffened.

"Enough chatter," Alek's father said from behind us. "We're here to shoot, not gossip like schoolgirls."

Conversation ceased with the command in his tone. I avoided looking at Alek's father, although I could feel him glaring at me for a few more seconds before turning back to his target.

"Shooting is easier than it looks," Alek explained, loud enough for only me to hear through my headphones. He slid the magazine of bullets into the bottom of the gun. "Just point." He pointed. "And shoot." He shot, which echoed throughout the room.

Even with my headphones taking the blunt of the sound, I could feel the vibration in my bones. I jumped, just slightly.

Alek paused for a second, scanning my face before giving me a small wink. "This is how the professionals do it," he said. He raised the gun again. I watched as his forearms flexed, tightening his grip on the gun as he pulled the trigger. Again. And again.

He didn't stop until the magazine emptied.

When my adrenaline subsided, I looked at the target.

He had shot multiple bullets, but only one thick hole remained on the target. And it was directly in the center.

A whistle came from the boys to our left.

"Impressive," they said. "Now let's see what type of damage your pretty little girlfriend can do."

Alek's jaw tightened, but he looked at me with brows

raised. My eyes widened, my head already shaking. I took a step back and he stepped forward, nodding.

"No!" I hissed at him. "Absolutely not!"

"It's easy," he replied. "Here." He stepped toward me and held the gun out.

Clenching my teeth, I stepped closer to him, aggravated. I knew this day would consist of more than just watching Alek shoot a gun at a target.

Alek grabbed my hand and placed the gun in my palm. It was heavier than I expected. I had to use my other hand to secure it in my grip.

I stepped up to the small table, raising the gun to eye level. He chuckled behind me, sliding his hands down my arms to cup my palms and shadow my movement. My breath hitched as he pressed his chest into my back until I could feel his heart pounding lightly in his chest.

He easily could have felt my heartbeat, too. Although mine raced wildly.

"Good," he said. He used his hands to adjust my grip, just slightly, while pulling back an inch. "When you're ready, move your finger to the trigger and pull slowly."

"Are you sure?" I breathed.

He laughed quietly. "Just try not to kill anybody."

It wasn't exactly a boost of confidence, but with Alek standing so close behind me, I didn't have a choice. I rolled my eyes, taking a deep breath to calm myself before I moved my finger to the trigger.

And pulled.

Alek's hands tightened around me, protecting me from the kickback of the gun.

When I looked at the target, relief flooded me. It wasn't in the center of the target—not even close.

But it did hit the target.

I spun around to Alek, unable to hide the smile on my face. "Did you see that?" I asked. "I actually did it! I actually shot a gun!"

He was smiling just as much as I was. "You sure did. You're a natural. Let's see you do it again."

I returned to my shooting position. This time, Alek let me hold the gun on my own. "Spread your legs," he ordered. I jerked back to him, anger flushing my cheeks. Alek only cocked his head, releasing a low laugh. He stepped a little closer, enough to make my heart leap into my throat. I craned my neck to look up at him, and he lowered his face to mine. "Spread your legs." His foot nudged the inside sole, urging my feet apart. "For balance, Lyra."

Embarrassment flooded me, and I cleared my throat as I turned back to the target. Alek leaned down and whispered, his breath tickling my skin, "Aim." I aimed. "And shoot."

I shot the gun.

I hit the target again, closer to the center this time. Adrenaline and excitement rushed over me. I couldn't help but turn to Alek, waiting for his reaction. His look of approval sent a thrill through me, and I stifled a smile as I turned back to the target.

We continued the same thing. Alek gave me a few tips here and there, but otherwise he freely let me shoot his gun at the target.

After a few minutes, the other demons in the room ignored us.

"Ready to go?" Alek asked after a while.

"I don't think my body can handle any more adrenaline." I rubbed my hand over my heart for emphasis.

He zipped up his black bag. "You better get used to it. Demons run on adrenaline."

I raised a brow. "Is that so?"

He grabbed my hand, mindlessly interlocking his fingers with mine, before starting toward the door. "Stick with me long enough and you'll see."

I smiled at him, and it wasn't at all fake. I had completely forgotten I was even supposed to be acting, I was supposed to *pretend* to be having fun. Because for the last thirty minutes, I was genuinely happy to be there with Alek.

"Where are you two off to?" His father stopped us before we left the building.

I noticed the way Alek stiffened. His hand tightened in mine, and he lifted his chin slightly as he replied, "I'm taking Lyra back home. We just came to shoot a few rounds."

His father stared back at him. I could see the similarities between the two of them now. Alek was only a few inches taller than his father, but their tanned skin matched, along with their black, flowing hair. Even the loose strand of hair that sometimes hung down Alek's forehead belonged to his father, too.

Something silent passed between them. I was sheltered, sure, but I wasn't a complete idiot. I watched as the demon king's eyes darkened. They didn't leave Alek, though. I half-expected him to say something to me, to acknowledge me in some way.

But he didn't

"Let's go, Lyra," Alek said to me. This time, we weren't interrupted as we left the building.

"What was that about?" I said once we were inside Alek's car.

"Nothing." His jaw tightened.

"Does he not like me or something?" I hated that I even asked the question. I hated that deep down, I cared.

My mother hadn't loved me for years. She hadn't even liked me. Maybe she thought she did, but chaining your daughter up and forcing her to stay with you isn't love. It's control.

"It's not you he doesn't like," he said. "My father isn't exactly a warm individual. We haven't gotten along since…" He stopped himself. "It's been a while. That's how a typical interaction goes between us."

His eyes were glued to the road in front of him. "He seems like a real nice guy," I joked.

Alek smiled, but it was forced. Over the few hours we had spent together, I had learned which of his smiles were real and which were fake. His real ones lit up his entire face in a way that made me want to smile too.

"Look," he said. "It's going to take more work than I thought to convince him this is real between us."

My stomach flipped. "Okay… like what?"

He took a long breath. "There's an event at Night Raven this weekend. I wasn't going to bring you but… it might be best if you're there."

"What type of event? Another dance?"

"No," he said cautiously. "It's not a dance."

The way he answered made the hair on my neck stand up. "Okay, then what is it?"

"It's a bit of an initiation. I can't explain much, other than it could be pretty intense. You'll be with me the entire time, and I won't let you out of my sight. Think you're up for it?" He looked at me for the first time since we got in the car.

I rubbed my sweaty palms on my jeans. "Do I really have a choice?"

Eight

I hadn't been able to get ahold of Natalie before it was time for the next event at Night Raven. I wanted to ask her about it, to see if she knew anything about a demon initiation ritual.

But I was going in completely blind.

"Is your father going to be here?" I asked Alek.

"No, he doesn't come to the bar unless it's an emergency. This is more of an intimate gathering with close friends and Night Ravens."

"Wow," I groaned, ignoring the nerves igniting in my stomach. "Sounds like the exact type of place I should *not* be."

"Nobody will mess with you, if that's what you're worried about."

I *wasn't* worried about that, at least not until he mentioned it, but the gesture of his protection was surprisingly sweet.

"And I have to be here because...?"

"It's not just my father who needs to believe we're

together. He has… minions. People who report to him. It wouldn't even surprise me if some of my own brothers were spying for him."

Wow. "Tight crew," I teased.

Alek rolled his eyes. "It would be seen as odd if we were together and I didn't invite you to this. People would get suspicious, and my father would be pawning me off to the next match he sees fit again. This event happens once a year, and it's sort of a big deal. So at least act like you aren't repulsed by every demon in here tonight."

"Fine," I grunted. "But if you make me do something weird like drink blood or summon an evil creature, I'm leaving."

The corner of his mouth lifted a centimeter before he recovered, re-assembling the emotionless mask that he wore whenever we were in public. "Deal."

Alek walked me into the bar through the front doors. Instead of the usual club music and the long line of freshly twenty-one-year-olds, the place was eerily quiet. "Is anyone here?" I asked as I stepped inside.

There was not a single person in sight.

"You think we would have our sacred, ritualistic Night Raven events where anyone with peering eyes like you could watch?"

I scoffed, "I don't have peering—"

"Sure, you don't," he joked. "Basement's that way." He pointed to the corner of the bar, where a black door that nearly blended in with the wall appeared. I hadn't noticed that before.

"Why do I have a weird feeling I'm walking into my worst nightmare?" I mumbled to myself.

A cool hand fell onto my lower back, sending chills down

my arms and up my neck. "Don't worry," Alek whispered in my ear. "You're untouchable."

Tonight would be the night that I found out exactly how true those words were.

As soon as he opened that hidden door, the loud thumps of the club music rattled my bones. *Yep, that sounds more like it.*

Alek stepped through first, grabbing my hand and pulling me behind him down the dark, dimly lit basement stairs.

I was half-expecting some sort of frat house, neon-lit cement room. But what I found instead was a large room, even bigger than the one upstairs, with a massive bar, leather and velvet seats, twinkling lights across the ceiling, and…

Demon. Dozens of demons.

"These are all demons?" I whispered to Alek.

His lips touched my ear when he answered, "Mostly, yes."

The realization dawned on me that I had been surrounded by demons my entire life. The creatures my mother warned me about time and time again, they looked like normal men and women.

Granted, these demons were infinitely more attractive than any of the men I had seen. But I had a very small frame of reference, and that was besides the point.

Alek was immediately greeted by someone, a tall man with blond hair and those same electric green eyes. They exchanged a few words I couldn't hear, then turned their attention to me.

"This is her?" the friend asked.

"Zac, meet Lyra. Lyra, this is Zac, one of my closest friends."

I let go of Alek's hand to shake Zac's. It was warm, and it matched his welcoming smile when he flashed his perfectly white teeth. "It's a pleasure to finally meet you, Lyra. I've heard so much about you."

I glanced back to Alek. "Talking about me much?"

Alek started to answer, but Zac cut him off. "Please, he can't shut up about you. Now I can see why."

"Lay off, Zac," Alek said. He placed a joking hand on Zac's chest and pushed him back a step. "I'm already working hard enough to keep the other guys around here at bay. Not you, too."

Zac stuck his hands up in surrender. "You got it, boss. Won't see anything but the utmost respectful behavior from me."

"Good," Alek said. "We're heading to our usual table. Grab some drinks from the bar and join us?"

"Right behind you," he said, slipping off into the crowd.

"He seemed nice," I said to Alek, who quickly grabbed hold of my hand again and stepped close to my side.

"He is. You can trust Zac. He's worked for me for years now, and he's never let me down."

I took note of that. Alek seemed to be on edge about a lot of the people in his life. His father, the other demons at the shooting range. Not Zac, though, which meant he was definitely trustworthy.

"Follow me. Let's go sit down." Alek began leading me through the crowd of demons toward the back of the room, where a large maroon velvet couch lined the back wall. "Here," he said, sliding into a spot at a large circle table.

I followed after him, sliding into the couch and looking out at the room around us.

"Is this table reserved for you or something?" I asked, noting the way that everyone else in the room practically avoided the space around us.

"Something like that," he answered with a smirk.

Once we were seated, I was able to take a close look at the company that surrounded us. The room was filled mostly with men, but a handful of women blended in with them. I found myself wondering which of them were demons, and which of them were… *something else.*

Zac slid in next to Alek, setting down three glasses and a large bottle of alcohol.

"So, are you ready for the blood bonding?" he asked as he made himself comfortable at the table.

He grunted when Alek elbowed him beneath the table. I waited for him to explain what the hell he was talking about, but when he didn't, I shook my head. Did he just say *blood bonding?* "The *what?*"

Alek cleared his throat and reached for the bottle. "No," he started as he poured my glass full to the rim. "I hadn't had the chance to explain that yet."

"Great," I mumbled. "That sounds totally normal and not at all freaky."

"Don't worry," Zac said, but the mischievous look in his eye told me to do just the opposite. "I think you're in good hands tonight."

My attention snapped to Alek. "What's the blood bonding?"

Alek only rolled his eyes and took a drink from his glass, as if it were annoying that I even asked. I lifted an eyebrow and waited for his response.

"It's something we've done for decades," Alek explained. "It's a way to share a bond. We blood bond when anyone new enters the group, it's a way to prove loyalty and show you're an established member of the legion. You bond with one member specifically, but we all see you as part of us."

"And what's my part in this?" I asked in a sharp whisper. "Because I'm not a demon, and I'm most definitely not a part of your *legion*."

Alek's eyes darkened. "Except that you are," he whispered with an equally sharp voice. "Because I told my father you were part of this legion. So unless you want to break our deal, you'll suck it up. Nothing will happen to you; I have a plan."

My jaw clenched instinctively. "I can't *actually* become part of your legion, Alek," I hissed. "You think my mother really won't find out about this? You're wrong!"

"I'm not wrong," he hissed back. "New legion members are kept highly confidential. Nobody will even hear your name for six months. Besides, this is all for show. Remember?"

I took a long breath, trying to decide if I could trust what he was saying or not.

Alek must have read my thoughts, because he leaned in and said, "If there was even a chance that your mother would find out, I wouldn't be doing this. I have something to lose here, too, sweetheart."

Shit.

I grabbed my glass and took a long drink of the sharp, bitter liquid. I was definitely going to need more of that.

The music cut a few seconds later, and an older man stepped into the middle of the room.

The entire crowd turned in his direction, aside from the

sound of a few glasses clinking against the wooden tabletops.

"Welcome, Night Ravens. It's time for our annual blood bonding night. Tonight is the night you'll prove your loyalty to the demon family and establish yourself as part of our legion. After this ceremony, our family will die for you, and you for them. This is not taken lightly, so if anyone is unsure about this decision, please leave now." He waited a few seconds. I shifted in my seat, waiting for an objection. To my surprise, nobody moved. "Good. You all know the rules. Have fun tonight. We're just getting started."

Alek's hand fell onto my shoulder. I didn't move it.

"You seriously weren't going to tell me about this?" I whispered in his direction. My heart pounded so fiercely, I could feel each beat in my ears.

"Relax," he whispered back, rubbing his thumb up and down my arm. "You're supposed to be enjoying this, remember?"

I ignored the feeling of his skin rubbing against mine and thought back to our plan.

If this was what it took to please his father, *I had no choice.*

I took another drink from my glass and focused my attention back onto the speaker in the center of the room.

"We are a brotherhood by blood, through and through. Our bond is the only thing that separates us from the monsters of this world. We are loyal, we are relentless, and we are free. Let's remember that as we celebrate each other tonight!" He raised his glass in a toast. "To the Night Ravens!"

"To the Night Ravens!" the entire bar repeated.

The music returned, and the entire basement of the bar seemed to erupt back to life. Music began beating so loudly again that I could feel every beat of the songs deep in my bones.

Alek didn't seem phased.

"Let's head to the bar," he said in my ear over the music. "There's someone here I want you to meet before this night gets started."

I didn't ask him to clarify. This night was overwhelming enough already. I slid out of my seat and waited for Alek to lead me through the crowd. We shoved past dozens of sweaty bodies now talking just a tad bit louder than they had been before.

"Lyra," Alek said as he pulled me to the bar, "meet Salem. Salem is my sister."

Salem stuck her hand out from behind the bar. "Lyra!" she shouted over the music. "It's nice to meet you! I've heard so much about you!"

"It's nice to meet you, too," I shouted back.

Salem was entirely different from Alek. She had short, choppy blonde hair and the tips were dyed a bright blue color. She wore a skin-tight crop top, and her sculpted abs peeked out from beneath.

And I was starting to wonder what Alek had been saying about me behind my back.

Salem scurried down the bar, getting the drink orders from the dozens of others waiting. Alek moved to stand behind me, his massive frame shielding me from the surrounding drunks as he placed an arm on either side of my body, resting his hands on the bar.

I tried not to think about how close he was standing. And how the hair on the back of my neck stood up, even though the basement was getting warmer with every hot body crammed inside.

Salem was back in two seconds, and she slid Alek and I two shots. "Here! On the house." She winked.

"*My* house, you mean?" Alek retorted.

Salem only smiled, and she was gone as quickly as she appeared.

I grabbed my shot and spun around in the tight cage of Alek's arms. "She seems nice," I said. "Much nicer than you."

Alek leaned toward me to grab his shot, and his chest almost brushed against mine. "Very funny," he whispered. "Cheers, darling."

He clicked his glass against mine, and we both threw the shots back. *Tequila.*

When I opened my eyes again, Alek was staring at me. "What?"

"For someone who doesn't get out much, you can take a shot like a pro."

I shrugged. "Natalie must be a good teacher." I left out the fact that I was beginning to enjoy the heated burn of alcohol moving into my stomach.

He raised an eyebrow, but his attention was pulled away by something in the distance that I couldn't see. His body stiffened immediately, but he didn't back away from me. I could have sworn he leaned in even closer to me.

The crowd seemed to quiet down just a touch, as everyone's attention pulled in the same direction.

"What's going on?" I whispered.

Alek's jaw tightened. "Nothing we'll have to worry about," he whispered back. His arms retook their positions on either side of me. "You're with me tonight. Don't forget that."

It sounded like a cliche, predatory threat, but there was a hint of something in his voice that I couldn't quite recognize.

I could smell the tequila on his breath mixed with sandalwood as he bowed his head next to mine. "Look at me," he whispered so close that his lips brushed my ear.

My eyes met his. His brows were drawn together, and his eyes were darker than I had ever seen them.

The sound of the chaotic crowd around us grew silent as I stared into his emerald ocean eyes.

"What is it?" I breathed.

He scanned my face slowly, as if he had all the time in the world. I watched as his gaze flickered down to my lips, then back up to meet my stare. For a second, I thought he was going to kiss me.

For a second, my heart stopped.

"This is how you greet your oldest friends?" The two men from the shooting range walked up behind Alek, breaking whatever tension had built between us. He held my stare a beat longer before turning to talk to them, but he stood directly in front of me so I was hidden from sight. The space his body left suddenly felt cold.

"Blade. Kyler," Alek greeted.

"Surprised to see us again so soon?" Blade asked.

"Not at all," Alek responded. "It's just like you to show up where you're not wanted."

Blade laughed. His friend didn't say a word. "We're still part of this legion," he said, his voice holding a dangerous edge. "Don't forget that."

I could have sworn I heard Alek growl.

"What you said the other day must be true. If she's still around, you must actually be dating. Tell me, how did she get so lucky as to take big, bad Alek off the market?"

Alek seemed to stand even taller. "She's not your concern."

They peered around him, both of them taking their time getting a good, long look at me. I didn't cower this time, even as every screaming instinct told me to run.

You're untouchable, Alek had said.

"Move aside," Blade barked. "Let me formally introduce myself, since I wasn't able to at the range the other day."

Alek hesitated, and if there hadn't been chills on my arms already, I was sure there would be now. He waited another second before he moved to stand beside me.

Now that I could get a good look, Blade and Kyler looked exactly how I imagined them to. They were both tall, although not as tall as Alek, and they each had a few dozen tattoos scattering their exposed skin.

But Blade's electric eyes blared into me, and I almost looked away.

He stuck his hand out for me to shake. "Alek here has been trying to find a woman to put up with him for quite some time, you know."

I glanced to Alek, who only directed his gaze at Blade. "I've heard," I answered.

"What's so special about you, then?" Blade asked, taking a step closer.

Alek's hand fell onto my hip. His fingers squeezed lightly.

"What makes you think there's anything special about me?"

He shrugged. "It must take a special girl to impress the demon king. And to be included in the blood bonding. What's different about you, new girl?"

My heart was beating so hard, I was certain they could

all hear it. I had never been talked to like this by anyone except my mother. He was trying to intimidate me. Manipulate me.

Not today. Not here.

I lifted my chin and put the biggest bullshit smile I could manage on my face. "I don't know, Blade. Maybe the demon king isn't used to seeing competent, successful individuals around his son. Certainly, neither of you cross those boxes."

What the hell, Lyra? Why did you just say that?

I relaxed slightly when I heard Alek laughing. I found myself leaning into his body. "Now leave us alone," he said. "And stay away from Lyra."

Before turning away, Blade and Kyler both looked me up and down one last time, their eyes lingering in areas that made me want to retreat.

Alek's warm hand on my hip stopped me from cowering.

This is all just a show, I reminded myself.

This was part of the deal. Alek's world of demons would be intimidating; I knew that when I agreed to this.

They had no idea who I really was. *What my worth really meant.*

I would be safe with Alek.

Right?

"Hey," Alek said, shaking my shoulder lightly. His voice was shockingly gentle. "You okay?"

I nodded in response, not trusting myself to speak.

"Come with me," he whispered. "We should get out of here before the blood bonding starts. Trust me, you don't want to be a part of that." Alek grabbed my hand and began pulling me through the crowd.

We were heading to the same door we entered from

when the same man who spoke over the music earlier started a new announcement.

The music cut.

"Demons and darlings, let the annual blood bonding begin!"

Nine

The music returned with a boom, playing even louder than the first time.

Cheers erupted through the basement, and the already-dim lights grew even darker.

Adrenaline pumped through my veins, telling me to run. To hide. To get out of here.

But Alek's grip on my hand didn't budge.

"Okay," I said. "What's your big plan?" I could barely see through the crowd, but a few screams in the distance made the hair on my neck stand up.

People were being bitten.

"Just relax," he said. We were standing next to a wall now, luckily somewhat out of the crowd. "I won't bite you. We just have to pretend like I did."

"How do I pretend that?"

Alek put his hands on my hips and pressed me against the basement wall, bringing his body dangerously close to mine. "Nobody's paying attention to us," he whispered. "Stay quiet."

He rested his forehead against mine, mimicking the intimacy of the other blood bonds happening around us.

Until a pair of hands grabbed his shoulders and yanked him away.

"Back off, Blade!" he yelled.

"Are you not planning on biting your date, Alek?" Blade hissed, grabbing my upper arm and yanking me toward him. I stumbled into his large, sweaty body with a yelp.

"It's none of your damn business," Alek spat.

His words were strong, but I could tell we were in trouble.

Blade's grip on me tightened as he held me in front of his chest. "It is, actually," he growled. "Because this is the *blood bonding*. So if you don't bite her, I guess I will."

I closed my eyes, bracing myself for the pain. For the teeth that would sink into my flesh.

But instead, Blade was shoved away from me. I opened my eyes to see Zac tackling him to the ground with a force so strong, their bodies blurred from the speed.

Alek was at my side in an instant. His superhuman strength became evident when he pulled me to his side. "Are you okay?" he asked.

"I'm fine!"

"She hasn't been bitten!" Blade yelled from the ground.

Panic rose in my chest.

I knew where this was heading.

Alek may have planned on sparing me, but dozens of eyes were lingering on us now.

And Blade had exposed us.

I moved before I could think, before I could stop myself. I had lost my mind; that was the only explanation for what I did next.

I grabbed the front of Alek's shirt and backed up until I was pressed against the cold basement wall once more.

"What are you doing?" he whispered. He braced his arms on the wall behind me, shielding me from the rest of the dark room.

"It's okay," I whispered back. "Just do it."

I couldn't see the shock on his face, but I felt him tense. "Are you sure?"

"If you don't, he will," I stated. We both knew it was true. "And I have a feeling it will be much worse if he does it."

He rested his forehead against mine. My hands wrapped themselves around his waist as he moved to grip my chin with both hands.

"This won't hurt," he whispered. He slid a finger down my neck, across my collarbone, and gently tugged the fabric of my shirt to expose my shoulder.

I shivered.

Alek placed a soft, gentle kiss on the exposed skin there. I leaned harder against the wall behind me, grateful it was there to hold me up.

And then Alek's sharp fangs sank into my flesh.

A shot of pain pierced through my body, followed by a heavy, unexpected wave of euphoria. My eyes rolled back, my ears filled with a moan that could've been mine, but at that moment, I didn't care. Alek's hands kept me standing as my legs weakened, knees giving way with the stars that sparked my vision. His grip tightened as his teeth sank deeper and deeper.

Heat of adrenaline rushed through my body, and a very different type of heat settled low in my stomach. *What was he doing to me?*

And as quickly as it had started, it was over.

Blade mumbled some sort of disappointment behind Alek, but neither of us turned to look. The music still blared through the basement, and I was thankful for the dark lighting that concealed how red I knew my face would be.

Whatever I had thought a demon bite would be, *it wasn't that.*

I glanced down at my shoulder, finding Alek's perfectly placed teeth marks and a small trail of blood.

But it didn't hurt.

"I'm sorry, Lyra," he whispered, close enough that only I could hear. "I swear to you I didn't plan on going through with this."

My entire body trembled, either from the rush of what had just happened or from the shock of euphoria I felt when his teeth were inside of me.

Was that normal?

"Um, it's okay," I replied. My head buzzed, a mixture of the emotions that flooded my body seconds ago and the drinks from earlier. My entire body swayed, and I was sure I would have fallen if it weren't for Alek holding me up with a strong hand on my arm. Alek lifted the shoulder of my top and replaced it to its original position, ignoring the blood that would definitely be smeared underneath.

"It should heal fast," he promised. "And at least now I won't have to draw my bite indentations onto you next time we see my father."

I tried to laugh, but it sounded foreign.

"Come on," he said, guiding me back to the door. "Blade should leave you alone now. Let's get out of here."

We walked back up the stairs and out the front doors of the club.

The cool air shocked my body, snapping me back to reality.

I didn't want to face the truth of what had just happened. Alek, *a demon,* had just bitten me, which somehow meant I was now bonded to him. I placed a hand on my stomach. *I was going to be sick.*

"Is this permanent?" I asked him, motioning to my shoulder. He opened his mouth to respond but shut it quickly.

That was the answer I needed.

"The bond will last forever, yes," he said.

"What does that mean?"

"It means you're one of us. It means you're protected. You can trust us, and we can do the same to you. That's what it means."

"But you were the one who bit me. Does that change anything between us?"

Alek ran a hand down his face and through his hair. "I don't know," he answered. "I've never bitten anyone before. I can't tell if what I'm feeling is from our deal or from…"

What he's feeling?

My mind raced. This was all happening so fast. *I wasn't actually part of his crew, was I?* I was a fraud. A phony. If anyone found out about this, I would be dead.

"Were you bitten once?" I asked.

We both sat on the empty concrete sidewalk outside the bar. "Ages ago, yes."

"By who?"

"My father," he answered.

"Your father? But isn't that…"

Alek shook his head and laughed quietly. "It was painful and necessary. There was nothing enjoyable about it."

I crossed my arms over my stomach. Did he know how the bite had made me feel just now? Maybe that was part of our magical tether. Or maybe I had imagined the entire thing. "So your bite was different?"

He looked at me, his eyes a shade darker than usual. "Why?" he asked. "Are you saying that you liked it?"

Fire erupted in my stomach. He was teasing me, I knew that. But the danger in his eyes excited me. I had never felt this before. I had never felt this wild, this free.

My life had been a cage of protection. It was hardly a life, really. I wouldn't consider what I had done the past twenty-two years living. Especially the years with my mother…

I shoved the memory away.

Alek waited for an answer.

"It…it wasn't what I expected," I responded. "And since when do you have fangs?"

Alek ran a tongue over his sharp teeth for emphasis. "They're not real fangs, just a predatory defense."

"So you go around biting your enemies?"

"Only when necessary."

I took a long breath of the cool night air and let it calm my nerves. It wasn't Alek that excited me, I reminded myself. It was this life. This danger.

This deal with him was risky. Yet somehow, I was less afraid of my mother than I was before I had met him.

Natalie was right. I had to stop letting her control me. I made my own rules now. I could protect myself.

"Let me walk you home," Alek said after a few moments. "I've put you through enough trouble today."

I let him guide me the few blocks to my apartment. I tried not to think about his teeth in my flesh. I tried not to think about his hot body pressed against mine, or the way his hands felt on my skin.

If only my mother could see me now.

"It's not that bad," I argued. Natalie stared at the bite mark on my shoulder in utter disbelief.

"Well, it's not good, Lyra. I can tell you that much."

I pulled my shirt back over the healing wound, kicking my feet up on my coffee table. Natalie refilled her wine glass, and I could feel the disapproval oozing off of her.

"I didn't have a choice!"

Natalie sat back and looked at me with those big, brown, puppy-dog eyes. "He forced you to do this?" she asked.

"Kind of," I explained. "But not exactly."

She shook her head in disbelief. "You have to be more careful, Lyra," she whispered. "If anyone sees this, if your *mother* sees this—"

"Yeah," I cut her off. "I know."

Natalie was the only other person in the entire world who understood these consequences. When we were younger, she was the one I would cry to about my mother, about what she would do to me. Natalie had been my shoulder to cry on in the darkest of times.

Natalie was also the one person who would wonder where I was if I went missing. But because she knew who my mother was, and because she knew who I was… there was nothing she could do about it. At the end of the day, we were both daughters of goddesses. We didn't play by the same rules as everyone else.

"I swear, Nat, he didn't mean to," I said.

Why did I feel the need to defend him? Alek knew exactly what type of situation he was bringing me into. He might not have meant for me to get bitten, but he sure as hell risked it.

"If you trust that he's in this for the right reasons, I'll believe you," she said. "But the second he hurts you, Lyra, I'll kick his ass."

There was no way she could kick a demon's ass, but the determination in her voice made me smile. "Thank you. For everything, I mean."

We watched the rest of our movie in silence.

I had just begun to forget about the absolute hell I was living in until my phone buzzed. I glanced down to see another text from Theia,

"Work is keeping me for another couple of days. I hope you're behaving, dear Lyra. I would hate to have to resort to chains once more, but those days are behind us. –T "

I was an idiot to have forgotten. My throat grew dry, and no amount of water in the world would solve it.

Theia was the tight, suffocating parasite I would never be able to outrun. I could play house with this new life as much as I wanted to, but that would never change my reality.

Even with a bonding bite from a demon, I was living on borrowed time.

I woke up with a text from Alek. *"Salem's on her way to get you. Dress casual. Wear good shoes."*

I jumped out of my bed and ran to my closet. *A warning would have been nice.*

Luckily for Alek, casual was all I owned. I slid on a pair of black leggings and a matching dark hoodie before securing my tennis shoes on my feet. I was barely able to slick my auburn hair into a ponytail away from my face before I heard Salem's car pull up on the street outside.

What the hell is going on here?

Salem waved at me as I jumped out of my window and approached her car. It wasn't as nice as Alek's car, but it fit her personality. I opened the door and slid into the passenger seat.

"I don't suppose you know what Alek wants?"

She took a sip of her energy drink and started driving. "With my brother? Who knows." I stiffened. "Look, I know you have a deal with Alek. Our father's an asshole."

I let out a long breath. "He told you about the deal?"

Salem nodded. "Yes, and I think he's a complete prick. If you want me to kick his ass, just say so."

I laughed. Salem was very different from her cryptic, menacing brother. I instantly felt like I could trust her, which was very rare for me. Besides Natalie, I trusted nobody.

Trusting people would get me killed. My mother had drilled that into my brain for the last twenty-two years.

"It hasn't been too terrible yet," I said. "Other than the blood bonding, which was very strange." My shoulder throbbed at the memory. "Besides, I guess I *did* agree to it."

"Well, if you change your mind and you ever want me to kick his ass," she said, glancing at me from the driver's seat, "you know where to find me."

Her car was exactly as I expected, with empty soda cans littering the once-beige floors.

I fought back my smile. "Do you know where we're going?"

"I do. But I've been specifically told not to tell you."

"Oh good," I muttered. "More surprises."

For about twenty minutes, Salem drove us through the city and into the suburbs. I had left the city more times in the last few days than I had in my entire life. Something about it felt so freeing, like there was an entire world left for me to explore.

I sat in that feeling for the rest of the drive, trying not to let my mind wander to the fact that I had missed out on so much in my life.

After a while, Salem pulled into a dirt parking lot. "We're here."

I glanced around, looking for some hidden building or anything at all that would be important, but besides one other car in the lot, it was entirely empty.

Salem pulled her car up to the other one, which happened to be a blacked-out Porsche. I didn't know a lot about cars, but I did know that was an expensive one.

Alek opened the door and stepped out.

"Are you coming with us?" I asked Salem.

"Nope. I'm just here to drop you off." Salem watched as I drew a long breath. "Look," she said, lowering her voice, "I know you don't trust him. You have no reason to. But if he swore he wouldn't hurt you, he meant it. He likes people to think he's all large and dangerous, but it's just an appearance."

I wanted to believe her. I really did. But the knot of nerves in my stomach told me otherwise. "Thanks, Salem."

As soon as I was out of the car, she drove off.

"Hello to you too, sister," Alek sighed as we watched her speed away.

I took a breath to calm my nerves. "You summoned me?" I asked.

Alek nodded, leaning against his sleek car and crossing his arms over his chest. He wore the same all-black outfit, only this time, he added a pair of black aviator sunglasses.

"I have a mission. I figured you might want to join me."

"What makes you figure that?"

"I don't know," he started. "But the fact that your mother is out of town and you seem to never get out of the city is a pretty strong hint. You seem like someone who could use the thrill."

I opened my mouth to argue his words, but he was right. "How did you know my mother was gone?"

Alek walked around to the passenger side and opened the car door. "I told you. I know things. Besides, I figured I needed some way to apologize after what happened the other night."

My body buzzed with the memory. The bite mark on my shoulder had been healing nicely, but every time I looked at it, I was flooded with the feeling of his mouth against my skin.

Accepting that as the best answer I would get, I climbed into the car. He shut my door before walking back to the driver's side.

"Are you going to tell me what we're doing?" I pushed.

He smiled as we pulled off, the muscles flexing in his forearms as he turned the steering wheel. "Part of being a Night Raven means looking out for our own. Today, you're coming with me to intercept an arrest."

I stared at him with a blank face, waiting for a better explanation. "Am I supposed to know what that means?"

His eyes flickered in delight. "It means one of us has been arrested. We're breaking him out today."

My jaw dropped. "What did you just say?" Alek smiled without looking at me. That same arrogant, idiotic smile. "Did you really think I would want to come with you while you committed a crime, most likely a *felony*?"

"I've done this dozens of times," he said, waving me off. "The cops are humans, remember? We're not. It'll be over before they even know what's happening."

My heart began racing. Hanging out around Alek and the demons was one thing. Breaking them out of jail…

"If my mother finds out about this—"

"What?" he asked. "What's your mother going to do? Why are you so afraid of her?"

I shook my head and gripped the leather car seat. "You don't understand."

"Then make me understand. Why are you so afraid of her, Lyra?"

That question was impossible to answer. Especially to him. I took too long to answer, and Alek eventually returned his gaze to the road.

"Fine," he said. "Don't answer. But this will be fun. You can trust me."

I kept my mouth shut as he merged onto the highway.

"Do you usually break out your prisoners in broad daylight?"

"Sure do," he answered. "That's when it's least expected."

I'm going to be sick.

Alek's phone rang, and he answered it using his car's Bluetooth. "What's up, Zac?"

"They're coming up behind you. Twenty seconds."

"Got it," Alek answered. "Same plan?"

"Same plan," Zac confirmed.

"Let's save this sorry son of a bitch."

I didn't have time to react. A police transport van passed us on the left, and Alek didn't waste a single second. He slammed on the gas, positioning himself directly behind the van.

"What now?" I yelled over the blood pounding in my ears.

"Didn't you ever hear that patience is a virtue?"

The van in front of us put his blinker on, slowly taking the next exit that also looked like it led nowhere.

"What's going on? Are they pulling over?"

Alek followed closely behind them. "Let's just say that the driver got a very urgent phone call regarding a potential ambush up ahead."

"Let me guess. It was Zac." Again, Alek only smiled. I groaned, "I can't believe we're doing this."

The car roared to life as Alek sped up behind the cop. Any thoughts forming in my mind left, replaced by my silent screams of panic.

"Do everything I say," Alek commanded. And then his car was screeching to a halt behind the stalled police van. "Get out of the car!"

I peeled the seatbelt off before throwing the door open and bursting into a sprint behind Alek. He was fast. Too fast. He wasn't even human, so how the hell was I supposed to keep up with him?

Zac was somewhere ahead of us, and I immediately heard yelling as the backdoor of the police van slid open.

One of the Night Ravens jumped out, running for the hills next to us.

Zac was tackling the singular police officer to the ground.

"You good here?" Alek yelled to him.

Zac picked the officer up by the shoulders and shoved him into the back of the police van.

"All good!" Zac hollered back.

I didn't stop running. My feet were pounding the hard ground beneath me as I caught up with Alek.

"Run, Lyra! Let's go!" he yelled.

He turned right and sprinted toward the tree line.

I had no choice but to do the same.

After just a few seconds, my lungs were screaming. The only time I had run like this was seven years ago, but I was running from something much worse.

"Hurry up!" Alek called from ahead of me.

Police sirens wailed behind us. "There are more?" I yelled, gasping for air.

He didn't have to answer. I glanced over my shoulder to see the three police cars pulling up. "What about Zac?!"

"Zac's a professional. He'll be fine," Alek assured me.

We sprinted through the woods until we found an abandoned building. It was hidden amongst the thickening trees, and without Alek, I would have run straight past it.

"In here," Alek breathed.

I couldn't speak. All I could do was focus on my breathing—oxygen in, oxygen out.

By the time we stopped running, I could hardly feel my legs. Alek grabbed my wrist and pulled me out of the sun.

The building seemed to be an old, abandoned warehouse of some sort. The wooden planks that created the walls were cracked and rotting. A few holes in the roof let enough light shine through that I could see Alek in front of me—although, I couldn't see much else.

"There's nowhere to hide in here," I said. My voice carried through the large space. I could hear the shouts of the other police officers growing louder and louder outside. They were probably halfway to us by now.

Alek's hands grabbed me, yanking me through a set of wooden doors that appeared to be a closet. He shut the door behind me, leaving us in pitch blackness.

The sound of my labored breathing filled the room. "Alek, they'll find—"

"Shut up," he hissed. He grabbed my torso and pulled me backward. I landed hard against his chest.

My first instinct was to step away from him, but one of his arms wrapped around my stomach, pinning me against him.

"Quiet," he whispered in my ear. "Try to relax. You're breathing too fast."

The sound of the warehouse doors opening in the distance caused me to yelp.

Alek's hands instinctively tightened on my body.

I wanted to scream. I wanted to tell him this was a terrible idea and that he was a complete dumbass for bringing me here.

But just as panic began taking over my senses, Alek's finger slid under the hem of my shirt. His finger moved slowly, sliding upward on my bare skin until his entire hand was flat against my stomach.

I leaned back into him with a gasp. His other hand moved up to my neck. He used his thumb to lift my chin, turning it slightly so my neck was exposed to him.

Every single inch of my body grew aware of everywhere he touched me.

His hand on my stomach moved higher, his thumb reaching the underwire of my bra.

My breathing slowed. Whatever wicked plan he had, it was working.

The footsteps in the warehouse grew louder and louder. Alek pulled me flush to him, ensuring we were hidden in the depths of the shadows.

But the footsteps grew heavier. Closer.

Just as I thought the closet door would burst open, Alek leaned down, his mouth finding the exposed area of my neck. His hot breath tickled me before his teeth gently grazed the delicate skin. I froze as his hands tightened around my torso.

And then I felt his tongue skimming toward the area of my shoulder where he had bit me.

Holy hell.

Fire erupted through my body. I tilted my head further,

giving him more room as his hands tortured my senses. His fingers remained teasing, gently lingering just under my bra but not crossing that delicate line.

Even though I wanted him too. *Shit*, I wanted him to.

I didn't even realize the footsteps were walking away, leaving our hiding spot in the darkness of the warehouse.

Alek's lips moved slowly across the sensitive skin of my neck. The memories of his fangs embedding my flesh flashed through my mind. I wanted it. I wanted *him*, and the wound from his teeth seemed to want it more. A heated, burning sensation ignited beneath my skin.

Alek didn't stop when we heard our followers leave. Instead, his hands gripped me even tighter, his fingertips now digging into my body with a new sense of urgency.

My head fell back onto his shoulder as his hands pulled my body tighter against him.

"Fuck, Lyra," he growled.

I didn't want him to stop. I leaned into him even more, surrendering fully to his touch.

His hands moved lower, dipping under the waistband of my leggings. An eagerness I had never felt before washed over me, taking control of my racing heart.

I became pressingly aware of his fingers lingering.

What the hell am I doing?

The realization hit me all at once.

I pushed myself off of him, pulling my shirt back down and retreating to the other side of the small closet.

"Why did you do that?" I asked.

"You needed to calm down," he replied.

"Not like that!" I hissed.

"Why not?" he asked, taking a step closer to me. "You didn't like my hands dragging across your bare skin?"

"No! I—"

Alek closed the distance between us, grabbing my chin and bringing his face close to mine.

"You didn't like me touching you? Teasing you?"

My heart raced in my throat.

"There's more where that came from, Lyra. I know you want to be touched. You forget that I am not human. I can sense the way your body reacts to me." He dragged his thumb across my bottom lip. "I could touch you all day long, if that's what you longed for."

He let go of my face, but neither of us stepped away.

"If you don't want me to touch you, Lyra," he whispered so close his lips almost brushed mine, "you just have to say the words. Tell me you don't like it when I touch you."

I froze under his grasp. I couldn't say the words. Not with him this close to me. Not after the way he just made me feel.

He knew it, too. He smiled before stepping back and opening the closet door.

"After you, darling," he said.

I practically ran out of the closet.

Alek was not my friend. He was not someone I should be locked in a closet with, and he was certainly not someone who should be touching me in the darkness.

But why the hell did it feel so good?

y new phone buzzed, vibrating the entire couch before I picked it up.

It was a text from Alek, who had conveniently changed his name in my phone to 'demon prince' sometime when I wasn't paying attention.

"How are you holding up?" it said.

I stiffened. The text was surprisingly nice, and that seemed out of character. It wasn't like Alek had ever been outright mean to me, but he didn't seem like the type to text and check in.

"Fine," I replied.

"Your knee healing okay?"

I couldn't help but smile when I read it. It had been weeks since I had fallen on the pavement and busted my knee, and Alek had seen me plenty of times since then.

Why was he asking now? Was it just to start a conversation? Was he thinking about me just as much as I was thinking about him?

No, Lyra, I told myself. He most certainly was *not.* He was just being polite.

Right?

"*It's pretty much healed,*" I typed back.

"*Good. And your shoulder?*"

I shuddered, and the bite mark on my shoulder heated instinctively. "*It's all fine.*"

A few minutes went by. Alek didn't respond.

"*Why do you care?*" I typed out before deleting the entire thing.

"*Why are you asking?*" I sent instead.

I set my phone down on the couch. I *shouldn't* care. I shouldn't care about whether or not he texts me back, or why he was asking me those questions.

I don't care.

I glanced down at the phone.

What was he doing? Why wasn't he texting me back?

It was completely absurd—thinking about him that much. I finally felt like I knew how those stupid little girls felt in all of those movies Natalie made me watch.

And it fucking sucked.

I stood up and walked to the kitchen before I could send another stupid text.

He doesn't care about you, Lyra, I thought to myself. *You're acting like a damn fool.*

The phone buzzed again. My body instantly reacted, moving to pick it up. If I had even an ounce of dignity left, I wouldn't have opened it. I would have waited an hour, or maybe two, before seeing what Alek replied.

But because I had not a single bit of dignity left in my entire body, I opened the text.

"*Wouldn't want my new toy getting bruised up.*"

My breath hitched in my throat.

I threw the phone back onto the couch before I could type anything back, leaving it there for the rest of the evening.

Every single thought I had that night involved Alek's hands on my body in the darkness of the abandoned warehouse.

I could still imagine the way his hands ignited across my skin. The way he held me, spoke to me.

I wanted him. I hated that I wanted him, but there was also a part of me that didn't care at all. Alek was everything I had been afraid of, yet he was everything I had been missing.

I glanced over to my phone on the couch. I should just text him. Text him and tell him how I really felt.

Alek clearly had no problem helping me with my situation. He wanted to touch me just as badly as I wanted him to.

So what the hell were we doing?

If he wanted me just as badly…

No.

Letting him touch me was foolish, and it wasn't going to go anywhere. This was all part of a deal. Letting him kiss my neck in the closet of a dark warehouse was not part of the deal, and it certainly wasn't going to help me.

Yet even still, the memory of Alek's hands on my bare skin lulled me into a deep, dreamless sleep.

Thirteen

The tapping on my window sounded different than usual.

I took my time crossing the dark living room, creeping toward the closed glass panel.

"Lyra," a familiar voice whispered. "Lyra! Let me in!"

I slid the window open, finding Alek standing outside. "What the hell are you doing here?" I hissed. "Someone's going to see!"

"Nobody saw anything," he said. "Now move aside."

"You're not coming in here!"

"If you want me to stand outside the window yelling at you, someone will definitely see."

I paused, debating my choices. Alek was stubborn, that much was certain. Even if I left him out there and ignored him, he would find a way to get inside.

If I just let him in, at least he wouldn't be on Theia's security cameras.

"Hurry up," I said, backing away from the window. "And don't touch anything."

Alek pulled himself up and through my window, landing on his feet inside my apartment.

"So this is how you spend your Saturday nights?" he questioned. I felt myself getting nervous as he looked around my apartment. He seemed so much taller inside.

My apartment was kept tidy at all times. My white furniture matched the white walls, and not a single thing felt out of place.

Still, my heart rate increased as he walked over to my color-coded bookshelf, running his finger across the spines of my dozens of romance novels. I waited for some sort of snarky remark about the titles, but Alek only smiled softly.

"Did you come here to creep into my apartment?" I asked. "Or do you actually need something?"

I prayed that Alek couldn't tell how nervous he made me. After the way he touched me, I couldn't look at him without wishing we were closer. I couldn't even be in the same room as him without wishing he was kissing my neck again.

Alek turned away from my shelves and took a deep breath. "My father wants to invite you to dinner."

"Okay," I said, mulling over the words. "And you couldn't tell me that over the phone?"

It was strange to see Alek tense up when he talked about his father. He was one of the most intimidating people I had ever met, which wasn't saying much, but he was still apprehensive around his own father.

But I was beginning to understand why. It was clear his father didn't like him so much.

"This will be different," he started. "He's going to be drilling you with questions. He'll be pushy and rude and arrogant."

"Nothing I'm not used to," I said with a smirk.

Alek crossed the living room and sat on the edge of my couch, resting his elbows on his knees and running his hands through his hair. "This isn't a joke, Lyra. We need to get our story straight."

"What story? We're in a relationship now. What else would he want to know?"

"He'll want to know how we met. He'll want to know about you, about your family." It became my turn to tense up. He noticed. "Is that a problem?"

"Talking about us won't be a problem. We'll just tell the truth, leaving out the part where we made a deal neither of us can back out of."

Alek nodded.

"But my family…" I shook my head. "There's not much to say. And my mother would be pissed if she found out about—"

"Like I've promised a hundred times, your mother will never know."

"What would he possibly need to know about my family? My mother is hardly around. I've never known my father. Story over."

Alek's green eyes blared into me with such intensity, it was almost as if they could see the truth.

I moved to sit on the couch, putting a safe distance between us. "I'll tell him my mother and I haven't been in contact for a few years. Work and travel have kept her busy. That should keep him from asking anything else."

I watched as he considered the words. "What if he asks you about her work? About what she does?"

I shrugged. This conversation was getting dangerously close to questions I could not answer. "How should I know? I'm the last person she would discuss her business with."

"Why?"

It was a simple question. An innocent one. Alek's tone held nothing but a safe amount of curiosity. Yet still, that question would be impossible to answer. Theia didn't discuss anything with me. Not a single thing. She especially didn't tell me about her work—about the veil. She told me I would learn more about it when it was absolutely necessary. Aside from protecting it, I didn't actually know what Theia did all day.

"There are more important people to discuss those things with, I suppose," I admitted. It wasn't entirely a lie.

But I wasn't in the mood for telling Alek my mother would lock me in a cage forever if she could get away with it. She would chain me up like a dog, only using me for the veil if it ever became necessary.

There was no use in building a relationship with someone who was born to die.

"Okay then," Alek said after a few moments. "We'll dodge questions about your family. What about you?"

I leaned back on the white couch and kicked my feet onto the coffee table. "What about me?"

"What do you do? What are your interests? Hobbies?"

"These really seem like first-date type of questions," I deflected.

"Yes, and considering the fact that he thinks we're dating, we need to get our stories straight. Answer the questions."

My mouth went dry. "There's not much to answer. I graduated college this year, but I'll never use the degree. I used to paint, but not so much anymore. I read a lot. I don't have many interests, and I don't have many hobbies."

Something flashed across Alek's face, but it was quickly covered by his darkened features. "Your mother is that strict?"

I wanted to trust Alek. I wanted to tell him what had really been going on.

But he wouldn't care. Nobody would. If they knew the truth, if they knew why Theia had kept me hidden all this time, they would understand. They would do the same.

I put a smile on my face, hopefully well enough that he wouldn't notice the pain underneath. "Let's just say she wouldn't be happy if she knew you were here right now."

Alek rested his chin on his hand. "You've never dated?"

"Excuse me?"

"You've never dated before? Your mother has never let you?"

"No," I answered flatly. "She hasn't. Not like I would be interested in it anyway."

He stared at me, unblinking.

"What?" I asked.

He didn't break eye contact as he said, "It's a bummer that you've spent so many years like this. There's so much life to live, Lyra. You're missing so many milestones."

I looked away, trying not to feel his words, trying not to feel the nasty truth that hid underneath them.

I had been avoiding those words my entire life. I had been avoiding those thoughts.

When my sixteenth birthday came around, I cried. I cried every single day for weeks. Because I wanted to live back then. I held onto so much hope. I wanted a car. I wanted to drive. I wanted to go out and have fun with friends I didn't have.

But the next year came and went.

And the next.

And my life never changed. My hope, however, changed drastically. It took me a long time to get over those possibilities. I had grieved an entire life—the life that could have been.

But that was no use, I told myself. A waste of tears and nothing more.

When I wasn't paying attention, Alek moved from his spot on the edge of the couch to come sit right next to me, putting only an inch or two between us.

"What are you doing?" I demanded, leaning away from him. I was still getting used to his presence, and that was much harder to do when he sat so close to me.

"If you've never dated anyone before, you'll have to learn a few things."

"I don't need to learn anything, thank you," I spat.

Alek grabbed my arm and pulled lightly, returning me to my upright position. His arm brushed against mine as we sat there.

"If you act uncomfortable around me, he'll know. He's looking for any excuse to call me out on my bullshit. Please, Lyra."

His hand still lingered on my arm. "Fine," I whispered. "What do you need me to do?"

"Well, first," he said, "I need you to relax." He grabbed my shoulders from behind and rubbed them lightly. I fought the urge to shudder each time his thumb moved across the bite wound. "Are you always so tense?"

"I'm not tense," I argued.

"See? Right there. That's you being tense. And stubborn."

I opened my mouth to argue, but Alek's thumbs found the perfect spot on my shoulders, digging lightly and massaging out the tension. "Much better," he said after I shut my mouth. "Now lean back."

I did what he ordered and leaned back, resting my head on the back of my couch. Alek adjusted his body to relax right next to me, resting his head parallel to mine.

"We're making great progress," he said.

"Really?" I teased. "You call this progress?"

He laughed quietly. "Step one is relaxing, just like you would if I weren't here. We have to be comfortable around each other. You look like you're hiding something when you're so anxious."

If only he knew.

"Fine," I said. "I'll try to relax in front of your father. What else?"

Alek lifted his left arm and rested it on the couch behind my head. I tried not to flinch at his movement but failed miserably. Alek took a long breath and leaned forward again, putting some much-needed space between us.

"I'm sorry," I muttered. "You just caught me off-guard."

His eyes snapped to mine. "Don't apologize, Lyra. Don't ever apologize for that."

I swallowed but held his gaze. The longer I stared into his eyes, the more nerves I felt flooding my stomach.

Alek turned his body toward me and leaned forward just an inch. "You can trust me. I know I'm just the psycho demon you met at the bar who forced you into this deal, but I won't hurt you. I'll never hurt you."

My heart pounded hard in my chest. "Okay," I breathed.

"Do you believe me?" he asked.

I nodded. *Yes.* I so desperately wanted to believe him.

"I'm going to put my arm around you now," he whispered.

I nodded again, letting him know I was ready this time.

Relax, Lyra, I told myself. *It's just Alek. It's not like he's seeing you naked or anything.*

He's touched you before.

Shit. That memory wasn't helping me relax.

Alek's arm found his way around my shoulders. He rested it there, letting me get used to the weight.

"See?" he whispered. His face was so close to mine, I could see each of his thick eyelashes that framed his eyes. "This is what normal couples do." With his free hand, he traced a long line up my arm.

"You're telling me this is how we'll be sitting when we get dinner with your father?" I breathed, trying to break the tension.

Alek smiled, and his perfect teeth only made my stomach sink deeper.

I wasn't supposed to be feeling this. His touch shouldn't have this reaction on me. He was a demon, and this was all for show.

But if that were true, why was he looking at me like that?

"Maybe," he whispered, inching closer to me. "Or maybe not. I like to be prepared for everything."

I didn't back away as he leaned down, resting his forehead against mine. My body erupted in sensation, every single one of my senses becoming aware of his skin against mine. His fingertips teased me. The movements likely came subconsciously to him, but I had never been touched like that before. So gentle, so delicate.

"Lyra?" he whispered.

"Yes?"

"Have you ever been kissed?"

"Yes," I answered quickly. Too quickly.

"I mean a real kiss," Alek explained. "And our deal doesn't count."

A wave of embarrassment flushed my cheeks. Silence passed between us before I answered, "No." Without pulling away, Alek let a strand of my hair fall through his fingers as he twirled it around. "Will you teach me?" I asked before I could process the words.

What the hell, Lyra? Where is this coming from?

Alek smiled, and I would have pulled away if it weren't for his hands on my body. Those damn fingertips.

"It would be my pleasure," he muttered. His hand moved up my arm and settled on my neck. He pulled away, just enough to look into my eyes. "Relax," he whispered.

That would be impossible.

Alek moved slow—torturously slow—as he lowered his mouth to mine. His soft lips touched mine gently, and my body froze. He stilled against me for a few seconds, letting me relax under his touch, before pulling away.

I took a breath. "That's all I've been missing?" I whispered.

Alek grinned, and I found myself unable to look away from his mouth. "No, Lyra, that is not what you've been missing."

His fingers tightened around my neck as his lips met mine again. He applied more pressure this time, and the heat in my body increased as I kissed him back.

I couldn't think about anything other than the way he touched me, the way his hands held me gently as his lips pushed against mine. I moved my hand to his arm, then his shoulder. His muscles contracted beneath my touch. His lips moved slowly, giving me time to learn his movements.

I mimicked him until it felt natural, our mouths dancing

together. My hand slid from his shoulder down to his chest. A low purr of approval was the only reaction from him.

As the seconds passed on, the kiss intensified. My entire body buzzed with electricity as his hands gripped tighter on my body.

Alek's tongue slid against my lower lip in silent invitation. I opened my mouth, letting him guide me into a deeper kiss.

And *holy shit*, it felt good.

My mind spun. Alek shouldn't be touching me like this. We shouldn't be doing this.

I pushed his chest away, just enough so our kiss broke.

Our breath blended together in the inches between us. "That," he started, "is what you've been missing."

He stared into my eyes, a small smile spreading on his perfect mouth.

Demon, my mind whispered. He's a *demon*, and you're *kissing him*.

I cleared my throat and sat up on the couch. "Well," I said, "let's hope we don't have to do *that* with your father watching."

Alek laughed as he sat up next to me. "Yeah," he mumbled under his breath, "let's hope not."

My face burned. The way Alek had touched me, the way he kissed me. Is that what I had been missing out on this entire time? My heart raced with adrenaline. I had never kissed anyone before, but somehow it felt so right. So natural.

"What are you thinking?" Alek pushed, interrupting my thoughts.

"I–I'm thinking… I'm thinking I'm a little behind on this.

And I should have learned how to kiss when I was a teenager."

His smile was soft. "You're perfect. Teenage years are for making mistakes and being stupid. You didn't miss any of that."

I stared into his eyes. My chest fluttered in a way it had never done before, sending a swarm of butterflies into my stomach. Alek was making me feel things I had never felt before; he showed me things I had never seen.

I tore my gaze away from him and stood from the couch, reminding myself that this was just a deal.

Just a deal. It meant nothing.

"You should probably go," I whispered. "I don't want my neighbors getting suspicious."

He paused for a few seconds before responding, "Right. Of course." I watched him scan the room as he leaned against the open window. "Goodnight, Lyra."

"Goodnight, Alek."

In one swift motion, he hauled himself up and out the window. I exhaled as I slid the glass shut behind him.

The second he was out of sight, my hand moved to my swollen lips.

Alek had kissed me.

CHAPTER
Fourteen

I didn't hear from Alek for two days. Two days, and then a text.

"Dinner at eight. I'll pick you up."

My gut twisted as I read the text over and over. This was it. This was the night we ate dinner with Alek's father.

I scrambled to find an outfit that was in any way appropriate for a dinner with Alek's father—the demon king.

He's not a real king, I reminded myself. He was just a regular guy who simply wanted to know more about the girl his son has been spending time with.

That, and the fact that he could probably kill me in the blink of an eye. But now that I thought about it, Alek could probably kill me in an instant, too. And he had yet to do such a thing.

Perhaps demons weren't all that bad.

Alek picked me up and managed to only make one snarky comment about the way I crawled through my window with a skirt and heels on.

Alek held the car door open for me as I slid in then shut

it behind me, walking around the vehicle to join me on the other side. With a deep sigh, he turned the car on and pulled away. We drove for a few minutes through the city until we approached a stone wall with a black gate.

"This is where you live?" I asked.

Alek drove through the gate and up the paved, circular driveway to a massive house sitting on the hill. Trees surrounded us, and the black stone of the building nearly blended into the darkness. Dim lights lit the driveway ahead.

"It sure is," Alek responded. His teeth clenched as the car halted to a stop.

"Why do you seem so nervous?" I asked him. "You're supposed to be the calm one here, remember?"

Alek looked up from the driveway and met my eyes in the dark car. "Let's just say you're not the only one with parental issues," he half-whispered. Alek's eyes searched mine for a few seconds before he cleared his throat. "But everything will be fine. Remember the plan."

I nodded and pulled down the hem to my black skirt. Alek slid out of his seat and walked around the car to open my door. I stepped outside and grabbed his arm, letting him lead me inside.

The inside of the house was just as fitting as the outside. Dark walls with red-velvet rugs littered the interior. Old, wooden furniture sat perfectly arranged around a large fire-place in the middle of the room. Although the tall ceilings seemed to go on forever, the home held a strange coziness that threw me off-guard.

"This way," Alek whispered.

I followed him down the long hallway ahead of us. I

couldn't help but imagine Alek growing up in a place like this… *living* in a place like this. It seemed so… so… *formal*.

Yet somehow, it made a lot of sense. Alek's all-black outfits would fit perfectly in this house, blending right in. Maybe that's what he wanted to do all along: blend in. I know I did.

"Father," Alek announced as we stepped into the dining room.

The space was massive. A long, wooden table sat in the middle of the room with a dozen or more chairs surrounding it. The center of the table held a row of lit candles, and art of all forms hung from the walls around us.

I tried not to stare.

My attention was pulled away as soon as Alek's father entered the room. Similar to Alek, he wore all black. Only instead of sleek, slim-fitting clothes, he wore a large black velvet robe that covered his entire body. A line of worry creased his forehead, and his dark eyes held something even more cruel than Alek's… if that were possible.

"Welcome," he said. I bit my cheek to hide the shock that he even addressed me at all. "It's nice to see you again, Lyra. Please, let's sit."

I smiled as Alek led me to the table, pulling my chair out as I took my seat. Alek moved to sit across from me, and his father between us at the head of the table.

Uncomfortable silence filled the room as servants rushed in, filling each of our glasses. Clinking porcelain echoed through the room.

Stay calm, Lyra. There's nothing to worry about.

"This is a beautiful home," I said, breaking the silence.

Alek's father's green eyes slid to mine. For a second, I didn't think he would respond. But he leaned back and placed his arms on the dining table as he said, "Built eons ago by our ancestors. Every family member has lived in this house for centuries now. It holds many memories."

"Wow," I breathed. "I'm sure it does."

I found myself holding my breath. Why was I so nervous? This was Alek's dad. He wasn't my mother. He couldn't hurt me.

Right?

"So, Lyra," he began again. I flashed a look at Alek, but he seemed just as nervous as I was. "You've been spending quite some time with my son."

The servants returned, this time bringing with them a plate of cheeses and assorted meats.

I swallowed. "Yes, I suppose I have."

Alek's father grabbed his fork and pierced a piece of meat, dragging it onto his own plate. "Alek is my son. And as my son, I find it is in my best interest to get to know the people he spends his time with. Don't you agree, Alek?"

Alek looked up for the first time. "Yes, Father."

"So tell me, Lyra, what do you find so interesting about my son?"

I froze. Alek had prepared me for a lot, but not this. Not this question. "Well," I started. I could feel Alek's eyes blazing into me from across the table. "I have to say that I find your son particularly… adventurous."

His father let out a harsh laugh. "Yes, I suppose he is. Although, I find myself surprised that someone as quiet as yourself is attracted to such a quality."

I took a deep breath and picked at a piece of cheese on my plate. "It can be refreshing at times," I admitted.

"How so?" he pushed.

"Alek has been showing me things I haven't had the

pleasure to experience myself. I haven't really gotten out that much recently."

"Why is that?"

I could feel the heat rising to my face. "A few different reasons," I admitted. "My mother prefers for me to stay out of trouble."

It was the truth, at least.

"Ah," Alek's father sighed. "So your mother is to blame here?"

"I wouldn't say she's—"

"Tell me about her, your mother."

I risked another glance at Alek. This time, though, he stared back at me with his jaw set. I looked back down at my plate and willed the redness away from my cheeks. "What would you like to know?"

His father shrugged. "Alek tells me your mother is very strict. Are you two close? Does she approve of this relationship?"

When I glanced at him, a small smile tugged at the corner of his mouth. He already knew the answer, he just wanted to hear me say it.

"My mother is very busy," I stated. "We don't have a lot of time to discuss personal life."

"Meaning…?"

"Meaning she doesn't know about the relationship, and I'm sure she would disapprove. It's her nature."

He nodded. "You're lucky, you know. Us demons are very secluded creatures. If Alek were anyone else, I'm sure someone would have run off to her and told her all about your adventures by now."

Panic began creeping up my back, tickling my neck. *Deep breaths, Lyra. You already knew this.*

"Yes, I suppose I am lucky."

He eyed me carefully. "Tell me, what exactly would your mother do if she discovered this relationship between you two?"

Why was he asking? More red, blinding panic crept in. Faster this time. My oxygen began fading. "Um…"

Lie, I thought. *They have no idea what she'll actually do. They have no idea what she's done in the past. He's simply asking a question.*

Lie, Lyra.

Images of chains and cement basements flashed through my mind. I knew what would happen. I would go back there. I would be forced back into those confines.

Alek's foot tapped against mine under the table.

I looked to him, and his eyes were surprisingly soft. *Answer the question, Lyra. They're waiting.*

"She would probably start keeping more tabs on me," I said over the lump in my throat. "And she likely wouldn't leave me alone anymore."

His father laughed again, quieter this time. "Well, we can't have that, can we? Who would keep Alek here out of trouble if you weren't around?"

I forced a smile myself.

"And your mother," he pushed, "why is it that she's so strict?"

They don't know, I reminded myself. *They don't know anything.*

I shrugged. "I'm her only daughter. I've always assumed that's the reason."

I didn't dare look at either of them. Why did he care? Why the interrogation about my mother?

He took another bite of meat. "Parents can be protective

over their children, yes. But your situation seems unique. I'm sure there's more reasoning than that."

This time, I couldn't stop the panic from flooding my body. He had to have known something. He wouldn't be pushing the topic unless he did.

"I think that's enough about Lyra's mother for now," Alek jumped in. "Why don't we let her enjoy some food?"

His dark eyes met mine in a silent message.

I had to get my act together. I was only making him more suspicious.

"Fine," his father agreed. "Let's talk about you. I assume business is continuing as usual?"

Alek stiffened, finally under his father's full attention. "Yes, Father," he responded. "The interception went well. Lyra came with me, actually. Night Raven has been profitable. Nothing new to report."

His father stared at him, unmoving. I took another bite of food.

"Lyra went with you to intercept?"

Alek stared at his father now, almost in a challenging way. "Yes, Father."

His father's nostrils flared. "And you thought that was a good idea?"

Alek swallowed. "Lyra's a big girl, Father. She can take care of herself. She was in no danger."

The energy in the room shifted. I focused on my food, not daring to speak up.

His father laughed again, but this time, there was no humor in it. "You've always been reckless, son," he muttered, "but that draws a line."

"She was perfectly safe. Besides, if Lyra is going to be part of this family, she needs to see what it is we do."

"Families have secrets," his father muttered.

"Yes," Alek retorted. "They do."

Alek didn't look away from his father. What had changed? Why was Alek standing up to him now, when he backed down so easily before?

I set my fork down. "It was fun, really. Alek protected me. We were in no trouble."

His father huffed, finally breaking their intense stare. "Yeah," he started. "I somehow find that hard to believe. When Alek is involved, there's always trouble."

"Don't talk about me like I'm not sitting right here," Alek spoke up. "You asked me to intercept, and I did. End of story."

"Except you brought Lyra with you. You know how that could have ended, Alek. What if she got hurt?"

Blood rushed to my cheeks once more. Alek's father's concern about my wellbeing was… strange.

"She didn't," he stated.

"It won't happen again," his father declared. "Understood?"

Alek's jaw tightened. "Yes, Father."

"Good. Now eat."

Alek stared at his father for one beat longer before he finally let out a breath and began eating.

The two of them confused the hell out of me.

We ate in silence for a few minutes. The servants came in and out without a sound, bringing more and more food to the table.

"So Lyra, I assume you're coming to the lake house this weekend? It's going to be a full moon."

"No," Alek interrupted. He set his fork down on the table with a clatter.

His father raised a brow. The entire room stilled, including me. "Excuse me?"

"She's not coming to that."

His father shrugged, clearly unbothered by Alek's interruption. "It's a family event. I don't see why not."

"It's too dangerous," Alek hissed. He leaned toward his father across the table as if I couldn't hear every word they were saying. Suddenly, I felt like an intruder in their home. "She's not ready."

"Ready for what?" I asked. They both ignored me, aside from Alek's jaw that tightened in response of its own.

"You're the one throwing her into danger," his father hissed back, finally losing an ounce of his composure. "If she can handle an interception, she can handle this."

My mind spun. What the hell were they talking about?

"Father," Alek's voice boomed through the room, louder than it had been all evening. "Trust me, she's *not* ready."

His father turned to stare at me. "You heard her, son," he said. I almost wanted to look away from those neon-green eyes. "She's looking for adventure."

ALEK WAS PARTICULARLY QUIET WHEN WE GOT BACK INTO THE car. "Are we going to talk about what happened back there?" I asked.

"Nothing happened. Nothing to talk about."

He drove with one hand on the steering wheel. I would have paid anything to see what he was thinking, why he was so mad.

"Well, I think that went okay, don't you?" I pushed.

"It was fine, Lyra," he muttered.

I tried not to show the hurt in my face at the venom in his words.

"I'm sorry," he admitted after a while. "It was a stupid idea for my father to even bring it up. It's not safe for you."

"Why not? Your father seemed to really want me there."

"Well, my father doesn't think clearly sometimes."

I didn't ask what he meant. Instead, I turned my attention toward the road.

Why was Alek being so cryptic? And why was he so upset that his father mentioned the lake house?

I wiped away the sweat from my palms and tried not to think about how many questions I received about my mother. That was normal, right? He was only attempting to make conversation, to get to know me. He didn't know anything. He didn't know my true identity.

Alek and I didn't speak the rest of the ride back to my apartment. I spent the time sifting through my thoughts, deciphering what had just happened. Alek didn't say anything else as I got out and walked inside, but the hair on the back of my neck stood up at the thought of what I was about to get myself into.

Fifteen

A couple of days later, Alek didn't seem as nervous about the lake house. In fact, he didn't seem nervous at all as he picked me up from my apartment and began driving us there.

I, on the other hand, was a nervous wreck. I hadn't stayed a night away from home since Natalie and I were kids. It had been years, and the looming paranoia of my mother finding out was growing stronger and stronger.

But she was still out of town. I knew that. I had no reason to worry, even though my paranoia had been at an all-time high since the interrogation about my family at dinner.

"How can I be sure you won't trick me into a weird ritual again?" I asked. I pushed away the rush of emotions that came with Alek's bite. My body had an odd way of reacting to that memory without my permission. "You won't be biting me again, will you?"

Alek laughed. "Don't worry," he muttered. "I won't bite you again until you ask me nicely."

I rolled my eyes, but my face heated anyway. "Just tell me what we're walking into here."

The suburban woods parted away, and we were suddenly pulling into a lot that overlooked the lake beyond. The surface of the water glittered with the reflecting sunlight. I couldn't deny the flicker of excitement that sparked inside me. The tires rumbled over the rough lot as Alek parked his car in the sand. By the looks of it, plenty of people had already arrived. Dozens of cars—all almost as nice as Alek's—packed tightly into the lot.

"This is our family's lake house," Alek explained. "It's a casual get-together that happens every year. Nothing you need to worry about."

I considered his words. "If I don't need to worry, why were you so freaked out when your father suggested I come?"

Alek put the car in park and shut off the engine. "I know I seem very reserved and responsible," he started. I choked back a laugh. "But the others don't exactly follow in my foot-steps. Every year, someone starts trouble."

"What kind of trouble?"

Alek sighed. "Do you know anything about the veil?" he asked without looking at me.

My blood ran cold. "You mean, the veil to hell?" I tried to stay calm. Why would he be asking me about the veil?

My mother had explained the veil to me years ago. For humans, death was simple. You die and you end up in one of two places. For everyone else, however, things happened a little differently. My mother explained to me that our type —the ones that weren't human—crossed over through the veil. The veil was simply an enchanted force that separated us from the others that resided in hell. It created a special afterlife for gods, goddesses, demons, whomever else they may be.

The veil, similarly to human deaths, led to either the good place or the bad place. Most gods and goddesses ended up in the good place. The demons, however…

"Yes, that veil."'

"I know the basics. Why?"

Alek's eyes met mine. "Some spirits can be summoned from the other side of the veil."

I waited for him to explain more, but he stared at me and waited for a reaction. "You're kidding," I stated.

"Not in the slightest. Every year, on this day, the veil is the weakest. And every year, some idiot attempts to summon a spirit."

I blinked. "Why would they do that?"

"There are many different reasons," Alek explained. "To speak to a loved one who has passed, to talk to old friends, to discuss business."

"Business?" I grimaced.

Alek pulled the keys out of the ignition and opened his car door. "If we're lucky, none of that will happen tonight. If you see anything weird, come find me."

"Got it," I said, stepping out of the car. "Avoid demonic summonings. Should be easy enough."

We began walking to the lake house. I could hear a few women laughing as they danced and plenty of men's voices. It was going to be an eventful night, indeed.

"And remember," Alek whispered as he put his arm around my shoulders, "you're with me tonight."

Heat swarmed my stomach. I know it was a simple gesture to him; he merely wanted us to be seen as a couple in front of everyone.

This was all part of the plan. This was our deal.

Still, my body ignited everywhere his skin touched mine.

I tried not to think about how close our bodies were as we approached the massive beach house. If I thought their first home was nice, this was a beach home straight out of a movie.

A massive white wrap-around porch greeted us. Zac stood on it, waving at us as we walked closer. "Alek, Lyra," he greeted. "Nice of you to join us!"

Alek laughed. "Did we have a choice?"

"Life's more fun when we pretend we do," Zac joked.

Alek's arm fell off my shoulder as we walked through the open glass doorway of the house. Unlike his family's home, the lake house was bright and spacious. White furniture littered the airy rooms, and the entire environment seemed to connect and flow with the beach energy outside. From where we stood, we could see the kitchen, the living room, and out the glass doors to the sandy beachfront behind the house.

Bottles of alcohol already littered the massive white kitchen, scattering the countertops and covering the large island in the middle of the room. Music from somewhere in the house rattled the walls, vibrating through the floors and up my legs.

"So this is it?" I asked Alek, raising a brow.

"Don't let the calmness fool you. When the sun goes down, the party really gets started."

"Fine. What do we do all night, then? Should I go hide in a closet somewhere?"

Alek walked to the fridge and picked up a beer. "No," he said. "My father will know if we aren't seen together. He has his spies, remember?"

I nodded. "So, what do we do?"

"Come on," he said, tossing me a beer and walking out of the kitchen. "It's a party. We do what any stupid twenty-somethings would do."

I didn't have a chance to ask questions. Alek was already walking out of the back door and down the massive steps to the lake down below.

I meant to follow him, but the beauty of the scenery caused me to stop in my tracks. It was only a lake, yet water seemed to spread across the horizon for as long as I could see. The water quietly lapped beneath me, creating a low roar of the elements. Seagulls flew overhead. I had no idea that seagulls even lived around here.

The last time Alek and I had visited the lake, it had been too dark to see. But here? I could see it all. It even smelled different, so fresh and earthy I would have never believed we were so close to a city. For a moment, I could have forgotten I was in a house surrounded by demons. I could have gotten lost in the peaceful scene around me.

But Alek called my name from the steps below, and that figment of my imagination quickly vanished.

Peace wasn't meant for someone like me. Peace wasn't part of my destiny.

The sun began to lower in the distance. A few guys tossed logs of wood onto a small fire in the sand. When I reached the bottom of the stairs, Alek waited for me with his hand held out. "Ready?" he asked.

"No," I answered honestly.

"Good," he said with a smirk. "Drink up. You'll feel better."

I took a swig of the liquid and tried not to gag. I would have taken the shots of tequila over that nasty stuff any day.

When we got closer to the fire, a few of the guys looked up. "There you are," one of them said. "We thought you might not show."

"Why would you think that?" Alek responded.

Someone across the fire cleared their throat. Alek stiffened before I could even see who it was, but once I did...

Blade and Kylar, the same demons from the bar.

Not Alek's friends. *Noted.*

"We wondered if you would be bringing your friend," Blade sneered. His eyes fell onto me, and I suddenly wished I was wearing a lot more clothing.

Alek must have sensed this. He let go of my hand and wrapped his arm around my waist, pulling me to his side.

I let him.

"Of course I brought her," Alek retorted sharply. "She's part of the legion now, remember?"

The smile on Kylar's face faded for half a second. "Trust me," he said. "I remember."

Zac walked up behind the boys carrying a box of beer. "Enough of the bullshit. Let's have some fun."

The tension between the group didn't fade, though. Not as the boys took a beer from Zac and began drinking. Not as Alek grabbed my hand and began pulling me away from the fire toward the edge of the lake.

"Wow," I said when we were far enough away. "Have they always hated you so much?"

Alek dropped my hand and sat down on the rocky beach. I did the same, making sure to keep a far enough distance between us. "No, actually," he said. His skin glowed against the lowering sun as he stared across the water. "If it weren't for my father, I'm sure we would still be friends."

I gaped at him. "You were actually friends with them?"

Alek smiled, flashing those perfect white teeth again. "It's hard to believe, I know. They all used to look at me differently. Besides Zac, anyway. We were all on the same team. We were all in this together."

"Then what changed?"

He shrugged his shoulders and shook his head. "Everything, I guess. One day I'm just a regular member of the pack. The next day, I'm named as my father's official heir and second in command. That changes things."

I pulled my knees to my chest and wrapped my arms around them for warmth. I liked to pretend I could actually relate to what Alek was saying. I, too, had a parent that distanced me from my friends. That made others look at me in a different light.

But Alek actually had friends that he lost because of it. That was the biggest difference between the two of us. Alek had something to lose.

I had nothing.

"I'm sure you can relate to that," he said after a few seconds.

"What?"

"With your mother working with gods and goddesses? I'm sure you've felt similar. Is that why you're such a loner?"

Right. I had told him Theia only worked with gods and goddesses, not that she actually was one herself.

"A loner?" I repeated, pretending I was shocked that he would even suggest that. "Wow, thanks."

"Come on, Lyra," he said. He finally turned to face me with that same, mischievous look on his face. The same look that was starting to grow on me. "We both know you're not a socialite. There's a reason we've all been living in the same town and nobody knows who you are."

More than you know, I thought.

"Fine," I admitted. "I guess my mother has had some influence on that."

Alek huffed. "We don't get to pick who our parents are, Lyra," he started. "But we do get to pick how our lives play out. We get to decide our futures, whether they want to believe that or not."

He held my gaze, unblinking. I wanted to tell him. I wanted someone to finally understand how untrue that was for me.

But what would that help? Alek wouldn't feel sorry for me. He didn't actually care. Watching the sunset with him in the back of a massive lake house made me forget that, but it was true. This was all part of Alek's master plan, and when he was done with me, I would never hear from him again.

I would be back in my cage, back in my own personal hell to live my life at the mercy of my mother.

And that thought terrified me more than anything.

CHAPTER
Sixteen

"There's something odd about you." Kylar's voice from behind me made me jump.

Alek had walked me back into the kitchen before he promised to be right back and left me alone.

It didn't take more than a minute for Kylar and Blade to find me. It was almost as if they had been waiting, lurking in the lake house until I was alone.

"What's that?" I said as casually as I could. I cracked the lid to another beer and took a sip.

Kylar approached slowly with his arms crossed, Blade a shadow behind him. "I don't know yet," he said. "But I have a feeling we'll be finding out soon."

I turned back around on the tall kitchen stool. "Is that so? What exactly do you plan on finding out about me?"

Kylar laughed, and the sound of it sent a chill down my spine. "That's what we're here to learn. Tell us what you really want, Lyra."

"Excuse me?"

"Tell us what you really want from Alek. Why are you here? Why are you pretending to be part of the legion?"

Blood rushed from my face. "I'm not pretending," I snapped. "And I don't have to explain myself to you."

The two of them stepped closer. I silently pleaded for anyone to walk into the kitchen, but I could hear the talking and laughter over the booming music outside.

Nobody would hear us.

"That's where you're wrong. You might be new here, but we're not. The Night Ravens are our family, and we protect our families from intruders. From outcasts." I took another drink of my beer. *Hurry up, Alek.* Kylar leaned forward and placed his elbows on the kitchen counter next to me. "So I'm going to ask you this one more time," he said. "Why are you here?"

A feral instinct washed over me. I wanted to run. I wanted to escape. I wanted to sink away into the shadows and hide.

But none of those things were options here. I straightened my spine and attempted to look strong. "I'm here because Alek invited me," I managed to say.

Kylar's mouth tightened. Before I could process what was happening, he grabbed my upper arm and shook me roughly. "Tell me the truth," he pushed, his lips curling back over his teeth, "or you'll regret ever being born."

I tried to yank my arm from his grasp, but it was no use. His grip tightened, and a yelp of pain escaped me.

A glass bottle flew across the room and shattered on the wall behind us, making me flinch.

Kylar immediately let go of me and backed up.

When I opened my eyes again, Alek stalked in our direction. His hands were in tight fists as he approached. "What did I tell you?" he hissed. Kylar put his hands up in surrender, but it was no use. Alek shoved him in the chest and pressed him against the wall. "I told you to leave her alone, did I not?"

"We're just getting to know her, that's all," Kylar replied. His words sounded genuine, but I knew better. And that hint of mischief in his eyes remained there, even as Alek held him.

Alek shoved him harder against the wall and bared his teeth. He was feral, animalistic. "Not anymore, you're not," he said. "Don't let me catch you two near her again." He released Kylar and stepped backward.

If Alek noticed the arrogant smirk on Kylar's face, he didn't show it. He ran a now-shaking hand through his hair. Part of me wondered if it was merely from adrenaline of the encounter, or if he was hiding how angry he truly felt. "Come on," Alek said to me as he took my hand. "I want to show you something."

Adrenaline still pulsed through my body, but I followed after him as he led me out of the kitchen.

"I shouldn't have left you alone," he half-growled. I gave his hand a light squeeze.

"I'm fine," I assured him, although I wasn't sure who needed the assurance more. Him or me. My heart still raced in my chest, and with each second that passed I began to realize how much worse that situation could have been. "Nothing happened."

"No, but it could have." His voice was so low that I barely heard it.

He didn't let go of my hand as he dragged me through the house and into one of the back rooms. He closed the door behind us, and as soon as he turned the lights on, my jaw dropped.

The room was entirely different than the rest of the house. Massive antique chandeliers and old frames covered the entire room, with one large leather couch in the center. This room reminded me of his home.

"What is this?" I asked. Distracted by the scene around me, my heart finally began to slow.

Alek began circling the room, looking at the photographs that hung on the walls. I did the same.

"Just a bit of history," he explained. "We like to keep a few memories here to remind us of what's important."

"You don't strike me as the sentimental type."

I studied the wall, taking in all the photographs. Some were group photos from long ago. Some were photos of the bar. Most were in black and white, but as we walked further, the photos became more recent.

Alek smiled. "Maybe not," he admitted, "but knowing I'm not the only one who has to live through this shit helps sometimes."

I came across a recent photo of Alek standing with another demon, a demon who looked shockingly similar to him. "Who's this?" I asked.

Alek cleared his throat. "My brother."

My head snapped towards him. "Your brother? I thought your father said you were his only son?"

"Yeah, well. Things change." He looked anywhere but the photo of his brother and slid his hands into the front pockets of his jeans as he shrugged.

Clearly, he didn't want to talk about whatever happened with his sibling. I fought the urge to reach out and touch his hand.

Alek stopped before a large, framed photo of a man. He looked young, and something about him seemed so familiar. "Is that a younger picture of your father?" I guessed.

"No. This is the man who was supposed to rule. He was in charge for decades before my father fell onto the throne."

"Really?" I asked. "What happened?"

He took a long breath before explaining, "He became too powerful. Too hungry. He wanted things that were impossible, and he didn't care who he had to hurt to get it."

I was familiar with that concept.

"So he was killed?" I asked.

"He was," Alek answered with a tight jaw. "And I regret it every day."

My eyes locked on Alek, who was still staring at the picture with unfading focus. "You killed him?" I asked in a whisper.

Alek nodded slowly. "It was for the greater good," he said, yet somehow, I didn't quite believe him. The pain in his voice told me there was more to the story.

"How does one kill a powerful demon?"

Alek looked away from the picture and met my eyes. "With help and with risks."

"I imagine your father had something to do with that."

His eyes darkened. "The things we do for our parents."

I should have looked away. I should have broken our gaze. But something behind his eyes sent a thrill of excitement through my body.

Alek didn't know the truth. He didn't know that my blood was sacred and that my mother had kept me hidden for so long because of it.

Yet somehow, when he looked at me, I actually felt seen. I

felt like he knew the truth, and that was something I had never felt before.

The sound of chanting interrupted my thoughts. I finally looked away from Alek, only to realize I had moved closer to him.

"What is that?" I asked, stepping back and turning my attention to the voices.

Chanting grew louder and louder.

The language was one I didn't recognize. Latin, maybe? Either way, the sound of the words made the hair on the back of my neck stand up.

"Come on," he said, leading me out of the room. "It's starting."

He didn't bother to wait for me. I followed directly behind him, eager to figure out what was going on.

When we reached the bonfire again, I halted in my tracks. "Shouldn't I be running away from the creepy chanting?" I asked Alek as he turned to face me. "Not toward it?"

I expected Alek to smile or crack some sort of a joke, but his face remained as serious as I had ever seen it. "No," he answered. "You should see this." He held his hand out to me. The chanting grew behind him, and oddly enough, so did the flames of the fire. "Do you trust me?" he asked.

I looked at his outstretched hand. Trust. That was something every bone in my body told me not to do. Alek was many things, but trustworthy?

I nodded my head. It wasn't even a question. Trustworthy or not, I was already neck-deep into his world. There was no going back now. I closed the distance between us and took his hand in mine.

Together, we approached the back of the small crowd.

"Stay calm," he whispered in my ear, close enough that

his breath tickled my cheek in the cold night air. I couldn't stop myself from shivering when his lips brushed—just barely—against my ear. "You're safe with me."

Stay calm? I peered through the crowd, desperate to see what everyone was chanting at.

When my eyes landed on an actual face forming in the fire, I could have sworn I was hallucinating. I blinked twice, but when I opened my eyes again, the face was still there.

One of the demons talked into the fire.

And to my surprise, the face in the fire talked back.

They spoke in the same, foreign language, all drowned out by the chanting that still continued around us.

"What is that?" I whispered to Alek.

His entire body had tensed, even his hand was stiff in mine. This made him uncomfortable. "Like I said earlier," he started, "the veil is thin tonight. Sometimes we can communicate with our ancestors who have passed, who have crossed to the other side."

"You mean… you're talking to the dead?" That was impossible… wasn't it? There was no way Alek's pack of demons could speak to the dead. There was no way they could communicate over the veil.

Alek's jaw tightened. "In a way, yes."

I returned my focus to the fire. "What are they saying?"

Alek listened for a few moments further before explaining, "They're talking about history. And our pack's plans."

"Plans for what?" I asked.

Alek looked at me but didn't answer. He knew something and wasn't telling me.

I was about to demand that he answer me when someone in the crowd screamed.

The fire grew larger, spitting flames into the air and causing the crowd to panic.

Alek yelled something to me that I couldn't understand before he was pulled into the crowd by both arms. He began yelling in the same, foreign language.

In the back of the crowd, I stayed put. I don't think my limbs would have moved if I tried. Terror and adrenaline and excitement all rushed through me. What I was witnessing shouldn't be possible. None of this should be possible.

The veil was impenetrable. That was what my mother had taught me.

But now I wasn't so sure.

Footsteps approached from behind me. Rough hands grabbed me by the arms, and something was thrown over my head, smothering my vision.

I tried to scream, but my voice was quickly drowned out by the ongoing chaos of the crowd.

No, no, no. This couldn't be happening.

"You're coming with us," a voice hissed close to my ear. *Blade and Kylar.* It had to be them.

I struggled against the tight grip, but it was no use. The hands lifted me off my feet and began carrying me toward the water, away from the crowd.

And away from Alek.

Shit.

CHAPTER
Seventeen

"**N**ot so tough without your boyfriend to protect you, huh?"

I could tell from the rocking and the sound of water that we were on a boat. Panic began taking over my senses, one by one. They were going to kill me.

I never learned to swim.

"Let me go!" I yelled. That only resulted in a fit of laughter from my anonymous companions. Kylar and Blade's voices were easy enough to identify, but we weren't alone. "He'll kill you for this!"

"That's the thing, sweetheart," one of the demons holding me said, "we're actually part of his legion, his pack. He won't touch us. You, however…"

The bag was ripped from my head. I blinked a few times, letting my eyes adjust to the new surroundings.

We weren't even that far from shore, but nobody was paying any attention to us. I could see the fire now, still blazing wildly in the crowd.

I could yell, but nobody would hear me.

"What do you want?" I asked. I tried to keep my voice steady, but it was no use. They wanted to see me weak. They wanted me to be afraid.

Kylar knelt in front of me. "We want you gone. We want you out of the legion."

"Why?" I asked. The water rocked the boat harder. "What have I ever done to you?"

Kylar's eyes darkened. "You're an obstacle, Lyra. Truly, it's nothing personal. But we need certain things from Alek, and you're in our way."

"What could I possibly be in the way of? I don't even know half of what goes on at Night Raven. Alek keeps his business to himself!"

Kylar put a finger on his chin, pretending to consider my question. "Alek's father wants him to be with you. The reasoning behind that is beyond me, but it's true. Alek holds his father's favor when he's with you. And you see,"—he motioned to the others on the boat—"that's not good for us."

The chill of the night rushed over my body. "Killing me isn't going to help you," I explained. "His father will hate you."

"No, no, no," Kylar teased. "We aren't going to kill you. It will be tragic, though, when you get a little too drunk at the bonfire and find yourself going for a swim in the middle of the night. It's much too cold, don't you think, boys?" The others nodded in agreement.

I didn't have time to argue. I didn't have time to talk sense into him. Before I could protest, the men holding my arms lifted me up.

And threw me into the frigid water.

The shock of the water forced the air from my lungs. I could have sworn my heart even stopped beating, just for a second. Every inch of my body was hit with the sharp pain of the freezing temperatures.

But I had to fight. I had to try.

I began kicking, propelling myself to the surface as best as I could. The air hitting my face was the best thing I had ever felt.

I sucked in a deep breath of air against my screaming lungs and tried to view my surroundings. The boat already approaching the shoreline was the only thing I saw.

And then I was under again.

Despite my fighting and thrashing, I couldn't stay above water. I tried to kick as hard as I could, but the water was so cold.

And my legs quickly grew numb.

My lungs wanted air. They needed oxygen, they needed anything.

I tried one more time, propelling myself as hard as I could to the surface.

But instead of moving upward, I sank deeper into the lake.

I held on as long as I could.

And then my world went black.

Eighteen

"Get up," a man's voice barked at me.

I blinked my eyes open. I was back in Theia's basement, but this was no flashback. I looked down at the shackles that typically chained my wrists. They had been snapped in half, the metal ripped apart.

Was I dreaming?

"You don't have much time," the voice said again. I looked up and peered through the darkness. A tiny ounce of moonlight flickered through that tiny basement window, illuminating a man's face before me.

I gasped and pushed myself backward, but he stepped closer to me.

I had seen him before. The dusty brown hair, the golden eyes. He was the man in the picture that Alek had shown me... that Alek had killed.

"What do you want?" I whispered.

"I want you to get out of here," he said. His tattoos were nearly identical to the ones I had seen on Alek's skin. "You don't have that much time, Lyra."

"What are you talking about? I can't escape here. She'll find me."

He glanced behind himself. A scream echoed in the distance. "Everything will change," he said. "You have to discover the truth."

My blood was frozen in my veins, and my limbs refusing to move. "What will change?" I whispered. "Why are you here?"

"Alek knows," he said. "Alek knows why."

"But Alek killed you," I whispered.

The man's face remained emotionless. "Alek knows."

He didn't say anything else. The moonlight disappeared as the man vanished from thin air.

Darkness engulfed me. I had no idea where I was or how long I'd been there.

When my mother appeared before me, I knew it wasn't a vision.

It was a memory.

My mother was crying. I had never seen her cry before, and it put me on edge. It was rare for her to let a single puzzle piece of her perfect, idealistic life fall out of place.

But she stood in my bedroom and cried.

My childhood bedroom was just as clean as everything else in my mother's life. The white walls matched everything else in our house, and my mother made sure not a single thing was left out of place.

"Mom?" I asked her. It was the last time I ever called her that.

"It's just us now," she said. She leaned her back against my bedroom wall and ran her hands over her face. Her mascara was beginning to run, leaving a black trail of sorrow behind on her porcelain skin. "It's just us now, and nobody is looking out for us."

I remember being confused. It had always been just us.

My mother crossed the room and sat next to me on the bed.

"They'll come for you, Lyra. It might not be for a while, but they'll come for you."

The seriousness in her voice sent a chill down my back. "Why?" I asked. "What do they want?"

"They want chaos. They want destruction."

"Who?"

She finally blinked away the last tear. "Demons, Lyra. The demons will come for you."

"Open your eyes, dammit!"

Someone was moving me, shaking my shoulders. I was no longer in the water, but instead on some sort of hard surface.

Alive.

I blinked my eyes open and immediately began vomiting lake water. I coughed and coughed, fighting against the water to get real air into my lungs.

But I was alive.

Alek knelt over me, now hanging his dripping wet head in relief.

"You scared the shit out of me, Lyra," he whispered. I realized he was also soaking wet, and we were on the beach of the lake.

I continued coughing for a few minutes until I finally quit choking on water.

"Your lips are blue," Alek said. "And you're freezing. Let's get you inside."

He moved to pick me up, sliding an arm under my knees

and pulling me to his chest. I didn't fight him on it. I didn't have the energy.

I ignored the lingering eyes that followed. Surely everyone had witnessed Alek pulling my unconscious body from the lake.

I couldn't help but wonder how many others wanted me dead.

The warmth of the house didn't help. I shivered relentlessly as my body tried to warm itself up. Alek brought us into a bedroom and kicked the door shut behind him. He walked us into the bathroom and set me on the edge of the bathtub.

Each breath burned my lungs. I huddled my arms around myself, as if that would help. As if that would bring me some sort of relief.

"Here," Alek said, wrapping a towel around my body. I could still practically *feel* how angry he was. His emotion radiated off of him in waves that only added to my shivering. "We have to warm you up before you get hypothermia."

I would have answered if my teeth would have quit chattering.

Alek reached behind me and turned the bath water on. I wanted to ask him how long I had been in the water, but I couldn't speak. I could only think about taking another breath. And another.

"I'm going to kill them," Alek muttered, more to himself than to me. "I'm going to fucking kill all of them for this."

A tiny ounce of warmth bloomed in my chest. Nobody had ever cared about me that much. Nobody had ever cared about my life that much.

I couldn't help but smile when I thought about my mother—about how pissed she would be if I died.

Her lucky day, I guess.

Alek began peeling the towel off my frozen shoulders, then moved to unzip my hoodie.

"No," I tried to say, but no words came out. I could barely move, much less object.

But Alek stopped and grabbed me by the shoulders. "You have to get warm, Lyra," he explained. "Let me help you."

I was in no position to object to help, and I didn't see many options. Especially considering I still couldn't feel my fingers.

Alek started again, moving slowly as he unzipped my jacket and peeled the wet fabric from my body. He did the same to my shirt, tugging it up and over my head before tossing it into the wet heap.

To my surprise, Alek didn't smile. He didn't laugh or make an inappropriate joke as he undressed my frozen body, peeling each layer of clothing away until I was dressed in only my bra and underwear.

The look of concern on his face, however, was unchanging.

"The water's warm," he promised gently. "It might sting at first, but that's the feeling of blood coming back to your skin."

I nodded and let him help me into the bathtub. Alek's hands didn't leave my body until I was fully seated in the water.

He was right. It did sting. But after a couple seconds, I could finally take a deep breath again. I rubbed my hands together beneath the water, willing them back to life.

Alek peeled off his own soaking wet shirt and leaned against the bathroom sink. His muscles flexed under his tanned, tattooed skin. I could see the veins in his forearms as he gripped the edge of the counter. He whispered something to himself I couldn't hear.

"Thank you," I managed to say, breaking the looming silence in the air.

"You don't have to thank me," he replied without looking at me. "I put your life in danger by bringing you here. I won't be that stupid again."

"They really don't like you," I said. "You should rethink who you allow into your legion."

Alek looked at me for the first time since helping me into the water. "You were dead a few minutes ago, and now you're cracking jokes?" His voice was stern, but a smile betrayed him. "You continue to surprise me."

I sank deeper into the water until my chin was nearly underneath. "That fire... the chanting..."

"Don't worry about that right now," Alek interrupted.

"But I am worried," I whispered. "Because the veil's not supposed to have an opening."

"It's not an opening. You have to think of it as more of a window. We can see them, and they can see us. But there's no passing through."

I was already shaking my head. "It's dangerous."

"Yes. It is. My legion's been doing it for decades now, ever since the veil was created."

I turned my attention back to the warm water, sliding down in the bathtub and letting the water cover the tops of my shoulders. He was getting too close. He knew too much.

If he could access a window in the veil, what else could he do?

What was he up to?

"You're safe with me, Lyra," he said. He walked over and

knelt next to the bath. "I meant it when I said that. I shouldn't have left your side today, and I never will again. I want you to trust me. I want you to feel safe with me."

I turned to face him, only to find his eyes inches from mine. "You saved my life today," I whispered. "I... I can never repay you for that."

I half-expected to see some sort of relief on his face from my words, but his green irises only hardened.

Alek looked away first. "I put your life in danger," he muttered. He placed a hand on the center of his chest, clawing at something deeper. "I could feel your fear, Lyra. I could feel your pain like it was my own. I can't even..." He turned his head even further so I couldn't read his expression. "You shouldn't forgive me for that."

I didn't expect the words to sting.

But they did.

Alek left the room, giving me privacy to warm my limbs back to their original temperatures.

Twenty

"Where have you been?" Natalie exclaimed as I climbed back through my window the next morning.

I shut the cold glass behind me and watched as Alek's car disappeared in the distance. "You wouldn't even believe me if I told you," I said.

Natalie wore a pink hoodie and sweatpants, and she swirled an iced coffee in her hand as she looked up at me from the couch.

"Have you been waiting here for me?" I asked her as I took in her tired appearance.

She sputtered, "Hell yes, I have! I need all the details! Was Alek as good in bed as he looks?"

I plopped next to her on the couch. "I don't know, nothing happened," I said. I tried not to sound disappointed.

"What do you mean 'nothing happened'? You spent the night at his lake house!"

Chills erupted over my arms at the memory of the cold

water. "Well, things happened. But none of them were good. His pack of demons made sure of that."

"Shit, Lyra. Are you okay?"

"I'll be fine. But I'm starting to feel like this isn't a good idea. Too much is happening."

She smiled at me. "Come on. You can't tell me you didn't at least have a little bit of fun getting out of the apartment."

Fun? I thought about the events of the night. I wasn't exactly sure I would call a night with Alek's demon pack fun. Entertaining at the very least, but not fun.

"If I'm being entirely honest, I wasn't sure I would even make it out of there alive."

"Too many hot boys?" she teased.

I slapped her arm playfully. "Alek has a few enemies who apparently don't like me hanging around. A few of them actually tried to drown me."

Her jaw dropped. "You're joking."

"Dead serious. If it weren't for Alek… I would probably be dead right now."

She leaned forward and set her iced coffee on the table so she could give me her full attention. "He shouldn't be letting you near them!" she hissed. A sudden protectiveness washed over her previous joking manner. "Alek should know better than that, Lyra. Demons are dangerous!"

"Yeah," I agreed. "They are."

She shook her head. "Maybe it's not a great idea for you to keep seeing him."

I shrugged. Like I hadn't already thought of that. "I don't think I have much of a choice. Until our deal is over, I'm locked in."

"That sneaky bastard," she muttered. I couldn't help but smile at her squinted eyes.

"He's just… I don't know. He's different than I imagined him to be."

I thought back to how Alek acted after I finished warming up last night. He could hardly look at me. I had drifted off to sleep on the large bed, and when I opened my eyes a few hours later, he was in the same spot—perched on the end of the bed and facing the locked door.

Any friendship I thought we had built was gone, like it never happened.

I couldn't help but wonder if he regretted ever getting closer to me. This was all part of a deal; it was all temporary.

Did he regret spending so much time with me? Did he regret even making the deal with me in the first place?

After last night, it was clear that I was a liability to him. I couldn't protect myself. I didn't fit in with the demons, even though I was technically part of the pack.

My hand mindlessly drifted to the scars on my shoulder. I could almost remember how it felt when his teeth dug into my flesh.

"You're not falling for him, are you?" Natalie asked, snapping me out of my trance.

"What? No! He's a selfish, egotistical demon who thinks he can get away with whatever he wants in this world. No, I'm not falling for him."

Her expression flooded with relief. "Good. You know that would be impossible. With your mother—"

"I know," I snapped. "You don't have to remind me."

The flash of pain on her face was only visible for a second, but it was enough for me to regret my tone. Natalie knew just as much as I did that my mother would never allow the relationship to continue.

Relationship. What a joke. Any thinking of that manner

would be useless. There was no relationship. There was no friendship.

It was only a deal.

She shook her head. "It really sucks sometimes."

I put my arm around her, around my friend. "Yeah, it does. But we don't get to be in charge of what happens in our lives."

Natalie huffed. "No, definitely not us."

We put a new movie on the TV and sat on the couch all day. Natalie stayed over while I cooked us lunch, gossiped about everything that happened last night, and listened to her ramble about the new boy she's talking to.

In the midst of it all, I caught myself forgetting. Forgetting that this was a prison for me. Forgetting that my life was being lived on borrowed time.

And in the midst of it all, I found myself not caring.

CHAPTER
Twenty-One

Two weeks passed. I didn't hear anything from Alek, and the one text I sent him to check up went unanswered.

For the first few days, I half-expected him to knock on my window every time I heard a sound. But when he didn't, I was left with a sick feeling in my stomach.

After that, I decided to stop caring. It was a dangerous game, one I couldn't afford to play.

Especially after what happened at the lake house.

The man I saw in my fever dream never returned. I had accepted the fact that I was picturing things, and the demon Alek killed had absolutely no business visiting me in my sleep. *A freak accident*, I called it.

I had begun to lose hope—begun to start forgetting about Alek entirely when a strange sound came from outside my window.

It wasn't a knocking, more of a thump and the sound of bushes rustling.

I stopped cooking immediately and grabbed the biggest knife from my kitchen.

Natalie always knocked. Always.

The lights were dim, but I ducked anyway, making sure I was out of sight to anyone who might be looking through the window.

When I got close enough, I slowly peered outside, just enough to see if anyone was out there.

"Lyra," Alek whimpered. I could barely hear him through the glass of the window. "Lyra," he repeated. He was only half-standing, half-slumped against the wall of my apartment building.

Shit. Something was wrong.

I dropped the knife and used both hands to slide the frosty window open. "Alek?" I hissed. "What are you doing here? What's wrong?" My eyes instinctively scanned the yard around him. It was a little past nine, but the sun was long-gone. With Alek's black clothing, nobody would see.

And nobody else was around.

He tried to lift himself through my window but could barely stand. I grabbed his upper body and pulled as hard as I could, causing us both to land on the floor inside with a grunt of pain.

I quickly got up and closed the window behind me.

"I need your help," he grunted. Alek was still lying in a heap, nearly in a fetal position with blood dripping to the floor.

He clutched his abdomen with both hands.

Adrenaline kicked in. I knelt next to him and surveyed the blood that leaked through the grip he had on himself. "What happened?" I demanded.

"Got stabbed. Couldn't make it home."

Alarms blared in my mind. "You got *what*?"

He shook his head. "It's nothing."

"Did they follow you? Does anyone know you're here?" I stood up and ripped my blinds closed just in case.

"No," he said. I was already on my way to the kitchen to grab a towel for the wound, but I could hear the smile in his voice. "You're safe, don't worry."

I ran back to where he continued to bleed out on the floor and pressed the towel above his hands. He quickly got the hint and grabbed on to the towel, pressing it to the wound himself.

How was I supposed to help him? Why did he come here? I wasn't a doctor, much less a *demon* doctor. And he was bleeding. A lot.

"What do you want me to do?" I asked. "What do you need?"

"I've lost too much blood," he said. "I need you to stitch it shut."

"Are you out of your mind?" I hissed back. "I can't stitch your *stabbing* wound!"

"You can," he grunted with more force, "and you have to. Or else I'll die, Lyra."

Shit, shit, shit. Where's Natalie when you need her?

"Fine," I said, running back to my kitchen. "I think I have an old sewing kit in here..." I dug through my drawers. Alek was lucky as hell that I had taken up sewing for a while a few years ago. He was very, very lucky.

I grabbed a bottle of rubbing alcohol and the tiny sewing kit before returning.

"This is going to hurt, you know."

"Yeah," he grunted. "It will."

My hands shook as I grabbed ahold of his blood-soaked

hoodie and pushed it up. I immediately saw where he was bleeding from.

And immediately cursed.

"I… I don't know if I can do this. What if I mess it up?" My hands started shaking.

"You can't mess it up, Lyra. I heal faster than humans, so I just need you to close the wound. Even if it's shit, it will work."

"Fine," I said, grabbing the bottle of rubbing alcohol and flipping the cap open. I pressed the towel to the wound one last time before pouring the liquid all over his abdomen.

He hissed in pain but didn't move.

With my shaking hands, I threaded the needle and leaned over him.

His toned body flexed under my touch, but he didn't resist. Not as I pressed the sliced flesh together with my fingers.

And not as I dove the small needle into his skin.

In fact, Alek was surprisingly quiet, aside from a few hisses of pain as I pulled the thread taut through his skin.

I worked as quickly as I could, stitching and wiping blood and stitching some more, until the entire wound was shut.

It wasn't pretty, but the bleeding had already slowed.

"There," I said. "Let me put a bandage over it so you don't bleed all over my apartment." I grabbed a bunch of white gauze and tape and quickly secured it over the wound. "And if this gets infected, it's not my fault."

I looked at Alek's face for the first time all night. He was staring at me—half in awe, half in delusional pain.

"What?" I asked him.

He didn't look away. "Nothing," he said. "It's just... I think I already got blood all over your apartment."

I shook my head and began wiping up the small pool of blood he had left. "Can you stand?"

I helped him stand from the floor and walk to the bathroom, where he began washing the blood off his skin.

I left him there while I got back to work on the apartment floor.

I wanted to ask him who the hell had stabbed him, and—more importantly—why he had come here.

After not speaking to me for weeks and not holding up his side of our deal.

But I brushed that urge off. Alek was a demon. He lived in a world I had only ever seen glimpses of. If he didn't want to talk about what happened, I should be grateful.

Yet still—that small, wicked voice in the back of my mind wanted to yell at him. Wanted to scream at him for leaving me here in this prison with no explanation, no understanding of why he had left me for so long.

"Thank you," he said, interrupting my thoughts as he exited the bathroom.

When I looked up, I saw him standing shirtless by the door.

"Um, you're welcome. Although you did scare me a bit."

"Sorry about that," he said. "I knew you were close and... like I said, I wasn't sure I would make it all the way home."

"None of the Night Ravens were around to help?"

Alek laughed, but something dark laced it. It wasn't his usual, contagious laughter. "Oh, trust me," he replied, "there were plenty of Night Ravens around. Just none to help me."

I stopped what I was doing and stepped forward. "Alek, tell me what happened. Who did this to you?"

He clenched his jaw and looked away.

I took another step forward. "Answer me." I don't know what came over me. I definitely had no business demanding that he tell me what happened. But in my defense, he did crawl through my window and bleed all over my floor. He's the one who showed up here after ignoring me for weeks.

At the very least, I deserved an answer.

"My father needed to make it clear who was in charge," he finally answered. His voice was hardly audible.

"You're saying your father did this? He stabbed you?"

His eyes found mine. "You're not the only one with a fucked-up family, love."

My heart shattered for him. I didn't want anyone to know the type of suffering I had known, but I did realize that being locked into a basement for years wasn't the worst thing to possibly happen.

At least my mother had never stabbed me.

"Oh my god," I whispered. "Alek—"

"You don't have to feel sorry for me," he cut me off. "It's part of the business."

"Getting stabbed is part of owning a bar?"

He smiled. "There's a lot more to it than owning a bar."

"Well, you're lucky I'm nearby. You should be more careful."

"I'll keep that in mind next time."

We stood there, staring at each other for what felt like hours. Alek's eyes scanned my face, flicking over each of my features while I stared back.

I didn't want him to know how much he affected me. I didn't want him to know that I had wondered where he went for the past couple weeks or even worse: that I had actually missed him.

"I haven't seen you in a while," he said as if reading my thoughts.

"No," I replied. "You haven't."

I shrugged and glanced away, looking at anything but him. I could feel the blood creeping into my cheeks.

When he took a step closer, my skin prickled in excitement. I didn't want to react that way, but my body acted without my permission.

"I'm trying to protect you, Ly," he whispered. "After what happened at the lake… it's safer if I keep my distance."

My heart pounded in my chest. Of all the things I was expecting him to say, that wasn't one of them. "What happened at the lake wasn't your fault," I argued. Why did I feel the need to defend him? He was right!

Alek shook his head. "Demons are dangerous, Lyra. You shouldn't be around us any more than you have to be."

"But what about our deal? What's the point if you can't even bring me around?"

He turned and began pacing, running his hands through his messy hair. "I don't know, okay? I don't know."

The stress in his voice made me pause. Maybe he really was torn up about this. But why was he so concerned? This was all still just part of a deal to him…

Right?

"Fine," I said after a while. "If that's what you think is best."

He tilted his head to the ceiling and smiled, as if thinking about how ridiculous this entire situation was.

That's what I was thinking, at least.

"I never expected for you to be so… involved."

"Involved?" He nodded a response. "You mean this?" I pulled my shirt to the side, exposing his teeth marks that were now scarring over my pale skin. "You never expected for me to be this involved?"

Anger crept its way into my words, lacing the edges of my voice. I couldn't stop it. He dragged me through all of this, showed me how exciting his life could be, and then decided it's too much?

Alek's eyes darkened as he turned to look at my exposed skin, at the marks he had left there.

"I don't know what I was thinking," he sighed. "It's too dangerous for you."

"I think we're past that," I replied.

I watched his throat bob as he swallowed. "Look at me, Lyra," he said, spreading his arms out on either side of him. My eyes obeyed, tracking down to his exposed torso and the gauze that covered his skin. "This is what you're getting into. This is what I've dragged you into."

"I didn't ask to be dragged in," I replied.

"Then you should be happy about this. You should be happy that I'm leaving you alone."

I clenched my fists, digging my fingernails into the delicate skin on my palms. "Are you kidding?" I hissed. "You want me to be happy?" Alek said nothing. "You swore to me this would be worth it for me, Alek. You told me you could show me how to *live*. You showed me all of this that I've been missing!"

He smiled, but it was a sad smile. One that made my chest ache. "Well, maybe your mother knows best, after all." His voice cracked.

His words were a slap in the face. "Don't you dare say that."

Alek's shrug pissed me off even more. "You're safe in here, Lyra."

"Safe, maybe. But I'm as good as dead."

"*This* is as good as dead," he replied, pointing to his stabbing wound. "*This* is what happens out there, Lyra! You get hurt. You get betrayed. It's not all fun and games!"

"I don't want fun and games," I argued. "I want to live. I want to… I want to…"

"What?" he pushed. "What do you want?"

I dropped my hands in surrender. "For the first time in twenty-two years, I actually felt something with you. Danger, anger, whatever. At least it was something."

His brows furrowed together, but only for a second. He quickly recovered. "I can't be responsible for you getting hurt," he whispered. "I wouldn't be able to live with myself."

I stepped forward, finally closing the distance between us. "You still don't see it, do you?" I whispered. Tears formed in my eyes, but I quickly blinked them away.

He needed to hear me. He needed to understand.

"I'd rather die out there with you than live for nothing inside of this prison with *her*."

His nostrils flared as he stared down at me. He was only inches away now. Every ounce of my being responded to being so close to me. He was a magnetic force, calling every part of my soul closer to him.

Closer to the thrill, closer to the danger, closer to *life*.

I waited for him to give in. I waited for him to tell me that he was sorry, that he was wrong. I wanted him to take me with him back into his world of danger and adrenaline. I wanted to feel something again, and I wanted him to be the one to show me how.

But Alek didn't say any of those things. Instead, he tucked a loose piece of red hair behind my ear and leaned down, just slightly, as he whispered, "Then you're not as smart as I thought you were."

He left through the window.

I locked it shut behind him before I let the first tear fall.

Alek texted me first the next day.

My heart sped up the second my phone buzzed. I definitely didn't expect to hear anything from him after what happened yesterday, and I hated the way I scrambled to read the message as soon as I saw his name pop up.

Especially since it wasn't even an apology.

"Show time," it said. *"I'll pick you up tonight. Be ready."*

I fought the urge to chuck my phone across the room. He had quite the audacity to text me with a meeting time right after telling me he was cutting me out of his life.

Apparently, the demon life wasn't so dangerous, after all. That, or his father was going to be here. Either way, I was getting out of my apartment today. And that was something.

I ignored the ball of excitement that built in my stomach as I walked to my closet and began searching for an outfit.

Had he changed his mind? Was last night completely out of character for him, or did he suddenly get over how he felt?

I brushed it off. It didn't matter what the reasoning was for Alek's whiplash behavior. If he wanted me there, I had no choice.

I was dressed in black jeans and a matching hoodie when he pulled up outside.

"You're looking more and more like a Night Raven," he chirped as I slid into the passenger seat.

"Yeah, well, I guess I better start acting like one if I'm going to survive around here, right?" I asked, referencing last night.

It was a challenge, but Alek only nodded. "Right," he agreed.

We drove in eerie silence. Until Alek finally cleared his throat ten minutes later. "There's right and there's wrong, Lyra," he said. I waited for more, but none came.

"And?"

He licked his lips and took a shaking breath. He almost seemed… nervous. "And in life, we have to choose. What is right? What is wrong? Sometimes it's not that simple."

His knuckles grew white as he gripped the steering wheel. A rush of caution flushed through my body, as if my instincts were warning me. Alek was a predator. He was inhuman, dangerous, and deadly. And here we were, speeding in his car while he clearly lost his temper.

"What are you getting at?" I asked, my voice as calm as possible.

"I've had to do things in life that most people would rank as bad. Very bad." He glanced at me from the driver's seat. "Do you understand what I'm saying, Lyra?"

It was my turn to take a shaking breath. "Are you talking about how you killed that demon?"

Alek laughed, but it was a cruel laughter. One that made me shiver. "That's one of them, yes."

I straightened in my seat. "You mean you've killed… others? Is that what you're trying to tell me?"

He returned his focus to the road, speeding up on the winding highway. "The amount of people I've killed doesn't matter," he said. "What matters is why I did it. Why they deserved it."

The blood rushed from my face. Was he trying to scare me? Was he trying to intimidate me? To show me that his world was as dangerous as he claimed it to be?

"So why did they?" I asked. "What did they do to deserve it?"

He pulled the car to a halt. There was nothing around us now besides a few trees. "Get out of the car," he said. "I'll show you."

I clenched my teeth and stared back at him. He wanted me to be afraid. I could tell by the way he stared at me— powerful and domineering. He wanted to be in control of this situation.

But I wasn't about to give him the satisfaction. It would take a lot more than a demon to scare me.

I had lived through enough fear.

"Fine," I said. I pushed my door open and crawled out of the car.

"Follow me," he ordered. And then we began to walk.

I followed him into the woods, deeper and deeper until we were swallowed by the trees. The road was long gone behind us, along with any hope of being found.

An eerie feeling washed over me. Every single one of my senses was on high alert—even though I knew Alek wouldn't hurt me. He may have wanted to scare me, but he didn't have the guts to hurt me. Especially after everything he told me last night.

We walked for a while, long enough that the clear dirt path disappeared entirely.

"Where are we going?" I finally asked when it seemed like he was trying to make us disappear. Maybe he was trying to make us disappear, sink deeply into the forest until we could both forget about all of our problems.

If only it were that easy.

"Almost there," he said.

I followed behind him. He walked quickly, clearly more agile than me, but slowed his pace enough so I wouldn't get lost.

At least he cared that much.

Seconds later, a dimly lit cabin came into view. One lantern outside the front door was the only visible light in the area. Alek waited for me at the front door.

I was only slightly out of breath when I caught up to him. But he didn't wait.

He twisted the doorknob to the cabin and pushed the door open.

"After you," he demanded.

Everything in my body told me this was wrong. That I shouldn't be here. Natalie and I had seen enough horror movies to know how this situation ended.

But I couldn't back down. Not in front of Alek. Not now.

I ducked my head and stepped through the door.

"What is she doing here?" a male voice seethed. "Alek, take her home!"

"She needs to see this," Alek retorted sharply, shutting the front door behind us.

My eyes quickly adjusted to the dim lighting. "What is

this?" I failed at keeping the horror from my voice. Two bodies hung from chains in the center of the room. I couldn't tell if they were dead or alive. Two demons—Night Ravens —watched Alek and I carefully as we stepped closer to the hanging bodies. "What's going on?"

Alek stepped inside. The Night Ravens straightened as he entered. "This is the price we pay, Lyra. We aren't good men." One of the demons handed Alek a knife. "We aren't good people."

For emphasis, Alek turned and sliced his blade across one of the men's torsos. He barely flinched. I was surprised he was even still alive with the amount of blood pooling on the wooden floor beneath him.

I froze where I stood.

"There is a very thin line between light and dark, Lyra. Between evil and good. Somewhere in the middle, there's a gray area." He stepped toward me, coming dangerously close with the bloody knife still in his hand. "Do you understand me now, Lyra?" he taunted.

"Yes," I replied sharply. "I understand."

"Good," he said. "Do these men deserve to die? Maybe. Maybe not. I might have a different answer than you. My father might have a different answer than me. These men crossed my father. They invaded our territory. That means they die. But I'm not the one who makes the rules, Lyra. None of us do. None of us get to decide who lives and who dies."

I stared at him, unblinking.

"We are only the servants to a higher power. Each one of us. I hope you understand that."

"I understand that more than anybody," I replied. I knew I should have shut my mouth. Just stand there and cower like he wanted me to do. But I couldn't resist. He thought this would scare me? He thought showing me his dark side would have me running away like a scared little girl?

He thought wrong.

"Kill them both," he ordered the Night Ravens without breaking our stare. I didn't look away, either. Not as the sound of metal slicing flesh cut through the air, and not as both of their bodies were dropped from the chains.

"She's really a Night Raven now," one of the boys joked.

"No," Alek responded, grinding his teeth as he spoke. "She's not. She'll never be."

I turned on my heel and stormed outside.

How dare he talk to me that way? How dare he bring me all the way out here to humiliate me?

No. I wasn't going to let that happen. Not again. I had been through enough humiliation in my life.

My feet carried me out of the cabin and back into the woods—back in the direction of the road. Although I had absolutely no idea what direction I was heading towards, I just needed to get away.

Anger pulsed through my veins. I hardly even heard him following after me until he yelled, "Lyra, stop! You'll get yourself lost out here!"

"I don't care!" I yelled back. "Leave me alone!"

He ran to catch up with me before grabbing my arm and forcing me to face him. "I told you to stop." He wasn't yelling, yet somehow his words rattled my bones.

I ripped my arm out of his grasp. "And I told you I don't care."

His nostrils flared. "You needed to see this."

I continued stomping into the woods. "You really thought this would mortify me? You really thought this would scare me off so I would run and hide and never come back?"

"That's not—dammit, Lyra! Can you slow down?"

His grip clamped down on my arm again, harder this time. "You humiliated me."

"I want you to know the truth."

"What truth?!"

"That I am bad, Lyra. I am not good for you! You might think this is all thrilling, you might think we have fun and get to live on the edge, but this is the reality of it!" He used his free hand to point back to the cabin. "We kill people, Lyra! People die every day because of us."

"People die every day without you, too."

"You don't get it."

My eyes were daggers, begging him to hear me as I said, "Don't get it? I see you, Alek. I see what you do. I may have been surprised to meet a demon in that bar, but I'm not surprised anymore. I know what bad people look like, trust me." I couldn't stop my voice from shaking. "You might think that you're bad. You might think that there is nobody worse in this entire world than you. Well, I hate to break it to you, Alek. But you're wrong. You don't scare me."

"No?" he taunted, gripping my arm even tighter and hauling me to his chest. "I kill people, Lyra. I'm a killer. I'm a demon, a monster."

"There are many worse things than death. And you might be a monster to them,"—I signaled to the bodies at the cabin—"but not to me you're not."

We stayed that way for a while, breathing the same oxygen in the chill of the forest night. I wasn't sure how my hand got to his chest, but I could feel his rapid heart dancing beneath my touch.

"Getting close to me is a bad idea," he breathed.

"What are you going to do about it?" I pushed. "Run away? Ignore me for weeks again? I'm in this, Alek. You can't force me out of your life now because you're afraid. You made this deal with me, and I accepted. Don't back away now because you can't handle it."

He leaned down, his lips coming mere inches from my own. "Afraid?" he questioned.

I tiled my head up to him. I wanted him to kiss me. I wanted him to show me just how much he wanted to be with me. Why was it so hard for him to stay away? Why was it so hard for him to keep me out of trouble?

"You're the one who should be afraid," he whispered. Before I could protest, he stepped away, putting a world of distance between us.

He left me standing there, heart racing and emotions wild, while he led the way back to his car.

He didn't look at me as he drove me back to my apartment. He didn't look at me as I opened the car door.

He didn't even wait for me to get into my apartment before driving away, screeching the rubber tires as if he couldn't get away fast enough.

Twenty~Three

Two days later, Zac knocked on my apartment window.

"I need to talk to you," Zac whispered from outside my window. After nearly giving me a heart attack, I had finally subdued my fight or flight response to the random visit from the Night Raven.

"Fine," I said, stepping aside from the window. "Come on in."

He pulled himself up and inside my apartment, just as graceful as Alek.

"Wow," he said as he surveyed the area. "When Alek told me you were on lockdown in here, I didn't think he really meant it."

I returned to my position on the couch, trying to act as casual as possible. "I might as well turn that window into my front door," I joked.

Zac's face didn't budge. He was typically the light-hearted one compared to the other Night Ravens I had been around. Seeing him so serious was rare.

And it put me on edge.

"What's up?" I asked.

Zac sat on the other side of the couch, as far away from me as possible. I looked at him then, really looked at him, for what seemed like the first time. He rubbed his palms on his black jeans.

It was odd seeing such a large man so nervous. Even compared to Alek, Zac was an absolute monster of a man. An uneasy feeling crept into my stomach. "We need to talk about Alek," he said.

"Okay, what about him?"

"He's trying, Lyra. He's… he's been put in a bad position with his father."

I straightened on the couch and glanced to where Alek's blood had left a small stain on the floor. I made a mental note to finish cleaning it. "Are you talking about him getting stabbed?"

Zac ran his palms down the front of his thighs once more and swore under his breath. "That's part of it, yes."

"You mean there's more?" It was my turn to curse under my breath. "Great."

"Look," he said, finally looking me in the eye, "I heard about last night. That was out of character, even for him."

I shifted in my seat. "I'm not so sure it was."

"Alek is dangerous, but he's not… he's not a bad guy, Lyra. His father controls him like a damn puppet." His voice shifted to a whisper as he finished his sentence.

"I know that," I replied softly. "It's obvious he's conflicted."

Zac let out a breath of relief. "Good. I—I don't want you to get scared off. That's all."

This entire situation was strange. He came all the way here just to make sure I wasn't afraid of Alek?

"Why do you care so much?" I asked, furrowing my brows.

He stopped tapping his foot and looked at me from across the couch. "Because," he started, "Alek cares about you, Lyra. He's going to try to push you away, and it's stupid and reckless of him to do anything other than that, but he cares. He's had a hard life. He deserves someone like you in his life."

I caught myself falling for his words before I remembered the harsh truth. "This is all temporary," I said, more to myself than to Zac. "If he's thinking anything other than that, he's a fool."

"It doesn't have to be temporary," Zac argued.

How cruel those words were.

"It does. I'm risking my entire life by even playing my part in Alek's little game. I almost died the other night at the lake house."

"And Alek's making sure that won't happen again."

I shook my head. Of course this was happening. Our simple deal was never so simple, was it? There were always going to be these dirty, tangled strings attached to it.

Had I gotten in way over my head?

"I still don't understand why any of this matters," I thought out loud. "I know Alek told you about our deal. This is for the approval of his father, is it not? Nothing more. Nothing less."

"It's not that simple, Lyra. And you know it."

"Why? What changed?"

"You were pulled into our world, into these traditions

and rules. You have enemies now. And because Alek marked you, your enemies are our enemies."

I laughed. "I'm not sure how true that is."

Zac surprised me by sliding himself closer to me on the white couch. "Hear me when I tell you this, Lyra," he started. "Alek will do anything for you. Don't let him push you away. He's had a tough life, and a really tough year. He doesn't know what's good for him, even when she's standing right in front of his face. Does that make any sense?"

Unable to form coherent words, I nodded.

Zac stood from the couch and headed back to the window. He gripped the window frame with both hands before turning to face me. "There's more that you don't know, Lyra. More that we can't tell you yet. There's a carnival not far from here tomorrow night. We'll be there. You should come talk to him."

I didn't have time to ask what he was talking about. He lifted himself out of the window and vanished into the night.

CHAPTER
Twenty~Four

"Someone's going to see us leaving this window one day," Natalie said as she crawled outside.

I followed her, pulling the window down and leaving just a few inches to crawl back inside. "Let's not jinx it," I replied. I pulled my black cropped sweatshirt down to cover the skin on my torso. "We've somehow been lucky this far."

"You're right about that one. We've been on a lucky streak lately. Aside from you almost drowning in the lake and everything."

I gently shoved her shoulder as we walked toward her car. She laughed and brushed me off.

Natalie's car was surprisingly messy for the daughter of a goddess. Similar to Salem's car, she had soda cans and half-eaten candy bars on the floorboard. She quickly leaned over and brushed off the passenger seat before I sat down.

"You should really consider keeping this cleaner," I said to her. "I don't even want to know what your room looks like these days."

Natalie laughed and pulled away from my apartment building, driving us into the city. "You haven't been to my house in years," she stated. "I could be a totally different person!"

"By the looks of your car, I doubt it." I snorted.

Natalie was right. When we were kids, I was allowed over to her house all the time. Because our mothers were so close, it was easy for me. This was before my mother was so strict, and before she lost herself in whatever crazy idea she now had of keeping my blood safe forever.

These days, I never went over there. It was much easier for Natalie to drive over to my apartment.

"Have you ever been to a carnival?" I asked her.

After Zac brought it up last night, I was dead set on not going. But after a couple of hours, the idea of seeing Alek again became heavy enough to sway my decision. Natalie, of course, was instantly excited about the idea.

"No," she answered. "Although I've been to plenty of parades. I think they're probably pretty similar. Food, crowds, music."

"Carnival rides?"

She smacked her lips. "Alright, they're pretty similar minus the carnival rides."

My chest bubbled with excitement. "I hope I can ride one of them."

"What you really mean is you hope you and Alek can make a trip over to the kissing booth." She made her best attempt at a kissing face.

"I already told you it's not like that!" I defended, but Natalie wasn't buying it.

She rolled her eyes. "I know the real reason you're dragging me here is for him. Don't worry, I get it. I've done plenty of crazy stuff for boys."

"Going to a carnival isn't crazy," I said. "And it's not for a boy. This is for myself."

"Right," she said with a snort. "Whatever you say."

I knew the carnival would be crowded, but I didn't think it would be *this* crowded.

Natalie pulled the car into the large dirt parking lot. Kids, teenagers, and adults of all ages wandered around us. I could see the lights and a few tall rides from the carnival a few blocks away.

"Are you nervous?" she asked as we began walking.

"No," I lied.

"Don't be. You should focus on enjoying yourself. Don't worry so much about Alek."

"I'm not worried about him." The carnival came into view ahead of us. Beyond the front gates, a chaotic crowd buzzed with energy. It felt both exciting and intimidating. Music, flashing lights, and sounds from what I assumed to be carnival games all mixed over the low roar of voices.

And that smell. *God,* it smelled amazing. My stomach rumbled in response to whatever food was responsible for that warm, delicious scent.

"Good," she said. "Because he's right over there. And he's coming this way."

My heart immediately dropped to my stomach.

I looked in the direction of the carnival and, sure enough, Alek was stalking in our direction. And he didn't look happy.

"What the hell are you two doing here?" he asked when he was close enough. He wore a black leather jacket and fitted black jeans. His hands were in tight fists at his sides.

Clearly, Zac didn't give him the heads up that we had been invited.

"We're here to enjoy the carnival," Natalie answered. "If that wasn't already obvious."

Natalie may have been the only person to ever act sassy to a demon.

"I can see that," Alek replied, crossing his arms over his chest. "But why?"

"Why not?" Natalie retorted.

"It's dangerous here. We have business to take care of."

"What type of business?" I asked.

"Demon business." Alek's eyes flickered over to me for only a second before returning to Natalie. "It isn't safe."

"If all of these other innocent humans are safe and enjoying themselves at the carnival," Natalie continued as she flickered her hair over her shoulder, "then I think we are, too."

I had to bite my cheeks to keep from smiling.

Alek was clearly pissed. For whatever reason, he didn't want us at the carnival tonight. But I could hear the shouts and laughter all the way from out here. I wasn't about to let him bully us into leaving just because they had demon business to take care of—whatever that meant.

"Fine," he said after a while. "But you're staying with me."

"What?" Natalie squealed. "We don't need babysitters!"

He gave her a sharp look. "I don't care what you do and don't *need*. If you want to be at this carnival so badly, you'll play by my rules. Let's go."

I glanced at Natalie, who just gave me a shrug before following behind Alek. I trailed after them, and the three of us made our way to the carnival entrance.

"Zac!" Alek yelled. "Come with me."

Zac stepped out of the small crowd of demons who huddled near the carnival entrance. He jogged over to us with a big, goofy smile on his face. "Hey, wasn't expecting to see you two here tonight."

"Oh really?" I asked.

"Wouldn't pass up a carnival!" Natalie replied at the same time.

Alek only rolled his eyes.

"The girls want to experience the carnival," Alek explained to him. "You're on Natalie duty. Don't let her leave your sight."

Natalie rolled her eyes. "I told you I don't need a babysitter," she repeated.

Zac stepped forward and rolled his shoulders back. He was good looking, I had to admit. Definitely soft on the eyes, even for Natalie.

She must have noticed this, too, because she looked him up and down before saying, "Let's go, I've been dying to ride the Ferris wheel."

And then she was tugging his arm, dragging him away from us.

"Nat!" I yelled after her, but she merely waved a hand over her head and yelled back,

"Good luck!"

Great.

"Want to tell me why you're really here?" Alek asked. His dark eyes blared into me, as if looking at me alone was enough to learn all of my secrets.

"Zac invited us. He told us you would be here, and that it would be fun."

"Really?" he asked, looking toward where the two of them ran off. "He said that?"

"Yeah," I explained. I shoved my hands into the pocket of my sweatshirt, suddenly very aware of the fact that I was stuck somewhere I wasn't welcome.

But this was a damn carnival, not a private party. I could enjoy myself here if I wanted to.

"Alright," Alek sighed. "Since you're here, I guess business can wait." He casually threw his arm around my shoulders and began walking us to the entrance of the carnival. "What's first on your carnival bucket list?"

"Seriously?" I stiffened under his arm. "You don't have to do this."

"You're here. I'm not letting you out of my sight. I need to hold up my side of the deal, anyway." He stopped walking and looked me in my eyes as he said, "We're doing this."

I didn't fight the smile that crept onto my face. "Fine. Well, I've never been to a carnival, so I'm not totally sure what to expect."

"I guess that means we'll have to cover it all."

"I guess so." I shrugged.

I let Alek lead me around the carnival. We spent the next hour walking around the entirety as Alek explained, in detail, what everything was. Corn dogs—which were apparently somehow very popular, games, the Ferris wheel, other rides that looked as if they could fall apart at any second.

I tried not to act nervous at the sheer number of people around us. I had never seen so many people at once before. The noises, the lights, the music. It was all so much.

"Hey," Alek said when he saw me staring into the crowd. "Everything alright?"

"Yeah, it's just a little overwhelming."

He smiled softly. "I can see how this might be a lot to take in. Here, I have an idea." He pulled me toward the Ferris wheel. "Ride for two," Alek demanded.

The worker in the blue striped shirt nodded and opened the gate, letting us into the next available seats.

"Are you sure this is safe?" I whispered as the worker secured the door behind us. "What if we fall out?"

"That's part of the thrill," Alek whispered. He put his arm around me on the swinging chair and leaned in close as he added, "The danger is what makes it so fun."

A chill ran down my spine. I tried to convince myself it was from the chill of the night air, but I also couldn't look away from Alek's eyes. Not until the ride started moving again. I cleared my throat and forced my eyes away.

"So," I started, "what type of demon business does the league have at the carnival?"

Alek shrugged. His hand fell loosely on my shoulder. "Business you don't have to worry about."

"Considering you won't let Natalie and I walk around here alone, I think I *do* have to worry about it."

"You really want to know?" he asked.

"I sure do."

"Not all demons are like us, Lyra," he started. "In this area, we have things under control. We have leadership. We have order."

"Under your father?"

"Exactly. But in other places of the world, demons create chaos. For no other reason than to piss off the gods and goddesses."

I considered his words. I had never really thought about demons other than the Night Ravens. In our small area of the world, the gods and goddesses left the demons alone, and vice versa. A demon was no match for the power of a god, but a legion of demons? It would be a fight.

"What does that have to do with the carnival?"

"Let's call it a turf war," he explained. "It happens every couple of years. My father holds power over this legion, and others challenge his position."

"Doesn't that mean they challenge your position too?"

Alek's brows drew together. "Yes, it does. Which is why you can't be walking around here alone."

"What do I have to do with any of this?" I asked.

A beat of silence passed between us.

His brows pressed together. "You're kidding, right?"

I waited for him to continue.

"To everyone else, you're mine. We've been in a relationship. I've brought you into this legion. Anyone trying to hurt me will try to hurt you first. You're an easier target."

I sank into the seat of the Ferris wheel, which was moving higher and higher into the sky. "Great," I mumbled. "More enemies. Just what I need."

"This will all pass soon," he said. "It's just petty, arrogant bastards trying to take something that doesn't belong to them."

I tried to pay attention to what Alek was saying, but my focus was captured by the carnival below us. "We're really high up here," I whispered. The wind began to pick up, rocking the chair of the Ferris wheel back and forth.

Alek's hand tightened on my shoulder. "Are you afraid of heights?" When I glanced at him, he was smiling.

"I don't know," I replied. "I've never been this high up before."

"Really?" he asked. "So if I do this…" He moved his

body backward and then forward harshly, causing our already fragile seat to rock.

"Alek!" I squealed. "What the hell are you doing!"

"Just giving you a taste of what you missed out on at all these carnivals when you were younger."

I held onto the outer bar tightly with one hand, and gripped Alek's thigh instinctively with the other. "Don't you dare do that again!" I ordered.

"Or else what?" he teased. "What, exactly, are you going to do about it?"

I had no idea what had gotten into him. After what happened at that cabin, after how he spoke to me, I was certain he'd had enough. This was all just a stupid deal to him, anyway. He didn't need to be nice to me. He didn't need to protect me at a carnival, and he sure as hell didn't need to make me laugh.

I was either an idiot, or Alek actually had fun around me.

"I wasn't sure you would even talk to me today," I said quietly.

"Yeah," Alek agreed. "I wasn't so sure I would, either."

His words hurt me in a way I wasn't expecting them to. "But why? What's with the complete change of pace? I thought things were going fine with our deal."

"Things were going fine," he agreed. "But there's… there's more that you don't know. About me. About my life. Things I can't tell you."

"Then tell me," I pushed. "Tell me what's changed your mind."

"Nothing's changed my mind," he said. He took a long breath and turned his head to the sky. "Being around me is dangerous for you. It took me way too long to realize that."

I knew that wasn't the real reason. Alek had absolutely

no problem putting me in danger after we first met. He never once mentioned anything about protecting me, or about me getting hurt.

"Fine," I said. I wasn't in the mood to argue with him about it, and if he didn't want to tell me the truth, then there was nothing I could do to change his mind. "Whatever you say."

Instead of focusing on how many people were at this damned carnival, I focused on everything else. The twinkling string lights above us reminded me of the stars that Alek had taken me to see that cold night. Damn. That seemed like ages ago now.

I had learned so much since then. I had changed so much.

We rode the rest of the Ferris wheel in silence. Alek didn't talk to me again until we were stepping off the ride. "Hungry?" he asked.

I shrugged, but my stomach chose that exact moment to rumble loudly. I hadn't eaten at all today, and the smell of carnival food was in the air. "I guess I could eat," I hesitantly answered.

"Good," he said. "Follow me. Your next lesson will be on carnival food."

I began following as tightly as I could behind Alek, but the crowd was absolute chaos. Alek was taller than almost everyone else, but I could only see a few inches ahead. It only took a few seconds before someone shoved me sideways, and I lost track of Alek.

I reminded myself not to panic. I knew the direction he was moving. If he got too far ahead, he would find me.

He would look for me.

I continued trying to maneuver myself through the thick

sea of bodies that blocked my path until a hand clamped down on my wrist from behind me.

"Look who we have here," a man's voice approached from behind me. I spun around to find a tall stranger approaching me.

Shit.

Twenty~Five

"Can I help you?" I asked.

The man looked me up and down slowly as he stepped closer—too close for my comfort.

"You can't," he slurred. His breath hit me like a slap across the face, dripping with the scent of alcohol. "But your little boyfriend can."

Alarms rang in my mind. I had to get out of here fast, especially if this was one of the demons Alek mentioned on the Ferris wheel. What had he called it? A turf war?

"I don't know what you're talking about," I retorted. I glanced around, but there were so many people everywhere. I had nowhere to run. Nowhere to go.

"It seems like you know exactly what I'm talking about," the man pushed. "Especially considering he's been flaunting you around here all night like his new piece of eye candy." His eyes flickered down my body again.

Every instinct I had told me to run. If I could just distract him long enough, I could find a way to get over to Alek.

Where the hell was he?

"Look," I started, "whoever you think you are, whatever you think you're doing, you've got the wrong person."

"I don't think so, honey," the man chuckled darkly. He took a step closer to me. I took a step back. "I think you should come with me. I'm sure your boyfriend will come find you once he notices you're gone."

He took one more step in my direction.

I turned and bolted.

I ran as fast as I could into the crowd, into the swarm of people who wouldn't help me. I had always assumed I was a decently tall girl, but I couldn't see a damn thing. I resorted to pushing and shoving bodies as I made my way aimlessly through the masses.

The man followed tightly behind me. I ducked and weaved through small spaces as much as I could, which only managed to slightly slow him down. We crossed over the entire center crowd of the carnival until I reached the other side.

I was trapped. A gate lined the entire back path behind the food vendors.

The man caught up with me in an instant, grabbing tightly onto my arm. A small scream escaped me. "Let go!" I yelled.

"I don't think so," he growled. "You might be just the leverage we need to—"

"Get away from her!" Alek's voice boomed through the crowd. I flinched away as he turned around, only to find Alek standing behind him.

If I thought he looked pissed off before, I was sorely mistaken. Alek practically smoked with anger as he grabbed the man by the throat.

He was taller than the stranger. Stronger, too. I watched

in horror as he punched the man directly in the face. The impact resulted in a sickening crack, and he fell to the ground.

But Alek didn't stop there. He jumped on top of him, cascading punches on his face one after the other. Someone in the crowd was screaming. It took me a few seconds to realize it was me.

Alek kept going, punch after punch until Zac appeared, pulling Alek away from the pummeled man.

"What the hell is going on?" Zac yelled. Natalie ran to my side, asking the same question.

"He had Lyra," Alek said. "He was… he was going to…"

A few of the other Night Ravens approached. Two of them grabbed the stranger by both arms and hauled him to his feet. His head hung backward, clearly unconscious.

Natalie gasped beside me, her hand covering her mouth in shock.

"We'll take it from here," one of the Night Ravens said to Alek. They began dragging the man away, getting lost back into the crowd we had just come running from. "Nothing to see here, folks," he announced to the small crowd that gathered around the spectacle. "We've taken care of the situation." After a few seconds, the bystanders began to lose interest, returning to the carnival.

I could feel my heartbeat in my throat. "What was that?" Natalie asked me.

"I don't know," I explained. "He came up to me out of nowhere. I have no idea who he was."

"This is why you shouldn't have come!" Alek yelled.

"Relax, dude," Zac said. He grabbed Alek's arm, but Alek quickly shoved him off.

"It's true! You being here causes problems, Lyra. Not just for me, but for my legion."

Embarrassment flushed my cheeks. "How was I supposed to know one of your freak demon enemies was going to chase me through the crowd? How are you possibly blaming this on me?"

Natalie slid her hand into mine, but it did little to comfort me now.

"I told you it's better if you stay away from me," Alek said. "It's not safe. If this doesn't prove that, then I don't know what the hell does."

Natalie was already pulling me. "Let's get out of here," she said, "before any other fights break out."

I waited for Alek to say something. To object. But he did nothing. He stood there, frozen, as Natalie pulled away from the crowd. Away from the demons. Away from the carnival.

And away from him.

▭

I HAD TRIED AND FAILED TO GET ALEK OFF MY MIND AND SLIP into some sort of sleep when my phone buzzed.

My stomach dropped when I saw another text from Theia.

"Work is keeping me a few extra days. I'll stop by when I get home. I hope you're being good. - T "

Twenty~Six

"Let me make sure I heard that right," Natalie said, eyeing me with caution. "You are asking me to come out with you tonight, and you want to go back to Night Raven?"

"That's right. Theia will be home soon. We might as well go out while we still can."

I wasn't going to tell her the real reason I wanted to go to Night Raven. Alek hadn't texted or called me at all; I hadn't heard a single peep since the carnival. It had been three days. Three days of silence. I wasn't sure why I expected an apology, or even a lame explanation.

I just expected something. Anything.

Natalie placed both hands on my shoulders. "Are you feeling okay, Lyra? Are you sure you're not sick? Because I never in my life would have thought you would ask me to go back there."

I shrugged and brushed her hands off my shoulders. "Salem invited us," I explained. "She's really nice, and it would be rude to blow her off. That's the only reason I want to go."

"Mmhm," she replied. "I'm sure it has nothing to do with your fake boyfriend who will most likely be there."

I tried to act natural. Alek had proven that he wanted absolutely nothing to do with me. *This didn't have anything to do with him,* I told myself. Although even in my own mind, I knew I was lying.

I wanted to see him again, even if that meant putting my pride aside and showing up at Night Raven.

"No! He won't even be there, and even if he were, I wouldn't care."

"Then why is your face red?" she teased.

"Oh, shut up." I walked to my closet and began looking around. "Salem said a really great band is playing tonight. It could be fun!"

"You don't have to convince me, hun. I'm in! I don't know what they put in those drinks, but I had the time of my life at Night Raven."

"Yeah," I groaned. "That makes one of us."

I had been keeping my explanations to Natalie vague. Not because I didn't want to tell her about Alek, but because a small part of me liked that it was hidden. I had never acted so wild in my entire life.

And I didn't hate it.

Natalie and I got ready for the night faster than usual. We were both excited to go out this time, which was rare. Typically, we wasted at least an hour with Natalie trying to convince me to go out with her.

We were well past that point.

Salem waited for us outside the bar. "Lyra!" she squealed

when we saw her. "I'm so happy you came!" She yanked me into a tight hug.

"I'm happy we came too," I replied, pulling back with a grin. I nodded to my friend. "This is Natalie. Natalie, this is Salem. Alek's sister."

Natalie extended her hand. "So, the mysterious Alek has a sister? That makes him far less mysterious in my mind."

Salem shook her hand. "After all the stories you'll hear from me tonight, he won't be mysterious at all."

We all laughed. A pure sense of joy filled my chest, a feeling that was foreign to me.

And the night had just begun.

Salem saved a booth for us in the back of the bar. Right across from the stage. "We've got a few minutes before the band starts," she explained. "But drinks are on me tonight, so let's get this night started, shall we, ladies?"

Natalie slid into the booth. "Salem, I think we're going to be best friends."

I knew the two of them would get along. I had hardly interacted with Salem, but she had an energy that instantly made anyone feel comfortable.

Nat had the same energy. It was part of the reason we had stayed close over the years.

That, and the fact that she knew my greatest secret.

"So, Lyra," Salem started, "I heard my idiot brother almost got you into some shit during a mission the other day."

I rolled my eyes, trying not to remember the way his mouth felt on my neck. "You could say that."

"I have to say, I don't think Alek's ever taken a girl on an interception. You must be pretty badass if he trusts you to tag along."

Never?

"After the way I almost blew our cover, I doubt he'll be inviting me on more."

"Please!" Natalie chimed in. "That man is head over heels for you. He'll be inviting you everywhere, Lyra. You just wait."

Salem nodded thoughtfully. "It's true. He seemed… less douchey lately. I believe we have you to thank for that."

She raised her glass, and we all clinked ours together.

"Cheers!" she announced. "To young love!"

"Oh whatever!" I interrupted. "This is just part of that stupid deal. As soon as he's done using me to repair his image, I'll never see him again."

Salam and Natalie made eye contact before Natalie said, "I'll believe that when I see it."

We spent the next hour drinking, gossiping, and listening to Salem's crazy drunk stories about the demon bar before the band finally made their way onto the stage.

"Have you ever seen live music?" Natalie whispered to me.

I shook my head. I had hardly even left my apartment, let alone to attend a concert.

"Buckle up," she continued. "You're about to have the best night of your life."

As soon as she finished talking, the sound of music boomed through the air. First a guitar, then drums. Soon after, the singer took the stage. I had never heard anything like it.

"Wow," I said, taking in the ambiance of the bar. "He sounds great."

I didn't recognize the song he was singing, but it didn't

matter. I let the music into my body, taking in every bit of it possible.

"He sounds better than great," Salem pushed. "Come on. Let's dance."

"Dance?" I questioned. Natalie knew I wasn't a big dancer. That first night at Night Raven had been the only time.

But we had never heard live music before.

"Come on, Lyra! Look out there…" I looked to the dance floor where she pointed and saw dozens of girls just like us dancing.

They looked so happy. So *free*.

"Okay," I agreed. "I guess a few dances won't hurt."

Natalie squealed in excitement, and we met Salem on the dance floor.

For once, I didn't care about who was looking at me. I didn't care about how I looked or how bad my dancing was.

The three of us moved to the middle of the crowd, dancing with the beat of the music.

The singer had a similar style to Salem, with piercings and black ripped clothing. The type of clothing my mother would die over. The type of songs my mother would kill me for listening to.

I relaxed further, surrendering to the music. Between my two friends, I had never felt safer.

My body knew what to do. I didn't have to think about the music or what movements looked normal. I found myself swaying slowly to one song, then jumping and screaming with Natalie and Salem at the next.

Time escaped me. The only sign of how long we had been dancing was the sweat that now dripped down my neck.

"Hey," I whispered to my friend. "I'm going to take a break. I'll be right back."

They both whined, but Salem ultimately said, "Your loss, Lyra. Don't be long!"

I shoved my way from the crowd and headed to the bar. *Water. I need water.*

"Never thought I would see you here of your own free will," Alek's voice approached behind me. I spun around to find him leaned against the back wall, arms crossed and eyes dark.

"How long have you been here?" I asked. My voice came out in a rushed breath. I became very aware of the sweat that was beginning to soak through my shirt.

I must have looked like a maniac to him.

"Long enough."

"Salem invited me," I said. Why did I even feel the need to explain myself? "And we're having a good time."

"Good," he barked. "I'm so happy that you're having a great time dancing yourself around this bar."

"Excuse me?" I pushed, stepping closer to him. "Are you angry with me?"

"Yes, Lyra!" he hissed as soon as I was close enough. "You're supposed to be *mine*. You're not a *single* girl in this bar, remember?"

My eyes rolled back. "How could I possibly forget?"

"I'm being serious. This is my bar. My legion members come here. What if someone saw—"

"Saw what? Me dancing with my friends? Listening to music?" His jaw tightened. "I mean, you tell me you're going to liberate me. You tell me that by being with you, I'll get a chance to live. What about this? I've never heard live music before. *Never.* Did you know that?" I couldn't think straight. Emotion, adrenaline, and alcohol blocked my ability to act rationally. "If I wanted to be a prisoner," I spat, "I would go find my mother."

I stormed away, leaving him at the wall and heading straight to the bar. "Ice water, please."

I mean, seriously? Alek knew better. Alek knew better and he chose to treat me that way anyway. He knew my mother was strict. He knew I feared her. He knew I ran from her. He knew I had never really lived.

He had admitted to giving me a chance. A chance at living. And now this?

My chest tightened. I wouldn't be a prisoner. Not again. I wasn't going back.

"Lyra," his voice came up behind me. "You're not my prisoner."

"Aren't I?" I turned to him. "I do what you want, when you want it. I go where you want me to go. I wear what you want me to wear. How different are you than her? What's stopping you from locking me up, just like she did?"

"Don't say that," he whispered. "Don't compare me to her."

"Why shouldn't I?" I took a sip of my water.

"Look, if you want out of this deal, fine. Leave. Run. Hide. Go back to your strict, locked-down life. But,"—he glanced to the door of the bar, where a group of Night Ravens staggered in—"I know you, Lyra. *I see you.* You don't want to hide anymore. What I said earlier was wrong, I didn't... The truth is..." His hand slid up my back to the nape of my sweaty neck. "I wanted to rip out the eyes off every man who watched you dance. Because I don't care how fake this is to you, Lyra. You're mine."

My stomach twisted and melted, responding to his

words involuntarily. His words affected me in ways they shouldn't have, because I wasn't supposed to be this attracted to him. I wasn't supposed to want him, to want to kiss him. But I did. God, I did.

His fingers tightened on my neck. "You can hate me. You can ignore me forever, if that's what you want. But please, don't blow this in front of them." I followed his eyes, only to find Blade and Kyler across the bar, already staring at us.

"You're not as tough as you think you are, Alek," I whispered back to him.

Every instinct in my body told me to back down, but the music began playing again, and the new version of myself came back with it.

I stepped out of Alek's grasp, leaving him at the bar and heading to find Nat and Salem.

"Lyra!" Nat screamed over the music when she saw me again. "What took you so long?"

"Line at the bar," I lied. "But I'm back now."

Salem and Natalie each grabbed one of my hands. We continued dancing like I never left, moving to the music like this was what we were born to do. Only this time, I felt the eyes on me. That one pair of blazing, predatory eyes that made the hair on my neck stand up.

I tried to ignore it. I tried to go back to how things were, but my body refused to relax. Refused to let go.

"What's wrong?" Natalie asked. She could always sense when something was wrong. "Are you okay?"

I grabbed her arms and pulled her close, pretending to dance with her more as I whispered, "Alek's here. And he's not happy."

"I knew it!" she yelled. "He's jealous."

"He's an asshole is what he is."

"Forget about him," Salem chimed in. She grabbed my arm and pulled me back to the middle of the dance floor. "This is your life, Lyra. Remember that!"

Damn right.

I closed my eyes and focused on the music. I focused on the feeling of freedom I had just moments ago. I focused on my friends who danced beside me.

Only this time, while I danced under the spell of the band, I grew aware of the man who couldn't take his eyes off me.

We danced through the night, stopping only when I thought my feet were going to bleed.

"See, Lyra? We should do this more often!" Nat yelled. The music finally wrapped up, and we found ourselves sliding back into the same booth.

I glanced around the bar. Alek was still here, only now, he sat at a table with Blade, Kyler, and Zac. And they didn't look happy.

I reminded myself I didn't care.

"Thank you so much for this, Salem," I breathed. "I needed this."

"We all did," she replied. "I haven't had much luck with girlfriends since I moved back here. Alek does a great job at scaring away all of my friends."

"I can see why," Nat mumbled.

"Well, you're welcome with us any time," I admitted. "Although Nat's usually the one dragging me out of the house."

"Really?" Salem asked. "Seems like I've seen your face around here quite a bit."

"You're welcome," Natalie chimed in.

I elbowed her before answering, "My mother is strict.

That's all."

Salem leaned forward, resting her chin on her hands. "How so?"

"She doesn't want me—"

"Socializing," Nat finished. "Living. Being seen in the flesh."

"Yes," I interrupted. "All of those things."

Salem eyed me, as if trying to decide how much of that were the truth.

If only she knew.

"So why don't you forget her?" she pushed. "Plenty of people do it."

"It's not that easy." I choked back the feeling of defensiveness that crept in from the darkness. Salem only wanted to help. I knew that. "My mother has connections."

"So what? What could she possibly do to you that would be so terrible?"

I stiffened. Where did I start? Salem wouldn't understand. Nobody would. Nat was the closest person to ever seeing inside that locked window, and that was only because she saw some of it up close and personal.

She must have realized this, too, because she said, "Lyra's mother is a force to be reckoned with, trust me. You don't want to get on her bad side. Lyra's life would be over in a second if it were up to that woman."

My throat stung. The sudden talk of my mother reminded me precisely how not free I truly was.

My mother would be back soon, and all of this would be in my past.

All of it.

"I need to use the bathroom," I muttered before slipping

out of the booth. They didn't question me as I slowly walked away. I needed air. I needed space.

But I would never be far enough. I would never be fast enough to run away from the memories I created in this place.

And that would haunt me forever.

Alek left the group of demons he was standing with and sauntered over to me.

"What are you doing?" I asked, half a whisper in the thin air that lingered between us.

Every part of me was wanting to lean in, to close that tendril of distance between us.

Alek was danger. He was thrilling and terrible and chaotic.

And he was free.

"Time to seal the deal, Lyra," he breathed. "If you're going to dance in this bar, everyone here is going to know who you belong to." His lips were so close to mine, they would have brushed if I moved even an inch. He knew it, too. He stayed that way for only a few seconds, long enough that the curious stares were now glued to us.

Every inch of my body burned with desire.

And then, with a wicked half-smile on his face, he kissed me.

His mouth pressed into mine, warm and gentle, as his hands found their way around my body. My mouth reacted naturally to his, moving in perfect unison with him as he led the way. He pressed closer to me, making sure not a single ounce of space was left between us. My hands found their way around his neck, pulling him closer to me.

It was a show. I knew that. But I still couldn't stop myself from getting drawn into his delicate touch and his needy mouth. Alek was my drug.

I kissed him back, wanting to be convincing to our audience but also wanting something more, something I couldn't even admit to myself.

A few yells and cheers from Alek's table of guys was our sign that it had worked.

Alek pulled away but didn't take his hands off me as his eyes met mine. "You're a great actor," he whispered. His voice melted with the same heat I felt. "I nearly believed that."

I could feel the heat in my face as I held his stare. "Likewise," was all I could manage to say.

Something stirred inside of me as his beaming green eyes flickered down to my lips once more.

Could he hear how fast my heart was beating?

And then it was over. Alek stepped away and walked back to his posse, leaving me alone.

I didn't wait another second before leaving Salem and Nat, bolting out of the bar, and rushing home.

Twenty-Seven

"You can't keep coming here," I whispered. "Someone will eventually see you."

"You left the bar alone. I needed to make sure you got home okay."

I pulled my sweater tight around my waist. I had changed out of my clubbing clothes and washed the hoards of makeup off my face, but somehow I felt more exposed in my sweater and sweatpants than I had in the tight dress. "Well, I'm obviously fine, so you can go."

Alek's unreadable face darkened. He stayed put near the window, not coming any further. "Don't shut me out, Lyra. Let's talk."

"I'm not shutting anyone out! You don't have to pretend like you really care, Alek. We fooled everyone in the damn bar tonight. Mission accomplished."

His jaw tightened. "You know that's not all I care about."

A sharp pain formed in my chest. Bitterness and jealousy swam through my mind, threatening to drown me. I tried to push it all away, I tried to rebuild those walls Alek had been tearing down, brick by brick. But I was in too deep. Could Alek tell? Could he see how much this hurt? "Well, it should be."

I turned around and walked into my open kitchen, grabbing a cup and filling it with water. I stood with my back to him, trying to collect my thoughts as I placed both hands on the counter.

"I didn't mean to snap at you. I lost my temper, and I'm sorry."

Alek took a few steps forward. I felt his presence as he approached behind me.

"Forgive me," he said. It wasn't a question as much as it was a quiet demand.

Chills ran down my arms.

"Why should I?" I questioned. "What's the point?"

Alek moved even closer. If I leaned back even an inch, I would be pressed against his chest. "I don't want to be your enemy, Lyra. I don't want you to hate me."

"Why not?" I whispered. "This is just part of the deal for you, isn't it? This is all just a way to get your father to do what you want. So why bother with thinking anything different?"

His hand fell onto my shoulder. "Do I really have to say it?"

My heart raced. "Say what?"

A knock on my front door interrupted us. Alek backed away instantly, and the tension between us disappeared in an instant.

"Lyra, it's me. Open up!" I knew that voice.

Theia was here.

"Shit," I whispered. I opened the small closet door in my kitchen and pulled Alek's arm. "Shit, shit, shit. Get inside."

"What?" he whispered back.

"She can't see you here. Hide! Right now!"

The bewilderment on his face didn't leave as he squeezed himself into the small closet. "Stay quiet," I reminded him, and I shut the door.

"Lyra, are you in there?" my mother asked again with a knock. "Come on, open up!"

I quickly scanned the kitchen and living room, making sure Alek had left no signs of his visit behind.

She wouldn't know. She wouldn't know a thing. She had no reason to believe anyone had been here, and she definitely had no reason to believe that person was a demon.

I walked to the front door and grabbed the knob, taking a deep breath before swinging it open.

"Hi, Mom," I said. I had to remind myself to smile. I was supposed to be happy to see her.

I definitely didn't need to give her any more reason to hate me.

She ignored me completely as she stepped inside and immediately began surveying my apartment. "I'm in town for the night and thought I'd come check up on my lovely daughter. How are you, darling?"

I rolled my shoulders back and lifted my chin. "I'm good," I responded. "I'm done with school now. I've been doing a lot of reading."

She nodded, looking over the small stack of books on my coffee table. "Good," she said. "Reading will keep you busy."

I shrugged. "How are you? How's work?"

Her heels clicked the tile floor as she walked into the kitchen. I silently prayed that she couldn't hear how loud my heart beat in my chest.

But she didn't pay any attention to the closet. She set her designer bag on the kitchen counter and finally turned her attention to me. "Same as usual," she said. She always answered those questions the same way—same as usual, nothing new, boring as ever. But we both knew none of those answers were truthful. We also knew 'work' was a loose term for what my mother did.

Being the Goddess of Light in the realm didn't exactly constitute a normal job.

But she didn't talk about it. I didn't ask.

"That's good," I eventually replied.

My mother stayed that way, staring at me without saying anything, for at least a minute. Her attention made me squeamish to say the least. I didn't want her looking at me. Hell, I didn't even want her talking to me. Her presence made me uncomfortable, even if it was in my own apartment.

My apartment that she paid for. My apartment that she controlled. Stalked with video cameras.

"You've been good lately," she said. "It seems from the video feed that you hardly even leave."

I swallowed. These conversations had a habit of going one of two ways.

"Like I said," I started, "I've been doing a lot of reading."

Her eyes blazed into mine, like a laser through dust. She had no reason not to believe me, I reminded myself. She didn't suspect anything. "That's good," she said. "I knew you would finally grow out of that rebellious phase. Doctors say it's an area of your brain."

"What?"

She nodded and pushed herself back up from the kitchen counter. "Your brain is fully developed now," she explained. "You won't go making silly decisions again. You won't go running off from me now."

I forced myself to smile at her joking tone, but we both knew how painful those memories were. "No," I explained. "I guess I've grown out of that."

She surveyed my apartment before locking eyes on the window. *That damn window.* "A little cold for an open window, isn't it?" she questioned.

I smiled again and gave her an agreeable nod. She sauntered over to the window, glancing outside for only a second before sliding it shut.

Every cell in my body screamed in panic.

She wouldn't know, I told myself. She would have absolutely no idea that I was entering and leaving through that thing.

Theia stepped forward and grabbed my face with her cold, boney hands and pressed a kiss on my forehead.

Every muscle in my body tensed.

"I'll be home in a few days," she said. "I'm proud of you, Lyra. Your blood holds more than you can ever imagine. It seems you're finally beginning to see that."

"Thank you, Mother," I whispered back. The emotions from her words were waves crashing on the surface. Did she not see it? Was she really so blind?

"I have to go, but I'll text you, okay?" She walked back to the front door, and I could finally breathe again.

"Sure," I replied. "Sounds good."

She shut the front door behind her.

I slid the lock into the bolt, turned around, and bolted to the kitchen.

Alek was already opening the closet door and sliding out. "That was close," he said. "I have a feeling she would be pissed if she caught me in there."

I laughed, but it came out as a breathy sigh. I ran my hands down my face and used the wall for support.

"Hey," he whispered, "are you okay?"

I opened my mouth to explain that I was fine, but the words didn't come out. Alek kept his distance as I finally straightened myself out. "She's… I just wasn't expecting her visit. That's all."

"I get it," he said.

"I seriously doubt that."

"So tell me, then," he said. "Explain it to me."

Shocked, I met his gaze. He was already staring at me in complete seriousness.

"My mother is… she's not exactly loving."

He smiled. "That much, I picked up on." His smile somehow loosened one of the growing knots in my stomach.

"I sometimes feel like I'll never be free from her grasp."

Alek pushed both of his hands into his jean pockets and shrugged. "What was all that she said about you running away? Maybe you could try that again." I could tell from his voice that the question was innocent, but I tensed up all the same.

"Yeah, well, maybe she's right. Maybe my rebellious phase is over."

"Over?" he repeated, taking another step. "Are you sure about that?"

The mischief on his face sent a chill down my spine.

"Running away did nothing but end up hurting me even more," I explained.

"You were younger then," he assumed. "And alone. You're not alone anymore."

Not alone. It didn't feel free. It felt too good to be true, actually. Because even if Alek wanted to say that, he didn't know the full truth. He didn't know my secret that forced me to stay alone. That would force me to stay alone forever.

"What did she mean when she said, 'your blood holds more than you could ever imagine'? Some sort of family genetics or something?"

I immediately stiffened, alarms going off in my mind. Alek had no reason to think anything was different about my blood. He was simply asking because of what he had heard.

Right?

I had to remind my body to relax in Alek's presence. "Um, yeah," I said. "My mother is very cryptic. She's always saying things like that."

If he didn't believe me, he didn't show it. He just nodded and walked across the living room toward the window.

He paused and turned back to me. "I don't want to pry in your family business," he started, "but you're an adult now, Lyra. If your mother doesn't treat you with respect, you can always cut her off. Leave. Start over. It sounds impossible, but it's not."

The blood rushed from my face. No, it wasn't possible. But how could I explain that? How could I explain that my mother will always find me? Always control me?

I shook my head. No, that was just what she wanted me to think. If I could get far enough away, maybe—just maybe —she wouldn't be able to find me.

"You sure you're okay?" he repeated.

"Yeah," I said, following him to the window. "I'm fine."

"Good," he answered. The tattoo on his neck flexed as he tilted his head to the side. He reached out to tuck a stray piece of hair behind my ear, the touch making my skin erupt in goosebumps. "Goodnight, Lyra," he whispered.

And once again, I was alone.

Twenty~Eight

Natalie was standing in my living room holding a duffel bag when I stepped out of the shower.

"What's this?" I asked, flipping my wet hair over my shoulder.

"It's a surprise." She stood at me with a huge smile on her face. "You're going on a small trip."

"What type of surprise?" I asked. "And where am I going?"

She scowled. "If I told you, it would ruin the whole thing."

"You're scaring me here, Natalie."

"Don't be scared," she said, perking back up. "This is a good thing."

"Is this an *Alek* thing?" I asked slowly.

"Maybe," she answered with a smirk that told me *yes*, this was an Alek thing.

Whatever it was, it had to be good. After the carnival, Natalie had changed her opinions about Alek. I didn't blame her. She saw the side of him that he had been so, so good at hiding.

She saw his dark side. His demon side.

She shoved the bag closer to me. "I can't go on a trip, Natalie," I said. "What if Theia comes back and drops in again? What am I supposed to tell her when I'm not here?"

"It's just one night. I'll be here the whole time just in case she stops by, but she won't. Because she's with my mother in Japan right now."

She pulled out her phone and showed me a text from her mother, confirming that yes, Theia was right there with her.

"It's risky," I argued.

"It is," Natalie answered. "But everything up to this point has been risky, Lyra."

"He doesn't even care about me. He made that very, very clear."

She took a long breath and walked over to sit on my couch. "I don't know Alek as well as you do," Natalie started. "I haven't been there for all of it. I've only seen a few glimpses. But what I saw at the carnival? What I saw at the bar the other night? He *likes* you, Lyra. And it's more than just whatever stupid deal you have together."

My cheeks flushed. "He doesn't," I insisted, even though I wanted to believe her words. "He's just a great actor." My mind wandered to his lips on mine, the way he kissed me in front of everyone. Was that all acting? Was that all part of the deal? Was there any, tiny part of the kiss that was real to him?

Of course not. None of this was new to Alek. None of this was special. *I* wasn't special.

"Then I guess we'll find out whether or not that's actually true," she muttered. "Because he's here to pick you up."

"He's *what*?"

Natalie stood up and walked over to my closet, picking out a sweater and a pair of jeans. "He's here to get you. You might want to get dressed. Everything else you'll need is in the bag."

"This better be a joke."

"Oh, I'm very serious," she replied. "And so was Alek when he insisted on surprising you with this. Get moving!"

I couldn't deny the flicker of excitement that ignited in the back of my mind. After all of this, after pushing me away and swearing to me that he wasn't good for me, Alek wanted to surprise me with a trip?

"Can you at least tell me where I'm going?" I asked Natalie as I got dressed and picked up the small duffel bag. I tossed her my mother's cell phone.

"Nope," she said with a smile. "But you'll thank me later."

My nerves had me smiling, too, as I crawled out of the window and walked over to Alek's car.

He stood just like he had stood every time before, with his back leaning against the passenger side door. "What is all this?" I asked, motioning to the duffel over my shoulder.

When I was close enough, he grabbed the bag from my shoulder and threw it in his trunk. "Get in and you'll find out."

I climbed into the car and waited for Alek to explain what we were doing, but he didn't. He silently started driving, pulling off my street and into the city.

"I owe you an apology," he said after a few minutes of driving.

"For what?"

"I didn't mean to treat you that way, Lyra. I let my fear

get the best of me. After the carnival… I wasn't myself. I wasn't seeing things clearly."

I definitely wasn't expecting an apology. Did he regret the kiss, too? Did he regret all of it?

"You don't have to run away from me, Alek," I said. "If you haven't noticed, I don't have much going on in my life. This is… even the danger is exciting to me. I know that's bad, but it's true."

He smiled. It was his real smile—the one I hadn't seen in ages.

"Well, I'm relieved to hear you say that. I guess after what happened at the lake house, I've started to feel responsible for you."

"You're not responsible for me, Alek," I said softly. "You have no idea how much you've done to help me." I reminded myself I was supposed to be angry with him. Maybe not completely pissed off, but I shouldn't be letting him off so easily. He was giving me whiplash with all of his mood changes.

But he was here. He was making an effort. And once again, he had the ability to pull me out of the cage of an apartment.

I had missed him. I had missed this.

"You deserve better," Alek said. "For whatever reason, I'm glad I have a deal with you. But you deserve better."

His words were flattering, but a void of emotions washed over his face. He was thinking something else; I just didn't know what.

I would give anything to know what he was thinking all the time. Alek was at war with something in his own mind. If anyone understood that, it was me.

"Are you going to tell me where we're going?" I asked again, turning my attention to the road.

"Yes," he answered. "I'm showing you the world."

My chest tightened. Half with excitement, and half with nervous energy.

Twenty minutes later, Alek pulled the car directly up to a private plane. "Is this for us?" I exclaimed. He threw the car in park.

"Let's go find out," he said with a wicked grin. I followed him out of the car. He grabbed my duffel bag and a bag of his own before walking toward the small plane. "Are you ready for this?" he asked.

"I have no idea!" My mind swarmed. Where were we going? Why was he doing this? Was this just him upholding his part of the deal, or was this part of his grand apology?

He nodded to an older man that stood next to the ladder and began walking onto the plane. I followed him, trying not to look completely dumbfounded at everything.

The interior was small yet luxurious, with a few white leather couches.

"The Night Ravens keep a private pilot around in case we have an emergency."

Fear flashed through me. "Is this an emergency?"

Alek dropped our duffels and relaxed into the long leather seat. "Not at all," he said. "But part of the perks of being the demon prince is having the private jet available to me."

"Sounds convenient."

"It is."

I stood awkwardly in the middle of the plane. "You better sit down before we take off. I'm not responsible for your injuries on this aircraft."

I sat next to him, making sure to put plenty of distance between us on the leather couch.

The plane began rolling slowly. I turned my body and stared out the window. We began moving faster and faster and faster until the weight of gravity on my body became so heavy, I nearly laughed.

And then we were in the air.

"I would stop looking out there if I were you," Alek said.

"Why?" We began rising, and we quickly cascaded over the tall buildings of the city below us. A wave of nausea hit me.

"Because you're afraid of heights," Alek said with amusement in his voice.

"Right." I quickly turned around and focused on anything besides how high we were flying.

"Do I get to know where we're heading yet?" I asked.

Alek stared at me. He had stretched his legs out in front of him and extended both arms on the back of the leather seats next to him. How could anyone possibly be this relaxed in a moving, flying object?

"I guess I could give you a hint," he started. He didn't take his eyes off me.

I wanted to squirm under his attention, but after all the time we had spent together, I decided to step up. To be confident. I stared right back at him, even letting my eyes flicker down to his lips. His chest. His relaxed body.

When my eyes returned to his, he was smiling.

"Don't tell me you're whisking me away to my final destination," I said. "Finally ready to get rid of me?"

He rolled his head back and laughed slowly. "I'm not ready to let you go just yet," he started. "And after the last couple of weeks, I'm afraid I've been slacking on my part of the deal."

"What does that mean?"

"That means we're doing something extravagant. We're going to Paris."

I stared at him a second longer, unsure if I heard him correctly. "Did you just say *Paris*?"

He nodded smugly. My heart immediately began racing in my chest. I had dreamt of leaving the city. I used to fantasize about getting far, far away from this place.

And with Alek, I was actually doing it.

"We won't be there long," he said. "Just a few hours. But at least you'll get to see it."

"I don't even know what to say," I mumbled.

"Say nothing. Consider this my apology for being a complete ass to you."

My chest warmed with an emotion I had never felt before. "Apology accepted."

Paris was colder than I expected. I pulled my jacket tighter around my body as Alek and I walked the empty, dark streets. Streetlights were few and far between, and while I knew Alek had no problem seeing in the dark due to his weird demon strengths, I was starting to get creeped out.

"Aren't there supposed to be, like, tourists or something?" I asked.

Alek placed a gentle hand on my lower back as we walked. "I'm not much into crowds," he said. "I figured I would give you more of the discrete tour. Besides, the tourists don't know about the best places here."

A massive rat scurried across the pavement in front of us, followed by a few dead leaves being blown after it.

"Discrete," I repeated. "Why does that not surprise me?"

"We're almost there. Keep an open mind," he said.

So I tried. I surveyed the old, brick buildings around us. Compared to home, this place felt ancient. Stones were falling off buildings. Old trees surrounded the streets. It was much, much quieter, which I definitely was not expecting.

When I pictured Paris, I pictured the Eiffel Tower. I pictured tourists and deserts and the French.

But this felt… it felt peaceful. It felt lived in. It felt warm, even though goosebumps covered my arms.

"This way," Alek said. He pulled me into one of the old, stone buildings. From the outside, it looked abandoned. Lost, just like many of the other buildings around us. Inside, the cement stairs inside were half crumbling, and I had to watch each of my steps as we walked up them.

"Are you sure this is safe?" I asked.

"After all this time, I would think you'd trust me at least a little bit by now."

I ignored him, and we finished cascading the multiple flights of crumbling stairs.

One man stood, ready to greet us at the top of the stairs. He had bright green eyes that nearly glowed in the darkness, similar to Alek's. "Sir Alek," he said. "It's a pleasure to see you again."

"The pleasure is all mine, Charles," Alek responded. The two men clasped hands briefly.

"I have a table for you and the lady, right this way," Charles said. He began leading the way up yet another flight of stairs.

Alek held a hand out, waiting for me to head up the stairs.

As soon as we reached the top, Charles pushed a door open to the roof. Suddenly, instead of being inside of an old, worn-down building, we were outside. There was one small table in the center of the rooftop, and a heater to warm us up stood directly beside it.

And beyond the roof was the prettiest, most magical view of Paris I could have ever imagined. The sea of stars above blended with the twinkling lights of the bustling city. People filled the streets in the distance, and even though we could see them, we were in our own, protected space here on the roof. I couldn't imagine anything more beautiful.

Charles and Alek exchanged a few words before he left us alone on the roof.

"I can't believe this," I said to Alek. I walked to the ledge, peering out at the city beyond. "This is… this isn't real."

"It's real," Alek assured me softly, moving to stand behind me. "Paris is one of my favorite cities. The history, the architecture. There's something comforting about it."

"Is this where you take all of your dates?" I teased. In the distance, I could see the reflections of hundreds of lights in the river below. I could see the Eiffel Tower, which twinkled with lights as beautiful as the stars.

"No," Alek said. "I've never brought anyone here."

My head whipped towards him. "Ever? That's surprising."

He laughed quietly. We both moved to take our seats at the table, where two glasses of wine waited for us. "Why is that surprising?" he asked. Instead of his usual leaned back demeanor, he leaned forward and placed both of his elbows on the table. As if what I was saying was the most important thing in the world. As if he were drinking up every word.

"Because you're you. I'm sure you have no problem finding women, and I'm sure it's simple enough for you to sweep anyone off their feet with a midnight trip to Paris." He smiled at me but said nothing. "What?" I asked.

"You're a very peculiar woman, Lyra Sol," he said. My cheeks heated.

"And what is that supposed to mean, Alekzander Black?"

"I'm the prince of demons. I don't date much. I may have had the appearance of a bachelor lifestyle, but it was just that. An appearance."

"Why would you want to appear that way?" I pressed. "If you weren't actually going crazy all over the city, why did you feel the need to fake date me to fool your father?"

He finally leaned back in his seat. "My father is... well, he's complicated. He doesn't like me all that much, if you haven't caught on to that by now."

I stayed silent for a minute. I didn't want to be the first one to bring up his brother, but I knew that was the reason. The way his father treated him in the few interactions I had witnessed had been absolutely garbage. I couldn't imagine the types of things that went down when I wasn't around. I mean, he had stabbed his own son!

"Why does he hate you so much?" I murmured.

Alek took a long breath but didn't look away. His eyes darkened before he answered, "I killed my brother."

My heart nearly stopped beating. "You *what?*"

"There was an accident last year. A demon ritual got out of hand, and he died. Crossed the veil. My fault, of course, so now my father wants nothing to do with me."

A flash of grief crossed his features before he recovered.

"Oh, my god, Alek, I'm sorry," I said. "I had no idea." Alek didn't want my pity, but I did feel sorry. He didn't deserve to be treated that way. Nobody did.

"It's my fault," Alek said matter-of-factly. "My father has every right to hate me. If situations were reversed, I would likely do the same."

"I don't believe that," I said.

"It's true. We do what we think is right at the time."

"And your father believed that stabbing you in the torso was *right*? You're grieving, too. You lost someone, too."

Alek shook his head and let out a breath. "I don't pretend like I know half of what that man is thinking," he said. His eyes grew cold as he focused on something in the distance. "But I do know that he loved Wrath more than anything. He'll give anything to get him back again, to see him one more time."

I didn't push it. This was the first time I had heard Alek talk about his brother, mention him by name. *Wrath*. I caught myself wondering if they had been close. It couldn't have been easy for Alek to lose his brother and then live with the guilt of the entire situation.

"For what it's worth," I started, "if redemption is what you're looking for, I think you've damn well earned it. You're not a bad guy, Alek. I've never thought that about you."

His eyes focused back on me. "You should. You should think that. As long as my father is in control, I'll have to do what he says. I'm his left hand until he says otherwise."

"But why?" I argued. "You could stand against him. You could make a difference if you—"

"That's all fantasy, Lyra. I mean, look at your mother.

Would you stand against her? Make a difference? Would you fight against her even if it meant losing everything?"

His words were harsh, but his voice was soft. I knew he meant well. "No," I sighed, slumping slightly in my chair. "I guess I wouldn't."

Charles returned with two plates of food. He quickly explained each item of the French cuisine before returning inside.

"I didn't mean to make this all about me," Alek said. "Let's talk about you. Talking about Wrath is just depressing."

"Okay," I said, picking up my fork. "What would you like to know?"

"Tell me about your mother," he said.

The alarms rang in my mind. I couldn't stop them. Even in front of Alek, who was clearly not a threat to me, I was on edge. "What do you want to know about her?" I asked.

Alek didn't know that Theia was the Goddess of Light. He had no idea why my mother was so strict, why my apartment was video-monitored, and why I couldn't text him using my own cellphone.

He knew nothing. He had never asked. Never pushed. Even though I knew he wanted to. I knew how my situation looked from the outside.

"Why does she keep you locked in that apartment so often?" he asked. "Why are you afraid of her finding out what you're really doing?"

I set my fork down, suddenly losing my appetite. "She's just strict," I answered.

"But why? Did you have a crazy rebellious phase when you were younger or something?"

He continued eating, completely ignorant as to how catastrophic these questions were.

Yes, I had a rebellious phase. If you would even call it that. I had escaped her increasingly tight claws and had ran —as far as humanly possible—until my feet bled.

Only, I wasn't just some rebellious teenager. I was my mother's purpose for surviving. My blood gave her worth. Gave her power.

Because my mother controlled the veil. And she needed my blood to do it.

But I couldn't tell Alek any of that.

Or could I?

Alek understood my need to live. My longing for adventure. He understood the darkest parts of me that I had kept hidden away. He saw it all, and he showed me the light. Which in his world, was just more chaos and darkness. But I loved it. I loved all of it.

Could I show him this? Could I share this burden with him? This man who was a stranger to me just a few weeks ago?

I stopped myself. No, I couldn't. Alek was a demon, and he had mentioned the veil more than one time.

But would he use me? After knowing how caged I had been? After knowing how tortured I had felt my entire life? How sheltered? I'd like to think he wouldn't, but when was I ever that lucky?

"I ran away from home a long time ago," I said. "After my father died, it was just my mother and I, so I could see how she would feel a bit insecure after that."

"Wow," he said. "Seems like she can hold a grudge."

"Yeah," I agreed, forcing a smile. "She can. It's a miracle she even allows me to live in that apartment alone. We've come a long way." He eyed me with brows drawn together. "What?"

"It's just… it seems like you'd be totally fine on your own. That's all. You're a beautiful, smart, witty girl. I don't see why you let your mother control you so much."

"It would be impossible not to. She has connections."

"That's right," Alek replied. "You mentioned that she worked for gods and goddesses. That must create a lot of pressure for you."

I blushed again. Of course Alek would remember a tiny lie I told weeks ago. And of course he would bring it up. "Exactly," I said.

It felt wrong lying to him. Especially because I knew he might have been the one person in the world who would really understand my situation.

His father controlled him, too. In a different way, Alek was also living his life in a cage.

Two caged animals begging to be let free.

Both too afraid to bite the hands that fed them.

How poetic.

We finished the rest of our dinner without discussing our parents. Alek mentioned a few of his favorite sight-seeing locations, where he used to wander in Paris, and how him and Charles had known each other for years.

"Are you ready for the real fun to start?" Alek asked. He stood up and held his hand out for me to join him.

Was I ever?

Twenty~Nine

"Skeletons?" I asked. "You mean this entire underground tomb is full of old bones?"

Alek shrugged his thick leather jacket off himself and hung it around my shoulders. I was already wearing a thin jacket, but the temperature continued to drop as we walked the narrow steps to the catacombs.

"Think about the history," Alek whispered. "Think about everyone who has lived before you, and everyone who will live after you."

Even with the extra layer of Alek's jacket, I shivered. "That doesn't help. I'd rather not think about the thousands of dead souls we're walking with."

He laughed quietly. Alek explained to me that these catacombs were typically swarmed with tourists during the day. Lucky for us, though, it was an hour after midnight. We were the only two in sight.

Which both relaxed me and put me on edge.

When we began walking down the stairs, I wasn't

worried. It wasn't until the sky disappeared above us that I started to second-guess where Alek was taking me.

Skulls became visible in the walls around us. Bones made up half the walls, and the dark tunnels before us looked anything but welcoming.

"This is your idea of fun?" I hissed.

"Try to relax," he said. "Just live in the moment."

We took the first turn in the tunnels, which removed any lingering moonlight from the stairs above.

I froze.

Alek's hands found my waist. "Don't be afraid," he whispered in my ear.

I leaned into his touch, half because I couldn't see a damn thing, and half because I wanted more of it.

"I'm not afraid," I lied.

"Good, because we're just getting started. This way."

He slid his hand down my arm and interlocked his fingers with mine. It was a casual movement, I knew it was.

But that didn't stop my entire body from erupting in goosebumps.

"What exactly are we supposed to be doing down here?" I asked.

"Respecting the bones that built these walls," Alek said. He stopped walking and pulled me close to him. In the darkness, I could hardly make out the shadow of his body. "Or maybe I just brought you here to scare you."

My heavy breath was the only audible sound in the catacombs. That, and the sound of dripping water far in the distance.

"Mission accomplished," I whispered. In the cover of the darkness, I slid my own hands up his sides. It was reckless and stupid, but something about the thrill of the catacombs fueled me.

We were alone down here. We were in a different world. We weren't here to put on a show to Alek's father, we weren't here to fool anyone. For the first time since I met Alek, this actually felt real. And not just for me.

Alek's hands drifted to the sides of my face. "It's odd," he started. "I feel safer down here. Even though we're surrounded by thousands of human bones."

He was so close now, our chests were nearly touching. My heartbeat rang in my ears, the scent of sandalwood growing more intoxicating with every breath.

"It's quiet," I replied. "It's hidden. That's rare for us, I guess."

I felt him smile in the darkness.

His thumbs swept over my cheeks. My hands slid slowly to his back. "Very rare, indeed," he agreed.

"Is this another trick?" I whispered. My heart fluttered with every torturous movement of his hands. "Is this another part of our deal? Of proving that we're together?"

"No trick, Lyra," he whispered. His lips were moving closer, taunting me with every word. "Not this time."

Alek's scorching lips found mine in the darkness of the underground. I pulled him closer, reveling in the encapsulating warmth of his body. He kissed me slowly, taking his time as he held me gently in his arms.

And I kissed him back. Nobody was around to watch us. Nobody would know. For the first time, this felt real.

Alek wasn't kissing me as a project or as a secret. He was kissing me for *me*. He kissed me because he wanted to.

Alek deepened the kiss with ease, sweeping his tongue across my lower lip. I let him guide me, showing me exactly what to do. Heat crawled up my body while chills erupted down my arms. Alek's touch was addicting, intoxicating.

I never wanted it to end.

Something between us shifted. Those gentle, taunting kisses grew deeper. I slid my hands up Alek's back as he pulled me flush against his body. His hands lowered, and he gripped the back of my jeans with one hand while he moaned into my mouth.

If it weren't for him holding me up, I would have melted.

Every part of my body burned with desire for him, for more of this. I had wanted this for so long, and we were finally alone. Finally doing what we should have been doing all along.

He kissed me in the darkness until we were both out of breath. I pulled away, barely enough to break our embrace.

"What was that for?" I breathed.

I felt his chest rise and fall, matching mine. Alek shrugged. "I wanted to see what kissing you felt like when you weren't acting," he said.

My heart twisted into a million pieces. I couldn't do this. I couldn't feel this way about him. Because as real as that kiss was, as real as Alek was standing here in my arms, this couldn't happen.

I wasn't free. This wasn't real. My brain knew that, but my heart refused to accept it.

"And?" I pushed.

"And you drive me fucking insane, Lyra."

I didn't ask him to clarify. I didn't say anything else as he led us back through the tunnels, toward the entrance of the catacombs.

We spent the next two hours walking through the streets of Paris. I was utterly shocked at the beauty of it all, but the best part was the fact that Alek didn't let go of my hand. Not once.

He didn't kiss me again. Not as he took me to stand beneath the Eiffel Tower, and not as we boarded the private plane back home.

But the last thing I pictured before I fell asleep that night were his lips on mine.

T hree days later, I left through the front door of my apartment for the first time in what felt like months. I could hear the buzz of the security camera tracking my movements as I walked.

I pictured my mother getting the movement alert on her phone and wondering where I was going. If I was lucky, she wouldn't check. Wouldn't ask.

My tennis shoes on the pavement became the only thing I focused on. I tried to clear my mind of all the shit that had happened over the last few weeks. I had come so close to death on more than one occasion, yet somehow, I had lived more than ever in my life.

I didn't have a plan.

After Paris, I was certain that what Alek felt for me was more than just a deal. I couldn't get him out of my mind. The entire trip was anything but casual, *and that kiss.*

I had been reliving the way he held me, the way he touched me.

It had been three days. Three days, and no word from

Alek. I had texted him a couple of times but got nothing back.

I fought that numbing feeling in the pit of my stomach that told me something was wrong.

Before I could comprehend whether or not it was a good idea, I turned around and headed for Night Raven.

What the hell was I going to say to him? Was I going to tell him that the deal was off, that I didn't want this to be fake anymore?

This was real to me. Maybe it was real to him, too.

I shook my head as I walked.

No way, that wouldn't work. A deal with a demon was impossible to break.

But maybe, just maybe, I could tell him my secret. Maybe I could tell him the real reason my mother kept me locked away. Maybe I could tell him that I've been nothing but a living blood bag my entire life, and that was the reason I had never lived.

Would he care? Would he even believe me?

He knew enough about the veil, so he had to know that the Goddess of Light was the one who could control it.

Who knows? Maybe he would want to help me.

It was a ridiculous idea, but after Paris, I was willing to try. I couldn't go back to living in that cage after this was all over without knowing that I tried everything, that I risked everything.

The front door of the bar was open.

I started to walk through, but I stopped when I heard voices from the inside.

"You're fucking kidding me," Kylar's voice started.

"This is serious," Salem replied. I could recognize her

voice from anywhere. "He knows she's the one. He's just waiting for the right time to ask her."

What the hell are they talking about?

"He could have told us sooner," Kylar replied. "We almost fucking drowned her in the lake. That would've ruined everything."

"If you two weren't such assholes, none of that would have even been a concern now, would it?"

A long pause strung between them. "Alek has to act fast. If he has any hope at dropping the veil and bringing Wrath back, it's the next full moon."

"I know," Salem sighed. "I think it's more complicated than just asking her."

"What's complicated about it?" Blade's voice chimed in. "She knows how to drop the veil. She has to. God, Alek is so soft. I would've had the veil down by now if it were up to me."

The sound of a fist hitting the table made me jump. "Well, it's not up to you," Salem said. "It's up to Alek, and he's taking his time. She's a fucking *girl*, Blade. She's not a weapon."

"Her mother's been hiding her like a damn weapon," he replied.

I couldn't believe what I was hearing. *They knew? Alek knew?* My deepest secret, the one thing I had tried my entire life to hide. And they knew. They knew I was the one who could drop the veil.

My blood was pounding in my ears, panic began morphing my senses.

"So this entire time he's been pretending to date her…"

"It's been a way to get closer to her," Salem answered for

him. A wave of nausea hit me. "That poor girl. She doesn't deserve any of this."

I wanted to back up. I wanted to run far, far away until all of this was behind me. But my legs were still frozen. This couldn't be happening. Not to me. Not after everything. Not after Paris.

"What a fucking idiot," Blade mumbled. They exchanged a few more words that I couldn't quite hear, until Blade said, "I take it the demon king knows about this?"

I leaned closer to the door, needing to know the truth. Needing to know how badly I had been betrayed.

"No," Salem answered. "He told Alek to get Wrath back. He doesn't quite give a shit how he does it. He knows nothing, and you two better keep your big mouths shut about it. I'm only telling you this now so you leave Lyra alone."

The two boys laughed, and I never felt more embarrassment in my entire life.

Alek had been using me this entire time.

"And this has been his plan all along. What a tricky bastard."

"It's a well-thought-out plan, Blade," Salem argued. "He even had special invitations made a couple of months ago to ensure Lyra would show up at the bar. He has this under control."

My breath hitched. Questions flooded my brain, making it hard to think. To breathe.

All of it was fake. Every kiss. Every touch. Every date. It was all a way to find out my deepest secret. Even showing up at the bar with Natalie that first night had been planned out, yet another way to sink his teeth in deeper.

Well fucking played, Alekzander Black. Well fucking played.

I pushed myself away from the wall, ready to run until I forgot about this horrible, wicked place. But my foot caught on the floor mat below me and my shoe scuffed the concrete.

Loud enough to give away my presence.

"Who's out there?" Blade hissed.

I cursed under my breath. There was nowhere I could hide. I wouldn't be fast enough to get away from them. Because at the end of the day, they were big, bad demons. And I was nothing. I was nobody.

Before I could run, Blade was out the door with a predatory grip on my upper arm. "How convenient," Blade started. "We were just discussing something important you may be able to help us with."

I clenched my jaw to keep from crying out in panic.

Blade dragged me inside without letting go of my arm. Salem immediately jumped from her seat at the bar table. "Let her go, Blade!" she yelled.

"What's the point? She just heard everything we were saying. We might as well get the truth from her right here, right now."

Kylar growled. "Your little boyfriend might be wanting to protect you," he hissed, "but not all of us can afford to wait for you to spread your pretty little legs and pour your secrets out to him."

My face heated.

"You have no idea what you're talking about," I breathed. No, none of this was true. Alek had no idea. He would find them here and he would kill them for this.

Right?

"Tell us how to bring Wrath back," Kylar growled.

I felt my palms bleed from the sharp slicing of my fingernails in clenched fists. I wasn't going to cry in front of them. Not now. Not ever.

"That's not possible," I said through gritted teeth.

Kylar's brows raised. "And how do you know that?"

Shit. I should have kept my mouth shut.

But they were idiots if they thought I was going to tell them anything more.

"Give up," Kylar hissed. "We all know you're the secret to opening the veil."

Thirty-One

"No," I stammered. "That's not true. Nobody knows about that, and you're all wrong."

"Let her go!" Salem yelled again. "Alek will kill you for this!" I couldn't look at her. She knew, too. She knew this entire time.

"Alek knows. In fact, this entire fake-dating scheme was a way to get closer to you. To find out exactly how to open that veil your mother is so adamant on protecting."

My chest tightened. *He's lying. He's lying. That's not true.*

The room shrunk around us. How long had Alek known? How long had he known about my mother—about the veil?

I took a step backward. Suddenly, Salem was not a friend of mine at all. She was a stranger, she was dangerous, she was a *demon*.

I needed to get out of there. I took a frantic step to the side, toward the bar door. But my back collided with a sturdy body.

"What the hell is going on here?" Alek growled. His

voice held something sharp that made my entire body run cold.

I spun around to face him. "You've been lying this whole time?" I asked. "You've been using me for the veil?" I searched his face for some sort of shock, some sort of denial. But his eyes became unreadable.

Alek held his hands up in surrender. His eyes flickered to Kylar once before returning to me. "Lyra, calm down. Let's take a second and talk about this."

"What else is there to talk about?" I pushed. The pain I had been feeling morphed into an unending flood of anger. "Your *friends* here filled me in on all of it. You've been pretending to need me for your fake relationship all while you've been trying to figure out my secret. Well done, Alek. You fucking win."

"It's not what it sounds like," he pleaded.

I scoffed, "Isn't it? Which part of it isn't true, Alek? I risked everything for you. I risked *my life* because you made me feel like someone in this fucked-up world actually cared about me. If you wanted to know my secret so badly, you should have just locked me up and tortured me for it. It would have hurt way fucking less."

I shoved past Alek and aimed for the basement door, but he gripped my arm and forced me to stop. His eyes were dark in a sea of unsaid words.

"At first, yes, I needed to know your secret. I killed my brother, Lyra. I was willing to do whatever it took to bring him back! My father ensured I would give it my best shot! When we heard about you, I sent those invitations. I knew Natalie would bring you with her to Night Raven. But that was before I got to know you, Lyra. That was before all of this! Can you let me explain?"

I shook him off. "No, Alek. You did a fabulous job convincing everyone that you actually cared about me." Tears blurred my vision. "You even had me fooled."

Nobody stopped me as I stormed up the basement stairs and out of the bar. The cold winter air slapped my skin, freezing the tears that now poured down my face.

How could I have been so blind? Of course Alek didn't want me. Of course he wasn't falling for me.

Who would fall for *me*? Who would possibly catch real feelings for *me*?

She was right. My mother was fucking right. I was worthless, only on this planet for one purpose.

My mind raced, imagining Alek laughing with his pack about how ignorant and gullible I had been. Did he tell them how scared I was when he bit me? Did he tell them about my stupid little apartment and my stupid little life? Had he told them about our kiss? About how he was my first?

Fuck. It had been so easy for him to infiltrate my fragile, protected life. I had practically handed him everything he wanted on a silver platter.

"Lyra, stop!" his voice called out after me. I ignored him, but his footsteps grew louder as he jogged up behind me. "Lyra, please talk to me." Alek stepped in front of me, cutting off my sidewalk path. I fought the urge to throw my fist into his face.

I quickly wiped the tears away with my sleeve. "What more do you want from me?" I asked. "Haven't you already done enough damage?"

Alek stepped forward and grabbed both of my shoulders. "I want to explain," he said softly. "I want to tell you every-thing. You deserve to know the truth."

The wind picked up. Cold air sliced across my exposed

skin, infiltrating my crumbling barriers. My sharp, shallow breaths sucked in painful breaths, but it was the pain that pierced through the growing numbness in my body.

The numbness I never thought I would have to feel again. The numbness I had been spending the past month growing out of.

"What truth?" I managed to ask.

"My father, he—he knows that Theia holds the secrets to opening the veil. He wanted to open the veil, and he wanted me to find out how to do that. After Wrath, I... I didn't see another choice. I didn't know you were still living in the city, Lyra, I swear it. When he told me Theia had a daughter, you were not who I was expecting."

"Why should I believe you?"

"I wanted to tell you so many times," he continued. "But I didn't know how. After a while, I knew I couldn't use you to open the veil. Not if you didn't want to help us. I care about you, Lyra! I didn't want to hurt you. I never planned for you to—"

"To what?" I interrupted. "To open the veil for you? That's what you really need, isn't it? That's the reason you've been pretending to like me all this time? So that you could discover how to open the veil. So you could bring back your brother."

Alek opened his mouth to respond, but no words came out.

My heart twisted.

"Right," I said. "Unfortunately for you, you were much closer to the secret this whole time. I'm right here," I said with my hands out. "I've been right in front of you this entire time!"

Alek shook his head. "I don't understand."

My entire world crumbled where I stood. All of the secrets I held, all of the years I spent alone, the days I had spent chained in the basement—they meant nothing anymore. What was the point?

Keeping those secrets got me nowhere. I had been so careful. So obedient.

Yet here I was. I had nothing else to lose. I had nothing else to give.

"I'm the secret," I breathed. Defeat weighed down each of my limbs. I was *so tired* of keeping the secret. "My blood opens the veil."

Alek's brows drew together. *What will he do now?* I wondered. *Is he still willing to take my secret straight to his father?*

"Your blood is the key?" he asked.

I nodded. "Now you know. If you want to take me as a prisoner and gift me to your father, go right ahead." Tears I had been fighting spilled down my face. "I don't care anymore, Alek. Theia was right."

"Right about what?" He stepped forward.

"My life has one purpose. My blood is my destiny. I don't deserve a life like everyone else. If this is my fate, so be it." Bitter, dark hatred crept into my chest. Not at Alek, although I knew I should hate him more than anyone. I hated her. "Better you than her."

A sob wrecked through my body.

Alek closed the distance between us, holding my face with both hands and forcing me to look at him. "Don't say that," he said. "That's not true. This doesn't have to be your life, Lyra. Not if you don't want it to be."

"Don't you see?" I questioned with a pathetic laugh. "I am the *only one* who can open the veil. If I am hidden, the veil stays closed. If you bleed me out right now and use my blood to open it, it's for the best. At least I won't have to go back there."

"Back where?"

"Back with *her*."

"She hurts you, doesn't she?" he asked. "Your mother is the one who gave you those scars."

I didn't have to answer. I shut my eyes, shielding myself from the pity I knew would be lingering on his face.

"Come with me," he pushed. "Come with me and we'll figure all of this out. You'll be safe from my father, and you'll be safe from Theia."

My eyes shot open as I backed out of his grasp. "No," I pushed. "I'm not going anywhere with you. Not after this."

"Lyra, please," he pleaded.

A flash of light surrounded us, making Alek and I both jump where we stood. "What the hell was that?" he asked.

But I knew. I had seen that white flash of emotion come from my mother one too many times.

The sound of traffic in the distance halted. Not a single bird chirped. Not a flicker of wind blew.

"She's here," I whispered. Icy, paralyzing fear I had never felt before rushed through me. "She's here," I whispered again.

I was frozen, unable to explain further. Unable to run. Unable to tell Alek to run.

I snapped my vision around us, looking for any sign. "She's come for me," I whispered. I could feel Alek's confusion as the light around us became brighter. I looked until it became blinding; Alek and I both hid our eyes at the last second.

Alek grabbed my wrist and pulled me closer to him. As if that would stop her.

I heard her before I saw her. "Hello, daughter," Theia said. "It seems you have been a very, *very* bad listener."

I froze where I stood. This was the end. Every moment in the last month, every taste of freedom. It had all led to this. I knew it was coming. Only a fool would think she could escape Theia's tight grasp.

"I'm not going back," I said aloud. Fear still weakened my voice, and it cracked as I repeated, "I'm not going back!"

She stepped into view before us, the dim streetlight reflecting off her porcelain skin. Her smile held the same hidden distaste for me that it always had. "I'm afraid you have no choice."

"You can't keep her locked up forever," Alek demanded. "We'll find her. We won't stop looking for her until we do."

Theia laughed, long and wicked. The sound of her caused my breath to hitch. "If you think you can stop me, you have a brutal awakening coming for you." Within two seconds, she was standing directly in front of us. Alek still held my wrist tightly, but my mother reached out and grabbed my free hand, tugging me in her direction. "This is family business, *demon*. Leave my daughter alone from now on."

She would kill him if she knew who he was. Who his *father* was. If she found out what I had just told him, he would be dead in an instant…

Alek's anger became palpable as my mother tugged me once more, yanking me from his grasp.

"Let us go," I spat at Alek. I hated him. I *wanted* to hate him. But at that moment, I didn't want him to die. I didn't want Theia to kill him.

Alek betrayed me. He lied to me, he made me think someone in this world actually cared about me and then he let my world crash around me.

But in spite of all that, he gave me one thing nobody else had: *hope.*

Alek would come for me. I knew that was true.

Not because he cared about me. Not because he might have loved me—no. Neither of those things were true.

But he needed me.

And now, he knew the truth. I had told him my deepest, darkest secret. The secret that gave my life a miserable purpose. *He knew.*

He would come. Sooner or later, he would come for me.

"I'm sorry," I said to my mother. I bowed my head, tucking my chin in surrender like I had done dozens of times before. *Be small,* I told myself. *Be submissive. Be nothing.* "I don't know what got into me. He just… they just…"

Theia ran a finger down my cheek. I bit the inside of my mouth to stop myself from flinching away. "Don't worry, Lyra. I'll keep you safe. I'll always keep you safe."

Hidden, she meant. *She'll keep me hidden.*

But at least Alek wouldn't be killed.

"Take me home," I whispered to her.

"No!" Alek yelled, a shocking desperation lacing his words. But it was too late.

My mother's power—light power—surrounded us, ready to bring us *home.*

Theia paced before me. Her black heeled boots clicked the cement floor with every step she took.

"I should have known better," she mumbled. "I should have known that you would disobey again. You're too selfish to see the good in the world."

"How is this good?" I asked. Tears streamed freely down my face, but I didn't care. Theia had kept me secluded in the past, but locking me up? In the basement? With chains?

She was losing her mind.

"You aren't a normal girl, Lyra. You don't get to live a normal life. I thought you would have listened to me by now, but after that little stunt you pulled last night, I guess not."

My heart raced just thinking about it. The few hours of freedom I had running free in the world before Theia caught me. The fresh air on my face. The sound of birds chirping as I ran with my bare feet on the pavement.

Theia stopped pacing and knelt before me. "Your life is nothing, Lyra! Don't you understand that? You were not born to be a normal girl. You were not born to have a normal life."

I clenched my teeth but said nothing.

Theia stared at me, her bright blue eyes searching for something. Dignity, maybe? Rebellion?

The truth was, I knew I wasn't going to get far. I knew Theia would find me. She always would, and she reminded me that any chance she got.

"You're going to stay down here now," she growled. She reached forward and tightened the chains on my wrists, tight enough to cause me to yelp in pain. "And I hope you remember this the next time you forget who you really are."

▭

THE BASEMENT LOOKED DIFFERENT THIS TIME. IT WAS SMALLER than I remembered. The shadows were darker.

Maybe it was because it had been so long since I was down here. It had been so long since Theia resorted to chains.

But I knew that wouldn't last long. I had been living my life on borrowed time, and the clock had run out.

"You can't keep me down here forever," I said. My voice was scratchy and dry, but I wouldn't dare ask for water.

"I can do whatever I want, child," she replied. I could barely see her figure in the darkness, but I knew she was there. I could feel the hatred pouring from her. "I shouldn't have left you. I was a fool to think you had changed. You'll never see the bigger picture, will you?"

"The bigger picture includes me staying down here forever," I reminded her.

"And what do you think those demons were going to do to you, Lyra? What do you think they wanted from you? They'll kill you if they find out the truth."

"That's not true. They actually care about me, unlike anyone else I've known."

She laughed, but there was no humor in it. "They don't care about you, Lyra. You're smart enough to know better than that."

I wanted to scream at her. I wanted to fight and kick and yell about how wrong she was. Alek did care about me. He had protected me and shown me things I never would have gotten to experience.

Unlike her.

"Why do you even care so much?" I whispered. "What's so terrible about the veil being opened that causes you to chain up your own daughter?"

A sharp sting of pain spread across my cheek, and the chain around my neck dug into my skin. "Watch your mouth," she demanded. "The veil will be the end to all of us. Do you understand that? We will all die if the veil falls. The demons and the other creatures from hell will run wild. There will be nothing left."

"They're not as terrible as you think."

Some of them had tried to kill me, yes, but not all of them. So many of them were kind. Empathetic. Caring. Even if I had to look past all of the egos and tattoos to see it from any of them.

"Those demons have you fooled, child," she sneered as she stood up. "I won't let you fall under their poison. They are wicked and evil creatures. Tell me, Lyra, how long have you been sneaking around with them behind my back? What do they know?"

"Nothing," I mumbled. "They don't know anything."

She huffed. "Well, I have to say I find that hard to believe. They know who you are, Lyra. They need something from you. Demons don't hang out with outsiders because they have pretty red hair, child."

A smile crept onto my face. "Well, it's a good thing I'm not an outsider anymore."

She stopped in her tracks. "What did you just say?"

"I'm not an outsider. I'm part of the legion."

She returned to her position kneeling before me. "What does that mean, Lyra? What did you do?"

I didn't have to answer her. My sweater slid off my shoulder, just enough to show her exactly what I was talking about.

I had been bitten. I had been blood bonded. There was no going back from that.

Her cold, claw hands gripped me tightly as she took a closer look. "I hope for your sake that this is a mistake, Lyra. I know you are not this stupid!"

I clenched my jaw once more. "Who knows? Maybe I am. I've been locked up all my life, remember?"

She slapped my face again, harder this time. The taste of sharp copper spread through my mouth.

"I've done all of this for the future of this world, Lyra. If you can't see that, then there's no hope for you."

I bit the inside of my cheek to stop myself from crying out in pain. No, there was no hope for me. Not anymore.

My fun was over. My freedom was gone. Theia wasn't letting me out of her sight this time.

And I knew I would never leave these chains again.

My hope quickly dissipated. That was what had kept me sane all those times before: the lack of hope. Accepting my fate. Accepting that I wasn't getting out of there.

The first few days, though, I had to admit. That tiny, relentless feeling that maybe, just maybe, Alek would come for me was the most torturous.

Not the chains. Not the cement floor or the ongoing attacks from my mother.

Hope.

Alek visited my dreams the first night. He pulled me from the basement, breaking away each of my chains as he held me close to him. *You're safe now*, he had said. *I won't let anyone hurt you.*

That one hurt the most to wake up from.

I lost track of what day it was. I lost track of how many times my mother attempted to bring me food, or how many times the sun set beyond the tiny window.

After a while, I stopped caring.

Theia was right. I was going to rot.

Was it worth it? Was the risk worth the possibility of being caught, of being chained up again?

My memories raced through everything that had happened over the last few weeks. Alek's lips against mine caused me to smile each time I relived the moment. I had never known it would feel so good to have the affection of someone else.

Even if it was fake. Even if it were merely part of a deal.

We had been playing part in a wicked, wicked game. I had risked more over the last few weeks than I ever had in my life. But in all honesty, I didn't have anything to lose. What was the risk if there was no leverage? It's not like Theia was pulling me away from a life. It's not like she was taking something away from me that I wished I had.

I had no future. I had no life. One purpose, she would say. I had one purpose, and that was to keep my blood hidden until it was needed.

So, I supposed it was worth it. The risk of the last few weeks… at least I had lived, even if just for a moment. I had held Alek's hand and run in the wild, away from danger. Away from our enemies. I had fought and cried and laughed.

Yes, it was all worth it.

My mind drifted in and out of consciousness. I didn't mind it. I preferred being asleep, anyway. At least when I was asleep, I had the chance of running into him again. At reliving some of those few, precious moments together.

I had the chance to taste freedom, even if it wasn't real.

The morning sun began filtering through that tiny, filthy window across the room. I stared at it, watching each small shred of light grow brighter and brighter.

It wasn't until a few moments later that I saw a figure blocking those tiny shreds.

I blinked. Was I dreaming again?

I blinked again. The sound of movement from outside caused me to sit up straight. No, I was definitely not dreaming.

And someone was outside that window.

For the first time in days, my heart began beating faster.

Someone was here.

I sat straighter, pushing myself against the concrete wall behind me and lifting my chin as best I could. The chains had become so heavy, weighing down more and more on my bones with every passing minute.

Whispering voices muffled from outside the window.

And then the entire thing shattered.

Broken glass fell into the basement, and those tiny threads of light returned. "Lyra?" a familiar voice asked.

Salem.

"Lyra, are you in there?"

"I'm here," I responded, my voice barely over a whisper. "I'm down here!"

I could hear a few male voices with her, but I could only see Salem's slim body from the outside of the window. "We're getting you out of here, Lyra. Just hold on!"

My stomach flipped. I could have vomited from the wave of emotion that rolled through me, but Salem's body sliding through that tiny window distracted each of my thoughts.

"She'll catch you," I warned as Salem landed on her feet and began surveying the situation. "She'll know you're here."

Salem knelt in front of me and took the chains in her hands, cursing under her breath. "We won't let her touch you again," she promised. "Alek, get down here. These chains are too strong."

Alek. My stomach erupted in excitement as his body slid, barely fitting through the window where Salem had just come from.

They had actually come for me. They actually cared.

He landed on his feet with a satisfying thud.

"What the fuck is this?" he muttered. He looked around the room, surveying the chains, the lack of furniture, and then—finally—me. "Your mother keeps you down here?" he hissed. "She did this?"

He joined Salem before me, his hand reaching up to brush my jawline as he surveyed the chains that held my neck. His thumb tickled across the bruised skin of my face. "Lyra," he breathed, barely even a whisper, "I had no idea."

"Get me out of here," I managed to reply. "Before she comes back."

"Shit," Salem muttered. "You don't have to tell me twice."

A loud grunt interrupted us from outside the window. Zac called out, "Alek, we've got company."

Alek cursed under his breath before standing up and running back to the window. He pulled a long knife from his belt and held it tightly in his hand. "Get behind me," he ordered Salem.

I was left helpless on the cement floor.

Zac grunted again, and through the small basement window, I could see a creature flash in his direction.

It most certainly wasn't human, and it most certainly did not belong in this world.

"What the hell is that?" I gasped.

Alek's jaw tightened. "It looks like your mother assigned you some protection."

And then he jumped out of the window.

Salem stayed behind, watching carefully as Zac and Alek fought the unworldly beast outside.

I could hardly believe my eyes.

We were going to die. My mother was sending paranormal beasts to protect me; she knew they would come for me.

Maybe this was all a trap. Maybe she had planned this all along.

Zac cursed and drew my attention back to the window.

It only took a few seconds of fighting for Zac and Alek to pin the beast. With a horrifying screech, they took it down.

I exhaled. "She must know you're here," I mumbled as Alek crawled back inside. "You have to go."

"I'm not leaving you," Alek demanded. "Don't you dare even suggest that, Lyra."

He grabbed the chains around my ankles first, snapping them apart effortlessly between his hands.

It surprised me at first, until I remembered that demons were stronger than the rest of us. They had supernatural strength, and it was probably easy for him to break something as fragile as a metal chain.

He did the same to my wrists.

And then his hands fell to the chains bolted loosely around my neck. "She deserves to die for this," he muttered as Salem kicked the chains away.

"Funny," I replied. "She would say the same to me."

Alek smiled, but I didn't miss the way his brows tightened in concern. He held my head with one hand and slipped his fingers under the chains with the other.

The feeling of his skin against mine distracted me, long

enough for him to twist his wrist and snap the chains apart.

And then, for what felt like the second time ever in my life, I was free.

"Can you walk?" Alek asked. I nodded, even though I wasn't entirely sure I could. He helped me rise to my feet. My legs were like water beneath me, but I had to move forward. To the window, out of here. I had to get out.

"Hurry up!" Zac urged from the window. "We don't have much time until the cameras are back on!"

Panic gripped onto my chest, squeezing tighter than ever before. Not again. I wasn't going to get caught again.

Salem jumped up and through the window, with Zac pulling her from the other side.

"Your turn," Alek said to me. "Grab hold of Zac." He gripped my waist and lifted me, propelling me in the direction of the window. Zac's hands were there in an instant, ready to get me out of there. Ready to help me.

He pulled my body from the other side, and before I could even think, I was lying on the grass outside.

The sun had never felt warmer on my face.

Alek was already grabbing my shoulders, pulling me back up from the ground. "Come on," he said. "We can't stay here. Your mother will scavenge this entire city looking for you."

"I don't doubt that," I croaked.

Salem gave me a tight hug before helping me into the passenger seat of Alek's car. "You deserve more, Lyra," she whispered to me. "You deserve to live."

I don't know why those words hurt me so much, but I bit back my tears as I let her guide me onto the leather seat.

Alek started the engine.

And drove us away into the night.

Thirty-Four

"You're protected here," Alek explained. "Nobody will hurt you. We can trust them."

Too late, I thought. Alek didn't take me to his house. Instead, Alek pushed the door open to our small, dark motel room. We had driven a couple of hours outside the city before neither of us could keep our eyes open.

To my surprise, though, the innkeeper had the same glowing green eyes as Alek.

"Thank you," I said as I stepped inside.

Alek nodded and closed the door behind us both. The room was what I expected it to be: one bed in the middle of the room, a small TV in the corner, and a bathroom that probably couldn't be trusted.

"We can stay here for the night," he said. "We'll figure out a plan in the morning when we're thinking clearly." I watched as he ran his hand across his face, pacing the small room.

"Why?" I whispered. "Why are you helping me?"

Alek stopped pacing and looked at me. He shook his

head and smiled lightly. "You have no idea what I would do to keep you safe, Lyra."

I froze. Something in his gaze darkened. His jaw clenched, and my gaze dropped to his tattooed body. The energy between us became palpable. I wanted to reach out. I wanted to close the distance between us and touch him. I wanted *him* to touch *me*.

My mind spun in circles. *But Alek betrayed me. He hurt me. He didn't care about me.* It was my *blood* he cared about. This entire time, he was after one thing. Alek knew my secret now. It wouldn't be long until he betrayed me like everyone else.

That was my destiny.

"I'm going to get us some food. Will you be okay here until I get back?" I nodded, not trusting myself enough to speak. "Okay," he replied. "Don't open the door for anyone. You still have the phone I gave you?" I pulled it from my pocket and held it up. "Call me if you need me."

I watched as Alek left the room, closing the door behind him.

In the deafening silence, I could hear my own heart beating in my chest. Could hear my shallow breathing. *Get ahold of yourself, Lyra.*

I set my phone on the bed and walked into the bathroom. My skin felt disgusting from the basement. I needed to wash off every last inch of dirt from that hell hole. Every inch of my body needed to be scrubbed clean from the trauma.

It would be impossible. I knew that much. But it was worth a shot.

I turned the motel shower water on as hot as it would go.

What the hell had my life turned into? Showering in a

cheap motel bathroom while a practical stranger found us food?

My stomach sank when I saw my reflection in the mirror. Dark circles engulfed my bloodshot eyes. My tear-stained face was paler than I had ever seen it, and bruises were beginning to form around my neck.

None of that scared me, though. What terrified me more than anything was the look of emptiness I saw in the mirror. Helplessness. Hopelessness.

Give up, a voice in the back of my head whispered. *Give up now and save everyone the trouble of saving you.*

I pulled my clothes off slowly. My muscles screamed at me with every movement, but I didn't mind. I welcomed the pain. Pain reminded me that I was still here. I was still alive.

Without pain, I had nothing. That had been the case for most of my life.

There were many times, of course, that I had turned the emotions off. I had decided not to feel. The numbness helped for a while, especially when I had chains on both of my wrists in the darkness of Theia's basement. Eventually, the numbness became obsolete.

Pulling yourself out of the darkness is much harder than surrendering to the pain.

I stepped into the scalding water, hissing as the heat rushed over my bare skin.

No amount of water would cleanse my past. No amount of water would make me feel *clean and worthy.*

I tilted my head back and let the water rush over my face. The heat washed the salty tears from my face, my neck, my chest.

I stayed there until the water turned cold.

The mirror in the bathroom was completely covered in

steam. I was grateful for it; I didn't want to see my reflection again. I didn't want to face myself again.

I grabbed a towel and wrapped it around my body.

Alek still hadn't returned with food, but I was thankful for the solitude. I left my clothes in the bathroom and moved to sit on the bed, fiddling with the remote.

I didn't know what to think about Alek. He betrayed me. This entire relationship was a lie. All of it. My mind flashed back to his teeth sinking in my flesh, his lips against mine.

It was all fake.

And not because he needed to convince people we were together. It was all a lie.

And the others knew about it.

That was the worst part, I thought—that Zac and Salem could look me in the eye and pretend to be my friends.

Did they feel sorry for me? Did they see me as the gullible prey walking directly into the predator's trap?

Or were they in on it? Maybe they, too, were part of this plan. For all I knew, it was their idea.

I shook my head. It was my fault for trusting them, anyway. It was my fault for letting them in. I should have seen it all coming. Salem didn't want my friendship, she wanted to see how deeply Alek had dug his claws.

And I didn't see a single thing.

The doorknob to the room twisted.

Shit. Alek was back sooner than expected.

My clothes were still filthy on the bathroom floor. I pulled my towel tighter around my body, ensuring it was tucked tightly under my arm as Alek entered the room.

"I hope you like Chinese," he announced as he shut the door behind him.

"Perfect," I replied.

Alek set his key down and moved to sit next to me at the foot of the bed. If he was in any way fazed by my towel-dress, he didn't show it.

I turned my attention back to the TV as he dug through the takeout bag.

"How are you feeling?" he asked in a light voice.

How was I feeling? I turned my head to look at him. "Tired," I admitted. My voice cracked.

I wanted to tell him everything. I wanted to tell him how hurt and betrayed he had made me feel. I wanted to tell him how badly I wanted to hate him for what he did, how badly I wanted to never see him again.

And I wanted to tell him how what hurt the most was thinking I could actually trust him. Thinking he would actually take care of me.

I cleared my throat to stop the rush of emotion from coming forward.

"Lyra," he said in a hushed whisper. Alek was no longer looking in the food bag. He moved closer to me on the bed, his arm brushing mine as he leaned in and tilted my chin toward him. "I'm sorry for everything. You deserved more than this."

His hand lingered on my chin. I became all too aware of his thumb brushing the skin on my cheek. My eyelids fluttered shut as I focused on the sensation.

"I never expected to have much of a life," I admitted. "Theia was always very clear on that. She made me repeat it over and over again when I was a child. And for a long time, I was okay with that. I accepted my fate."

Alek's thumb brushed over my cheekbone.

"What changed?" he asked.

My eyes met his. "You did," I admitted. "That first night

at the bar, I never expected to meet you. I never expected to start living my life. Somehow, I finally began to see everything I was missing out on. I didn't care that you were using me to impress your father; it was better than being locked inside forever."

Alek was so close now, his breath tickled my cheek. "Do you regret it? Do you regret meeting me?"

My breathing hitched. *Did* I regret it? Did I regret getting out of my apartment for once and feeling like a real college girl? Did I regret letting Alek show me how to live? The fear, the adrenaline, the risk. Those were the pieces of living that made me feel.

It had been so long since I had felt anything.

And now, I feared it was all over.

"No," I answered honestly. "I don't regret any of it. Even if it was all fake—"

"It wasn't fake," he interrupted. His free hand moved to my bare shoulder, and a chill ran down my spine. "Every fucking day, I wanted to tell you the truth. Every single goddamned day." Our breathing blended together as he leaned closer. Shit, he was close. I couldn't back away, though. I didn't want to. His lips brushed against mine as he said, "I'm on my *fucking knees* for you, Lyra Sol."

Thirty-Five

Alek moved first—or maybe it was me. His lips moved against mine with all the emotion he had been holding back. His hands scoured against my body, against the bare skin of my arms and my neck.

My body moved without my permission. I pushed against him, tangling my hands in his hair as I crawled onto his lap. My body burned with the need for more of him. Our mouths became one, working together with the same purpose.

And it felt so *right*.

Alek held my body against his as he leaned back in the bed. He pulled us backward and twisted, flipping so that I now laid beneath his body.

My heart pounded. Could he hear it? Could he tell how badly I had been wanting him?

Alek pressed against me. The weight of him brought the blood back to my limbs, back to my body. The numbness in my chest slowly dissipated, replaced by the fire he breathed into me with each touch.

He used one arm to brace himself above me, and the other to pull my bare leg up and around his waist.

I didn't object. I had wanted him for so long now, my desire turned to something much more intense.

I *needed* him.

With my leg hooked around him, I pulled on his black t-shirt. My hands ran up the length of his spine, then back down again.

Alek pulled away and met my gaze. "You're so much more than a blood bag to the veil," he breathed. "You have no fucking idea how special you are. I don't deserve a woman like you."

Tears pooled in my eyes. Alek quickly kissed them away.

"I wish you would have told me the truth from the beginning," I managed to say. "I–I've been protected and sheltered from so many things, Alek. But you?" I brushed my thumb against his lips. "I dropped my walls around you. I let you in."

"I know," he whispered.

"You *made* me let you in."

He leaned his forehead against mine. "I would take it all back if I could. All of it." He lifted his head again and his dark eyes met mine. "I love you, Lyra. I fucking love you. I'll protect you with my life if that's what it takes."

A sound I didn't recognize escaped me. Love. Love was never mine to have. It was a foreign concept, something I only heard about when Natalie rambled on.

I certainly got no love from my mother.

Was this love? Was Alek's feeling for me love?

My heart pounded in my chest. *He was here.* Alek was the one who pulled me out of the basement. But he did so much more than that.

Alek showed me the light. He showed me how to live. He forced me to take one step after another, even when I saw no reason in moving forward.

I didn't know much about love. But I did know that I never wanted to be apart from him.

"I love you," I whispered back.

Alek pressed his lips against my forehead. My eyes shut as he moved, kissing my cheek, my nose, my chin.

"Alek," I breathed. He lifted my chin with his hand and kissed my throat, leaving a trail of kisses down my neck.

He hummed a response but didn't stop what he was doing. The towel around my body loosened as Alek moved lower, setting my body on fire as his mouth explored my chest.

Both of my legs wrapped around him now, the towel becoming less and less of a barrier between us.

I wanted more of him.

Alek felt it, too. "Tell me to stop," Alek whispered as he inched the white towel lower and lower. "Or I'm going to show you exactly how fucking much you've been torturing me."

His hands lingered in a silent question, waiting for my command.

"Don't…" I murmured. "Don't stop."

A low growl escaped him as he picked up where he left off, teasing me with his kisses. Somewhere between us, the towel disappeared. Alek's hands roamed my body, cupping my breasts as his mouth found the delicate skin there, licking a torturously slow circle.

I sucked in a sharp breath and arched toward him, giving him more of me.

Alek's touch filled my soul, lighting a fire to the places

that had been hiding in the darkness. For the first time in my existence, my body buzzed with *life*.

I grabbed the back of Alek's shirt and pulled. He took the hint and easily tugged the rest of it up and over his head.

My hands found his bare chest. A groan escaped him, sending vibrations down my arms. I dropped my hands, letting them graze the tattoos over his torso until they looped around his jeans.

Alek leaned forward and grazed his teeth over my neck. "You drive me fucking crazy," he whispered. "I've wanted this ever since the blood bonding, ever since I first tasted you."

A new wave of heat fell over me as I remembered the way his teeth sank deep into my flesh. It was supposed to be painful, I remembered, but it was the furthest thing from pain.

Did he know how badly I wanted him then? Did he want me then, too?

His teeth grazed my collarbone, followed by a hot kiss. I couldn't stop the moan that escaped me.

"Tell me what you want," Alek said against my skin. "Just say the words."

He knew. He knew exactly what I wanted.

His teeth skimmed my skin once more, and this time, he didn't pull away. He froze, waiting for my command.

Waiting for me to say it.

"I want you to bite me," I admitted. I wrapped my hands around his bare back and held his body closer to me.

Another satisfied growl rumbled through him, and his sharp teeth sank into me.

Similar to the first time, another wave of euphoria washed over me. Ecstasy filled my entire body, originating from his mouth on my shoulder. Alek's hands pinned my bare waist to the bed beneath his body, and the weight of him against me only fueled the inferno burning at my core.

The pull of Alek's mouth caused me to arch against him. My towel had fallen away, and the only thing separating Alek's body and mine was the pair of jeans hanging low on his waist.

I slid my finger down his torso once more and tugged at them, showing him everything that I wanted.

Alek pulled away from my shoulder and quickly obliged, pulling off his jeans. A drunkeness lingered in his eyes now, mirroring the same fiery need that fueled me.

"Are you sure about this?" Alek asked.

My chest welled with love, more love than I had ever felt before. "I've never been more sure."

I could feel Alek against me, how equally eager he was for this. He pulled one of my legs around his waist before pausing, as if silently asking for permission once more.

My hands gripped his waist and pulled him tighter against me, answering that silent question.

Alek kissed me with a new ripple of passion as he pushed himself inside of me, giving me everything I had been wanting so badly.

His own mouth muffled my moan of pleasure, encapsulating my senses as he moved against me.

"Holy hell," I whispered.

Alek moved to kiss my jaw, my neck, my collarbone. His tongue flickered over the sensitive area of his bite as I moaned once more.

"You're mine," he said as my body began flooding with a torrent of heat. "You've been mine since the very beginning."

I felt his chest rumble against mine as we both found

euphoria together. Alek collapsed onto the bed next to me, holding me close in his arms.

We stayed that way, silent in the darkness of the motel room. There I was, running from my mother as my entire world was about to collapse, yet I had never felt more exhilarated. Never in my life had I felt more safe. Never in my life had I felt so loved.

"I love you, Alek," I whispered as my heartbeat began to slow down.

In the midst of my dwindling consciousness, I felt him smile. "I am unworthy of your love, Lyra, but I'm too selfish to turn it away."

Thirty-Six

Alek brushed his thumb against my cheek, pulling me from my dreamless sleep. I opened my eyes to find him staring at me with a wicked grin.

"What?" I asked. My voice croaked, and the morning sun was just beginning to filter through the blinds of the motel room.

He shrugged and brushed a gentle kiss onto my forehead. "I feel different," he said.

"What do you mean different?"

His chest rose and fell as he laughed, and I soaked up every single piece of this moment in time.

"My entire body is buzzing, I feel... powerful." His thumb brushed my cheek again. "It's your blood. It has to be."

I considered his words. "My blood?"

"Think about it," he said. "I felt the same way after the blood bonding. When I bite you... your blood does something to me, Lyra. It thrills me. It could be your goddess blood."

I didn't quite know how to react to his words. Was he trying to tell me my blood made him more powerful?

"I really hope you're not trying to confess that you're actually a vampire," I joked.

Alek smiled and leaned down to press a hot kiss on my throat. "Trust me," he whispered with a husky voice, "I am very much alive. And I don't actually drink your blood, but one single drop is enough to…"

We were both still very naked, but I didn't care anymore. Alek drew his hands slowly down my body, showing me exactly how much he wanted me.

I was glad that biting me had the same effect on him as it did on me.

"Is that normal?" I asked, although with his hands on my body it was nearly impossible to speak. "To feel that way after biting someone?"

I felt his chest rumble as he brought his lips close to mine. "No," he answered firmly. "It's definitely not normal."

My cell phone buzzed on the wooden nightstand.

I pulled myself up just enough to see Natalie's name displayed across the small screen.

The phone Alek had given me had ten texts, all from Natalie.

I skimmed them all, only landing on the last one.

"I tried to stop them, Ly! They're coming!"

My blood froze in my veins. I re-read the message three times to make sure I had it right. The horror must have been dripping from my face as Alek looked at me.

"What is it?"

"Natalie texted me. She said they're coming."

"Who's coming? And how does Natalie know anything?"

"I don't know. Natalie could have talked to Theia or

heard something from her own mother. Does anyone know we came here? Did you tell anyone?"

Alek shook his head. I could see the tightness in his jaw as he debated our options.

"Nobody knows where we are." He instantly pulled himself out of bed, grabbing his shirt from the floor and pulling it over his head. "But we better move just in case."

I took the hint and did the same, quickly dressing myself and running my hands through my messy hair.

I didn't think about last night. I didn't think about Alek's hands on my body, scavenging every inch.

I shut the door to the bathroom and splashed the cold sink water onto my face. I stayed there for a few seconds before Alek knocked lightly. "Ly?" he asked. "Open up."

My hands shook as I cracked the door, just enough for him to see my face.

"Hey," he said with a calm voice. He tripped the wooden door and pushed it open the rest of the way. I let him. He reached out and held my face with both hands, running his thumbs across my cheekbones. "You okay?"

I nodded, but my throat tightened. Alek leaned forward and placed a light kiss on my forehead. We stayed like that for a few seconds. He still smelled like old pine, even after all of the traveling yesterday and the night we had. I breathed him in and tried to relax.

"We'll be running forever," I stated.

"Maybe," he replied. "But at least we'll be living."

I pulled back and looked into his deep, green eyes. "Is that what you want? What will really happen to you, Alek, if you turn on everything? Your father needs me to open the veil."

Alek shook his head, his thumbs making another sweep

across my delicate skin. "I was on board with the idea when you were just a stranger, Lyra. But you're not a stranger anymore. I can't drag you back there for my father to use however he pleases."

I gripped his wrists. "We'll be running from very powerful people."

Alek's smile was contagious, even as we were about to run for our lives. "Doesn't that sound exciting? Come on. We should get going."

Hand in hand, Alek led me to the motel door.

Alek opened it, and sunlight flooded the room.

"I wondered when you two lovebirds would decide to wake up."

Thirty-Seven

Theia leaned back against the hood of her car with her arms crossed.

"What are you doing here?" Alek demanded.

"I think the better question is what are you doing here?" she pushed back. "And why are you with my daughter?"

"I'm saving her," he replied. He tugged on my hand lightly, pulling my body behind his.

Theia laughed. "Saving her?" she repeated. "You call using her to drop the veil 'saving'?"

Alek shook his head. "My father's ambitions are not my own. Your daughter deserves more than sitting chained up in a basement somewhere."

Heat rushed to my cheeks.

Theia pushed herself from the hood of the car and stepped forward. Her eyes dragged over Alek's body, taking in every feature for the first time. "Oh, Lyra," she said without taking her eyes off him. "You really fell for this?" She stepped forward again, moving inhumanly fast, and gripped Alek's chin. He growled but didn't fight back. "This pretty-boy act?" My heart pounded faster in my chest. "You made it too easy for her, didn't you?" she asked him. "You made it too easy for my daughter to walk right into your little trap."

Alek shook his head and ripped himself from her grasp. "Your daughter makes her own choices now."

"Does she?" Theia's gaze fell to me. "Please, tell me. Did she make her own choices when you bit her? When you forced her into becoming part of your rancid 'pack'?" Alek's jaw tightened. "Right. That's what I thought."

"Alek was only doing what he thought was right," I finally spoke up. It wasn't the entire truth, but it was true enough. There was no way in hell I was going to admit I knew about his plan to drop the veil.

"Well," Theia continued, "you sure continue to surprise me, daughter. I spend my entire life protecting you, and this is how you repay me?" She motioned to Alek. "By sleeping with the enemy?"

My face flushed. "Alek is not my enemy."

"No?" she asked. "Then tell me, Lyra. Did he happen to mention the fact that he killed your father?"

I repeated the words in my head. "What?"

Alek's grip on my hand tightened. Theia nodded, a satisfied smile growing on her face. "That's right. Your father—the one I never speak of. He wasn't a nobody, he was a demon. A powerful one. The most powerful one to exist in years, actually. And your friend here is responsible for his death."

My heart pounded in my ears. No, this couldn't be happening. My mind raced back to the lake house, to the photographs in the room.

The one photograph that looked so familiar. So... *similar.*

"Lyra," Alek started.

"Stop," I said. "He was my father?"

He swallowed before answering, "Yes. He was."

Emotion rushed through my body. Alek had somehow managed to keep yet another secret from me. "You knew this whole time, and you didn't tell me?"

He turned to face me. "I wanted to tell you, Ly. I wanted to tell you so badly at the lake house, but so much happened that day and… I didn't want to scare you."

"Scare me? I'm the descendent of a demon, Alek! I think I should be told information like that!"

Theia laughed quietly. "Like I said," she started, "Alekzander Black is many things, but your friend is not one of them. He killed your father because he held too much power, and he'll do the same to you to get what he wants."

"No," I said. I pulled myself from Alek's grasp. Everything was happening too fast, too much. Too much was going on, I couldn't think straight. I just needed to think.

Alek reached forward again, but I pulled back.

"This is what she wants," Alek hissed. "She wants to split us up."

I glanced between the two, between the two people pulling me in entirely opposite directions. Freedom or prison. Life or death.

How the hell did we get here?

"You killed my father because yours told you to do so," I said. "Why should I believe you won't use me to drop the veil, too? What's changed? How can I believe this isn't still part of your scheme to gain my trust so I'll drop it and bring back your brother?"

I closed my eyes to try and force the tears away, but I failed.

Alek's jaw tightened. I hated this. I hated everything about it. I trusted Alek. Even after everything, I had trusted him.

But what now? Where did we go from here?

"Come home with me, and we'll forget all about this. We'll start over somewhere else," Theia pushed. She took another step toward me.

But Alek put his body between us. "Don't do this, Lyra," he said. "She'll lock you up like she's done your entire life. You'll never live!"

"She'll die with you!" Theia yelled. Alek moved quickly —too quickly that I almost didn't see his hand move to his belt. He pulled a knife and held it between them.

Between us and her.

"No," he answered. "She'll live with me. The only person here who wants her dead is you."

She laughed again, taking in his knife. "You have no fucking idea how wrong you are, boy."

My heart dropped to my stomach as Alek leapt forward, knife out before him.

Theia dodged it easily—gracefully, even.

But Alek quickly recovered.

"You don't want to fight me," she said. "You don't want to do this."

"Yes," he hissed. "I do."

Think, Lyra. I had to do something. I couldn't just sit here and let her kill him.

Yes, Alek was a demon. He was strong, superhumanly so. But Theia was the Goddess of Light. She was not going to lose this fight.

But Alek had my blood in his system. He told me he had felt stronger, more powerful.

We had a chance.

Another car pulled up in the parking lot.

The rubber tires screeched to a halt.

Salem's bright blonde hair was the first thing I noticed. Her and Zac both leapt from the car.

Theia noticed this, too. Their tattoo-covered bodies gave it away. Night Ravens.

She held her hands out and threw a bolt of light at Alek's feet. "Stay back!" she yelled. "Stay back or I'll kill him!"

This time, it was Alek's turn to laugh. "I'd like to see you try, bitch."

Theia only scowled. Alek jumped toward her again and aimed the knife toward her chest. This time, she protected herself with her magic. With a yelp of pain, Alek's knife clattered to the ground.

And Alek was on the ground next.

He was conscious but clutching his right arm.

Zac and Salem immediately jumped in.

Again, Theia blasted her light, fighting them off.

No. This wasn't happening. This couldn't be happening.

Not again. I was done running.

I was done fighting.

Alek had shown me this life, he had shown me what I had been missing. I had been ignorant before. Being locked away wasn't so bad because that's what my entire life had been.

I hadn't known any different.

But now? Everything was different. I couldn't go back. I could *never* go back.

Salem grunted and jumped on Theia's back while Zac fought her off.

But they weren't going to last.

Alek's knife was on the concrete ground a few feet away.

I walked over and picked it up.

A strange, comforting wave of calmness washed over me. Theia wanted my blood. The only reason I had been locked away, tortured, and punished was because of my blood.

They key to everything, she would say.

The Night Ravens sought the same thing, although they didn't know that yet. The entire reason Alek had sought me out in the first place was because of it.

Which meant, ironically, that my blood had been both my biggest curse and greatest blessing.

I couldn't live like this. I didn't have to.

Without me, there was no way that veil would open. There was no way the demons could use me as a weapon, and there would be no reason for Theia to keep me locked away.

In euphoric clarity, I saw exactly what I needed to do.

I twisted Alek's knife in my hand. It was heavier than I thought it would be.

He stared at me from the ground, finally understanding what was happening around him.

I held the knife in my right hand.

Dropped to my knees.

And dug the metal into the flesh of my left arm.

Everything stopped. Theia stopped fighting. Salem and Zac stopped, too, and I think I heard Salem scream.

The sound of blood rushing through my veins filled my ears.

I looked down at the blood, at the warm, red substance that had cursed me for twenty-two years.

How wicked it had been. The one thing that kept me

alive for so long was the thing that had left me wanting to die so many times, too.

"Lyra!" Alek yelled.

"Stop!" Theia screeched.

I paused for a moment. The four of them were frozen in fear as they watched the blood drip from my fingertips.

Good. They should be afraid.

They were losing the one thing they wanted so badly.

Not me, of course. No. *My blood.*

Even Alek wanted my blood, even though he didn't know that's what he was on the hunt for.

They all wanted it. It was, after all, my only reason for existing on this planet.

"Why?" I asked, although I couldn't stop my voice from cracking. "This is what you all want, isn't it? My blood?"

Alek pushed himself to his knees and held both hands in front of him. "Lyra, put the knife down."

"You don't know what you're doing!" Theia yelled. "You have no idea!"

Tears threatened my eyes. I let them fall. "I do have an idea," I replied. "I think I know exactly what I'm doing, Mother." The blood continued to drip from my fingertips. "I'm tired. I'm so damn tired of living for everyone else. Of living locked away just to keep your little secret."

Salem and Zac stiffened behind her. I didn't care anymore. I didn't care if they knew. I didn't care if the whole damn world knew.

"You want to drop the veil so badly?" I turned my attention to Alek and held out my bleeding arm. "Here you go. My blood is the key. What you all have been looking for this whole time."

Nobody moved. Nobody spoke.

"What?" I pushed. "This is what you all want, right?"

"You're acting insane, Lyra," Theia said, taking another step forward. And another.

"Stay where you are," I yelled. "Don't come any closer!"

"You're hurt," she said. Her voice was so quiet, I almost thought she cared. I almost believed her deceiving look of pity. "You're important, Lyra. I know your life hasn't been fair, but I need you. I need you alive."

I tossed my head back and laughed at the sky. "Quite the sentiment, Mother. Thank you for caring so much about your daughter's wellbeing."

Alek rose to his feet and stepped forward, just a pace ahead of my mother. "I don't care about your blood, Lyra," he said. "I don't care about any of it. The veil, my father. I'll forget them all. I'll forget about all of it if you put the knife down and come with me."

My grip on the weapon only tightened. "Why would I believe you?" I asked. "How can I believe anything you say?"

The scene before me swayed. I was losing blood—too much blood.

"Because, Ly," he said. He took another step toward me. Or was it me moving closer to him? "I love you."

My mother screamed—a violent, hungry screech of anger and built-up emotions. I lifted the knife once more, but this time, I aimed it directly at my own chest. "Don't you dare come any closer!" I yelled at her. "Don't!"

For the first time in my entire life, I saw fear on my mother's face. She stopped in her tracks, not daring to move any closer.

"Good," I breathed. "I'm leaving here with Alek. You won't look for me. You won't look for us. If you do, I'll make sure I end up as good as dead. You need me alive so badly? Well, this is the only way." I surprised even myself with the power that laced each word. "Do you understand?"

Theia clenched her jaw and nodded.

My vision blurred again, and I stumbled sideways.

But Alek was there to catch me. His strong arms tightened around my body and pulled the knife from my grasp.

"You're losing too much blood," he said, but I hardly registered the words. Salem and Zac were both nearby, both talking to Alek in a rushed voice.

And then everything went black.

Thirty~Eight

The first thing I noticed when I woke up was the familiar smell of sandalwood.

I blinked my eyes open slowly. The room I was in was dark and cool, and I was on a large bed with silk sheets.

Definitely not my apartment. And definitely not Theia's basement.

"Alek!" Salem's voice rang through the room. "Alek, she's awake!"

I instantly sat up in bed, which caused my head to spin. The walls matched the darkness, and it became very clear that I was somewhere in Alek's house.

Wait…

I scanned the room again. Aside from a black dresser, a velvet armchair, and a fireplace in the corner, the room was empty. Not to mention it was pristinely clean and tidy.

This had to be Alek's room.

Alek and Salem switched places, and he closed the door behind him as he entered. "Hey," he said. He stood by the door for a moment, staring at me with his hands tucked into the front pockets of his black jeans. "How are you feeling?"

I glanced at my arm. Someone had wrapped it in thick bandages. I didn't even try to move it.

"I feel fine, all things considered." He gave me a sympathetic smile. Alek had never been one to show sympathy before. "What happened?" I asked.

He walked over and sat on the edge of the bed. His bed.

"After you threatened to bleed yourself dry, your mother backed off. For now, at least. She vanished before we could ask any questions."

"That seems… unlike her."

Alek shrugged. "We were able to get you out of there. You've been here recovering ever since. You did a number on your arm."

I replayed the jumbled memories in my mind. Theia had just let us leave? Let them leave with me? That didn't make any sense.

And if we were at Alek's house… "Your father—"

"He's agreed to let you heal before we discuss anything further."

I began pushing the covers off my body. "No, he'll use me, Alek. He'll force me to open the veil and—"

"He won't force you to do anything. Not while I'm around." His voice was firm, but I couldn't be too sure. Alek's father had forced him into much worse.

Killing my father, for one.

I was sure I should have felt some sort of pain or grief, but I had really never known my father. Any memories of his existence had been washed away by the trauma of my life.

Alek reached out and grabbed my wrist, turning my

bandaged arm over so he could look at it. "You're a fucking idiot for this, Lyra, you know that?" His voice cracked.

"I didn't have a choice," I whispered. "It was the only way to get Theia to leave us alone."

He pulled my hand to his lap. "Don't do that again," he said. When his eyes met mine, any lingering joke had vanished. Dark, desperate seriousness dripped from his features in a way that wiped the smile from my face. "Ever."

This time, I couldn't stop the tears from falling. I remembered what Alek had said as I sliced that blade—his blade—through the delicate skin on my forearm.

I love you.

My heart twisted. "I don't... I don't know how to live like this, Alek. Twenty-two years and I've never had a plan. I've never had a way out."

He wiped a tear away with his thumb, but his hand lingered gently on my neck. I leaned into the warmth of his touch. "You have a way out now. I won't let you go back to her."

I took a shaking breath. "Why?" I asked; it was the question I had been holding onto longer than I had realized. Ever since the lake house, when he jumped into that freezing water to pull me out. "Why do you care? I mean, my presence in your life hasn't exactly been beneficial."

Alek brought his other hand to my neck too, putting the slightest amount of pressure under my chin that made me lift my head up. "I meant what I said yesterday, Lyra," he whispered. Alek's forehead pressed gently against mine. "This isn't temporary for me. It may have started that way, it may have started as a simple ploy to get my father what he wanted. But not anymore. You're part of me now in a way that I can't even explain. I can't go a single fucking minute without thinking about you."

My tears fell harder.

"I love you, Lyra," he said. "I love you, and I'm not going to let another greedy, power-hungry bastard lay their hands on you again. Got it?"

I nodded against him. *Love.* It had been a foreign concept to me for so long, I was starting to think it never even existed. But now? I was starting to believe. That small, expanding feeling of hope fluttered in my chest.

"Your father won't be happy about this," I reminded him. "The whole reason you're even close to me is so you can expose my secret."

Alek pulled away, just enough that he could look in my eyes as he answered, "I've been tired of my father's orders for a while now. I'm not the only one. Change is on the horizon; I can feel it."

"What does that mean?" I whispered as if his father could hear us. "You'd defy your father's orders?"

He laughed and kissed my forehead gently. "I've been doing that for years, Lyra. This doesn't seem like a particularly great time to stop."

I laughed with him. An odd, warm feeling spread through my chest. I couldn't help but wonder if this was how my entire life would have felt if I wasn't locked away in Theia's basement.

"Get some rest," he said softly. "I'll come find you in a few hours."

"Alek?" I questioned, pulling on his hand before he could let go. "Will you stay with me?"

Something flickered across his face, something relieving and dark and heartbreaking. But amongst all of that, Alek nodded. "Of course, I'll stay," he whispered. He walked around the bed and crawled atop the thin silk sheets.

It was crazy. It was absolutely, undeniably insane. But I felt safer with him near. He had saved me. He had fought for me. And I knew, deep down, that he would do it again.

I let him pull me closer, and I rested my head on his chest. His heart rate was slow. Steady.

Nothing like mine.

"And Alek?" I said again. His hand drew lazy circles on my back.

"Yeah?"

"I don't want to die. Not anymore. I want to *live.*"

His fingers stalled for a second. I wanted to take the words back as soon as I heard them aloud, but on the other hand, he needed to know. He needed to truly understand just how dark things had been in that basement, just how little light I had left inside of me.

Alek had taken that dull flame and ignited it, had shown me a way out of an endless, destructive hell.

"I know," he said after a few seconds. His fingers resumed where they had left off. "I don't want you to die, either."

Alek stayed that way with me for hours, until my heartbeat settled to a low drum that matched his. Until I no longer feared him leaving. Until his fingers tracing my back turned to a lullaby.

And, for what felt like the first time in years, I slept. And I did not dream of the chains in the basement.

Thirty-Nine

"Lyra," a familiar voice pulled me from my deep sleep. "Lyra, get up."

I blinked my eyes. Alek was no longer with me, no longer in my bed. But similar green eyes find out mine in the darkness.

Alek's father stood beside me.

I immediately pushed myself to a sitting position. "What's going on?" I asked. "Where's Alek?"

"Alek's waiting for us downstairs. Come, come." Alarms went off in my mind, but Alek's father seemed calm enough. He wasn't angry, but he seemed to be in a hurry for whatever reason.

I was too groggy to analyze the situation. Too groggy to fight it.

I pushed the covers off myself and followed him down the hallway.

Everything was dark. Tiny, old lanterns in the hall lit the path as he led me further and further into their mansion.

My brain was telling me something was wrong, but I didn't know what. And where was Alek?

"Where are we going?" I asked.

"Shh, shh," he responded. We were almost running now, scurrying through the darkness like the rats in the streets of Paris.

Now I was definitely panicking. But I had nowhere to go, no way out of this mansion without Alek.

We walked down a long staircase into the basement. Everything was still dark, and my bare feet padded along the freezing cold floor. I followed Alek's father until we came to a large door.

He pushed it open.

I followed him inside.

Everything was dark except for a small fire. The walls were black, and I could hardly see Alek's father as he closed the door behind us.

"What is she doing here?" Alek demanded. My attention snapped to his voice. In the darkness, I could barely make out his figure.

"What's going on?" I asked.

"She's part of this, son," his father explained. "Whether you like it or not, we need her."

"Leave her out of this!" he yelled. My eyes began to adjust. I could make out an older woman near the fire, along with Alek and his father.

Something wasn't right. Every ounce of my body knew this was wrong.

"It's a full moon," I explained. If Alek's father had dragged me down here, it only meant one thing. He wasn't going to wait for me to heal. He wasn't going to let Alek talk our way out of this. He wanted me to open the veil. And he wanted me to do it right now. "You're dropping the veil."

"She's smarter than you let on, son," his father said.

"My mother will come," I insisted. "She's the protector of the veil. She'll know if anything even begins to happen."

"Oh, I count on it," his father said. "But what you don't know, Lyra, is that today is a very special day for us. For your mother, too. You see, on this day, every hundred years, the moon is not simply full. The moon is in an eclipse. It has a weakening effect on magic everywhere, which to most people would appear to be a bad thing."

My hands began to shake.

"But it's not a bad thing for us, Lyra. Do you want to know why?"

I shook my head. "No."

"When your mother, the Goddess of Light, comes for you, she will not be able to stop us. She will not be able to fight us with her power. She won't even be able to whisk you away into thin air like she's done before. No, she'll show up here only to realize she is stuck. Without her magic. With no defenses. This will allow for us to drop the veil without her interruption, and with the witch's help here, there's nothing she can do to stop it."

That couldn't be true. It was impossible for a goddess to lose her magic. It was only a myth. They had to be wrong. A small part of me hoped they were right, though. To see my mother powerless... I had wished for that more times than I could count.

"This," Alek's father continued, "is Narcissa. A witch who has worked with us for decades. She's prepared to help lower the veil, and she's been studying the ritual for decades. All we need from you,"—he stepped closer—"is a vial of your blood."

I backed away as far as I could, until my back was pressed against the wall behind me. "No," I said. "You can't drop the veil. It's too dangerous."

"We aren't dropping it for long," the older woman, Narcissa, explained softly. "Just long enough to get back what belongs here. Marcus has everything under control."

My eyes found Alek's in the darkness. "You can't bring him back," I said. "You cannot pull a dead soul from the veil. That's not how it works!"

"That *is* how it works," Alek's father—*Marcus*—held a hand out to stop Alek from walking over to me. "And you'll help us do it. You don't have much of a choice, girl."

"Why can't you accept that your son is gone?" I pleaded. "Wrath is dead. He's passed onto the veil. You can't bring him back!" I couldn't hide the desperation from my voice. Why didn't they understand? Why couldn't they just let go?

"He is my son!" Alek's father yelled, rattling the walls around us. "He did not deserve to die. I needed him here, and I still do. I'll get him back if it's the last thing I do on this planet."

The hair on my neck stood up. "Lyra," Alek pleaded. "Please." I couldn't tell what he wanted from me. He had been so adamant on protecting me, on not using me for this. But it seemed like he didn't have much of a choice, either.

See, Alek and I were similar in that way. Puppets. It was our parents controlling the strings.

A single tear fell down my cheek. "I can't do it, Alek," I said. "It will cause too much damage. The veil hasn't been opened in—"

"I don't care what the consequences are," Alek's father

barked. "I don't care if the entire fucking world falls apart because of this. You'll do it. You'll do it because you don't have a fucking choice."

Another tear fell. The hope that had been building inside of me over the last few weeks was beginning to dissipate, along with any feelings I had of getting past this. Of getting away from this life.

I was already shaking my head. "I can't," I breathed. "I'm sorry, I can't do it."

"Narcissa, begin the ritual. Now." Narcissa nodded and knelt on a small altar before the fire in the center of the room. She started to chant quietly, growing louder and louder with each foreign word.

"What is she doing?" I asked.

"Father, stop this!" Alek yelled. "You cannot force Lyra to bring Wrath back!"

"Maybe not," Marcus argued. "But she'll bring you back."

I screamed, and somewhere in the room, Alek did too. Marcus marched over to him and gripped his head tightly with both hands.

Alek's eyes met mine for one torturous second before his own father snapped his neck.

And killed him.

Alek's body fell to the ground with a thud. I rushed to his side, holding his head in my hands. "Alek!" I yelled. "Alek, wake up!"

"He's not waking up," Marcus barked. "There's only one way to get your precious boyfriend back. Lower the veil, and bring them both back."

Tears streamed freely down my face, dropping onto

Alek's warm body. "No," I whispered. "No, this can't be happening."

What type of sick father would kill his own son?

"Bring them back!" Marcus yelled.

I was openly sobbing now. My heart had been cracked open and ripped out, leaving me lifeless on the floor of the demon mansion. He had killed Alek. He had actually killed him.

My flash of grief morphed to uncontrollable anger. I screamed again, but not a scream of fear or uncertainty. It was a warrior's cry of agony.

"Bring. Them. Back!"

Tears streamed freely down my face. I didn't bother wiping them away as I stood from Alek's lifeless body.

Alek was dead. Actually dead.

I shook my head as I looked toward the woman— Narcissa. My mind had already been made up, was made up from the second Alek's body fell to the ground. He didn't deserve this. He didn't deserve any of this. In many ways, he was equally as much of a victim as I was.

"How?" I asked, not to Marcus, but to the woman whom I knew could help me. Narcissa. She was already holding her hands out in front of her. "How do we bring them back?"

"Come here, child," she said.

I did as I was told and walked over to where she knelt near the fire.

"Give me your hand."

She began chanting again, louder this time. The energy of the room shifted, and a cooling sensation fell over my skin as the fire grew and spewed flames into the air.

"What are you doing?" I asked her. If she heard me, she

made no indication to answer me. She kept her eyes closed as she chanted louder and louder.

I had to blink to make sure I was seeing this correctly. A long, shimmering wall rose from the floor of the room. It was translucent, hardly visible to the eye, but I could see it. I could feel it.

I knew exactly what it was. Narcissa had summoned the veil.

In all the years I had been alive for this one purpose, I had never laid eyes on the veil. I had never been this close. Very few witches even possessed the knowledge to bring it forth.

But here, in the basement of the demon mansion, was the veil.

"Oh my god," I muttered. Alek's body began to turn to ash, actually disintegrating before my very eyes. I could hardly see him through the shimmering light, but my chest ached. Marcus stood silent behind us.

"Now we need your blood," Narcissa said.

She picked up a knife and sliced the blade deeply across my palm. I didn't even flinch. A numbness had begun to spread across my entire body, blocking me from the pain I should have been feeling.

We were interrupted by a massive, blinding flash of light that took over the room. Narcissa and I both shrieked, covering our eyes.

"What do you think you're doing?" Theia's roar of anger quickly replaced the flash of light.

I froze. I knew she stood behind me, but I couldn't move. I couldn't look her in the eyes.

Marcus was right. My mother had shown up. Now I was hoping what he said about limiting her powers was true.

"I'm bringing my sons back," Marcus barked. "You cannot stop me, Theia. Not even if you wanted to."

I shivered as Theia's high-pitched, screeching laugh echoed off the walls. The shimmering light of the veil disappeared.

Alek's dead body came into view once more.

Everything stopped.

I spun around to face her, to face the woman who had ruined everything for me.

"Let us bring them back!" I yelled to Theia, meeting her blazing eyes. "We'll open the veil, bring them back, and shut it again. It will be as if it never happened!"

When her eyes settled on me, I could feel the hatred. I could feel how disappointed and disgusted she was in me. But I didn't care. I didn't care what my mother thought about me, or about what I was doing. I was bringing Alek back. I didn't give a shit who stood in my way.

"Your powers are weak," Alek's father started. "You can try to keep the veil closed, but you will not succeed. Lyra's blood is all we need to finish the ritual."

I glanced back at Narcissa.

She nodded.

My attention was drawn back to Theia when she let out a roar of anger. I glanced at her just in time to see her launch herself in my direction.

And then Marcus sunk a blade into her torso.

I gasped.

She fell to the ground.

"Do it!" Marcus yelled with a wild look in his eye, blade still embedded into Theia's stomach. "Do it now!"

I should have cared more that my own mother had just been stabbed, I realized.

But I only felt a bubble of satisfaction.

"Here," I said, holding out my bleeding hand to Narcissa. "Do it."

She began chanting again, and within a few seconds, the shimmering wall of the veil was back.

I could feel its power calling to me in a way I never had felt before.

"How do we know it will be them who come back through the veil?" I asked.

"This is their home," Marcus answered from the back of the room. "You crack that veil, and they'll come."

I hoped he was right. With every single ounce of my soul, I hoped.

I became vaguely aware of Theia's muffled laughter in the room behind us. She wasn't dead, so that was something. Although part of me wished she was. She would never forgive me for this, would never let me live this down.

Narcissa was yelling now, chanting words in a language I couldn't understand. She gripped my palm and flipped it over the fire. The heat burned my skin, but I didn't care. She needed this. I needed this.

Alek needed this.

Come home, Alek. Come back to me.

I watched in awe as the sheer, shimmering light of the veil parted, like a doorway.

"There it is!" Marcus yelled. "It's open!"

Narcissa didn't stop chanting. I didn't stop silently hoping that this would work, because we had no choice. This had to work.

Alek had to survive.

"Come on, Alek," I whispered. "Come home to us. Come back."

Theia's laugh grew louder in the background. Narcissa's grip on my arm loosened, her entire body began shaking and her eyes rolled into the back of her head.

The chanting stopped.

The room went silent.

Come on, Alek. Come home.

I was about to give up. I was about to accept the fact that once again, I had lost. Once again, I couldn't save anyone. Once again, I thought I could be someone I wasn't.

But then, in the midst of the swarming clouds of darkness, I saw it.

Someone moved beyond the veil, walking.

I couldn't see exactly who it was until they stepped through that small, magic doorway of the veil.

Alek carried a body over his shoulder.

Alek was alive.

As soon as they were beyond the reach of the veil, the shimmering wall disappeared.

Narcissa collapsed next to me.

The fire before us sputtered out.

"Oh my god," I said, running to them. Alek dropped his brother—Wrath—onto the ground. With a thud.

Marcus rushed in our direction.

Alek stumbled, catching himself on the wall. I was there in an instant, my bleeding hand moving to catch him, to support him. "Hey," I whispered. "Hey, you're okay. You're okay. It worked."

He was staring off into the distance, looking at something that wasn't there.

"Alek," I said, louder this time. I grabbed his face and made him look at me. It wasn't until his eyes met mine that his labored, frantic breathing began to slow.

"Lyra," he said, grabbing hold of my shoulders to stabilize himself. "You're here."

"I'm here," I cried. "You're back. You're okay."

Wrath began coughing on the floor beside us.

"Son!" Marcus yelled. "Son, wake up!"

I turned in time to see Wrath blinking his neon-green eyes open. He looked similar to Alek, with slightly paler skin and less tattoos.

A chill ran down my body. This was unnatural, I knew that. But many things in this world were unnatural. Many things in this world were wrong, and yet the universe allowed them to happen.

My blood was the key to dropping the veil for a reason. Maybe this was my purpose all along. Maybe I had been put on this planet, in Theia's hands, so that life could work out to exactly this situation right now.

Alek leaned down and pressed his forehead against mine. "You saved my life," Alek said.

"Technically, I brought you back from the dead." A wrecked sob shook my body. "But close enough."

Alek's father was now hugging Wrath on the ground. They were okay. Wrath was okay.

Alek tilted my chin up and kissed me. He wrapped his strong arms around me and held on, as if he would never let me go. As if he owed me the world.

Even after everything we had just been through, even with my heart still pumping adrenaline into my body with every passing second, I felt safe with him.

I knew Alek would protect me.

Theia's laughter started up again in the back of the room. Alek broke our kiss, and we all turned to see Theia staring at us all from her slumped position on the ground. Blood seeped from her hands, pooling on the floor around her.

It wasn't easy to kill a god. Theia would be fine, and we would all be worse off because of it.

"You idiots," she muttered. I could have sworn I felt the ground shake beneath us. "There is a very delicate balance between life and death." She coughed and had to catch her breath. I could have sworn I felt the ground beneath us rumble. "You have no idea what you've all just done."

The wind whipped my red hair around as I held on tightly to Alek. His motorcycle was the latest addition to my new life, and he insisted on taking it everywhere we went.

I didn't mind. It gave me more of an excuse to hold onto him. His muscles flexed under my grip as he pulled the motorcycle to a stop in front of Night Raven.

"Not so fast," he said before I could climb off. I stayed in my position on the back of the motorcycle as Alek stood up. He pulled my black helmet off my head and set it on the handle of his bike before returning and tucking my loose strands of hair behind my ears. "Did I ever tell you how much I like riding this thing when you're sitting behind me?"

"Hmmmm," I mumbled. Alek pushed my legs apart with his knee and stepped between them. "I don't think you have. Maybe you should repeat it."

Alek gripped my chin and leaned down, planting a hungry, aggressive kiss on my mouth.

Two weeks had passed since Alek's own father snapped his neck. Two weeks since I lowered the veil enough to bring him back and since I had seen Theia bleeding in the basement of their mansion.

Two weeks of pretending life was normal.

Alek pulled away from our kiss too soon and began tugging me toward the doors of Night Raven.

"Come on," he said. "They're waiting for us."

My lips slowly spread into a smile. "Or… we could stay on the motorcycle and do more of that."

Alek threw his arm around me. "I would love nothing more than to kiss you in every place imaginable, but then we would never leave the bedroom."

Heat pooled in my stomach. I took a deep breath and tried to hide my surely bright red face as we walked through the front doors of Night Raven.

"There you two are," Natalie called out from the bar. Her and Wrath were drinking while Salem whipped off the counter from behind the bar. "We were starting to think you'd forgotten about us."

"Forget about you?" I repeated, walking over to Natalie and throwing my arm around her shoulders. "With your loud mouth? Impossible."

"How are you liking the new bike?" Wrath asked. It had been two weeks, and I still couldn't get over how similar he and Alek looked. If it weren't for the difference in tattoos and the lighter shade of hair, I would definitely get them confused.

"Take it for a spin sometime and see for yourself," Alek joked.

"Careful," Salem chimed in. "He gets his hands on that bike and you'll never see it again."

We all laughed then. It didn't take long at all for Wrath to feel like he had been here all along. He was funny and smart, and he seemed to have virtually no side effects from being on the other side of the veil.

Even though Alek insisted on checking every single time we were together.

"Now that he's the king of demons, I think he can buy himself his own bike whenever he pleases," Alek said.

Wrath rolled his eyes. Their father had been more than happy to give up his position as king of demons. It was odd seeing him so attached to Wrath, especially when he didn't seem to give a shit about Alek.

Salem slid me a drink across the counter, but it began to shake.

Everything in the bar began to shake, actually.

Alek was at my side in a flash. "What is that?" I asked.

It had been two weeks. Two weeks since Alek died. Two weeks since I brought him and Wrath back.

Two weeks since Theia had been seen.

And two weeks since the balance between life and death had been altered.

More glasses began to shake. Natalie held onto the bar to stop from falling out of her seat.

Somebody stormed in through the front door. It was a middle-aged man, but he looked very familiar. I knew I had seen him before.

My blood ran cold. It was my father. My *dead* father.

"You." He pointed a finger at me. "You have to fix this."

The balance… the veil…

"Oh, my god," Natalie whispered behind me. Alek's hands tightened on my body as those familiar shadows of panic began to creep closer.

We had disturbed the balance. The delicate, life-altering balance.

And now, we would pay the price.